I Hear You!

I Hear You!

A novel of the supernatural by

Norman O'Banyon

I HEAR YOU!

iUniverse books may be ordered through booksellers or by contacting:

iUniverse
1663 Liberty Drive
Bloomington, IN 47403
www.iuniverse.com
1-800-Authors (1-800-288-4677)

ISBN: 978-1-4917-9370-1 (sc)
ISBN: 978-1-4917-9299-5 (e)

Print information available on the last page.

iUniverse rev. date: 06/27/2016

The football game was going just right. The Southfield-Lathrup Chargers were an equal match for the Clarkston Wolves, especially since they had recruited a giant two hundred twenty pound fullback. He had accounted for both the Charger touchdowns. Larry, at 6'1" 195, had been busy at linebacker for the Wolves. He had racked up six solo tackles and swatted several passes incomplete. Clarkston was leading by a touchdown in the fourth quarter, but the Chargers were moving the ball against a weary line. The mammoth just kept pounding into them for three or four yards every play. Larry was pretty sure they would score again if they kept running the ball. He could only play his position, keeping a close watch on the quarterback's eyes. A trick pass after all those running plays, could catch the Wolves off-guard.

Three more running plays, and then the quarterback's eyes told him it was coming. A receiver had broken free from the line and was racing up the sideline. Larry broke on the play, anticipating where the ball would reach the speedy end. He got there first, plucking the ball out of the air an instant before it reached its intended target. Larry pulled the ball in tight and returned it a dozen yards before he was pushed out of bounds. He wasn't the hero of the game, but had made a significant contribution to the victory. Of course there was a torrent of profanity and accusations that he had interfered with the receiver, but no yellow flag had been thrown. A few more insignificant plays ran out the clock, and Clarkston rung up another one in the win column.

It wasn't a play-off game, there was no great significance on the line, but a Friday night victory was always a reason to celebrate. The players and fans rushed out onto the field with typical exuberance, jumping and cheering like crazy. It was pretty easy to get caught up in their frivolity.

"Great catch, Crown!" Steve Lucas, the quarterback shouted as he smacked Larry's helmet. "You iced the game for us! Great interception!" He ran on to join a cluster of jumping, screaming girls.

The locker room was a continuation of the celebration. Adrenalin coated testosterone makes a noisy treat, until the coach came through handing out compliments for outstanding plays. He stopped near Larry to say, "That was great anticipation, Crown. I saw the quarterback fire that pass before I noticed that you were already moving to defend it. Great job! That would have tied the game for sure, and with that fullback, we couldn't have held them out for two. You saved the game for us. Fine job!" He turned to praise the beat up linemen. They had stood tall against a considerable opponent. Maybe Larry could feel a little heroic after all.

He had just finished packing his grass and mud stained jersey and pants in the laundry bag for his mom to wash, thinking that at least this week there was no blood on them. Steve Lucas called from the doorway, "Hey, Crown, we're going to Jiffy Burgers for something to eat. Come on by if you want to."

It was unusual for him to be included in the quarterback's post-game activity. Maybe that play was more important than he thought.

There were two sedans parked in front of Jiffy Burgers, and fourteen pickups. Larry made it fifteen. The place was crowded with happy kids. He made his way past booths filled beyond capacity. The counter was filled as well. But toward the end there was a standing cluster of his auto shop buddies who invited him to crowd in with them. "We can't promise that you'll get anything to eat. The waitress hasn't been around for several minutes."

"That's O.K. I've got to get going anyway. The shop is going to let me work on my car tomorrow, so I've got to get going early." He would have left, but someone asked him about his shop project, a subject he was glad to share. "I got a sweet deal on a pair of bucket seats from the same wrecking yard that helped me find the Buick Capri engine and tranny." While most of his auto shop classmates were working on fresh exhaust systems, or new brakes for their truck, Larry had undertaken the total rebuild of a '51 Volvo PV444. If his calculations were accurate, it would be finished in time for graduation. His scarlet and black paint job would be a sensation.

A sweet voice at his elbow asked, "Larry, could you give a girl a lift home? My buddies must have figured I was the odd-girl-out, so they abandoned me." Silvia Shepherd was in his U.S. History class, and he deemed it an honor to even be spoken to by her.

"Of course, I'd be glad to. It's so busy here I couldn't even get a coke anyway," he answered with a grin.

The diminutive lady looked into his dark eyes and said, "We've got some Royal Crown in the frig at home, and the folks are at the Lewiston Eagles tonight, so there is no one to bother. I'd be happy to split one with you." Her smile and gracious offer were impossible to refuse. He had no way of knowing what else she had in mind.

She directed him to drive east of Clarkston, near the bluff overlooking the Snake River. On the way they talked about the game, and her friends. She had a lot of friends. Finally she pointed to a large home with a circular driveway. It was very elegant, which made him feel even more uncomfortable. When Larry said he would just say "goodnight," Silvia insisted on sharing the R C cola. He had been so very gracious it was the least she could do.

In retrospect he wasn't sure of the chain of events. He had been seated at a counter with her beside him. That's where the first kiss occurred. Her fragrance was sweet, like tropical flowers. Then he was standing and she was pressing against him in a most sensational way. She whispered that she was wearing no panties. She asked him if he had a condom, and when he shook his head, it didn't seem to matter to her. He lost his virginity on the family room carpet.

She gave him another gentle kiss, saying that she needed to rinse out, and her folks would be home soon, so he might want to leave. As quickly as the wonder began, it was over and he was driving home trying to make sense of the whole episode.

Everything changed, and nothing changed. Walking through the halls he only looked for her face. Sitting in History he focused on her curls, and wanted more than anything to walk with her or talk with her, but none of that happened. He was still invisible to Silvia Shepherd. She was surrounded by a cadre of devoted friends that prevented him from getting close enough to catch her eye. If she smiled in his direction, he was embarrassed to find that it was meant for someone behind him. Nothing had changed.

Their football season ended with eight wins and five losses. By Thanksgiving he had installed the new twelve volt harness, battery and lights on the Volvo; but he couldn't get the memory of warm soft skin and her breath out of his thoughts. By the Christmas break he had installed the rack and pinion steering and new anchor points for the leather seats. He got special permission to use the shop during the long break even though there was no heat in it. He fabricated the drive shaft to match up with the universal joint, and prayed that she would remember him. Perhaps she would call. Everything had changed, and nothing had changed. He was still invisible.

By the time school resumed in the New Year, 1961, he had replaced the brake pads, Master cylinder, and shocks. He was grateful for a good hay season last summer that allowed him to earn enough for this project. He had mowed, baled, and delivered four large fields of alfalfa to the High Valley Hay Center in Ellensburg. By depositing all his checks in a bank account, he was assured he wouldn't squander the cash like most of his buddies seemed to do. He painted the engine compartment flat black, and then sent the bumpers and valve cover to be chrome plated. Without understanding the terminology or process, Larry was able to transfer the energy generated by his depression over Silvia's lack of response, into the creative renovation of his auto shop project. The Volvo would be a beautiful classic.

January crept by. There was a three day snow event that closed the school. In February the Army recruiter from Lewiston visited the school and Larry took some material to show his folks. His dad was interested in the conversation, but his mom wanted nothing to do with the thought that her boy would be far away in armed conflict. Dad won out when he said there are far more places that are peaceful and educational. In March there was a new set of white sidewall tires, and the school was whispering a rumor that Steve Lucas had impregnated Silvia Shepherd! No one was surprised that he, a ladies' man, would do that, but Silvia was the school poster child for integrity and moral correctness. They were voted King and Queen of the senior prom even though her tummy was beginning to show. Larry chose not to attend.

April was a busy month. With the help of Mr. Hodges, the shop teacher, the engine was placed on fresh motor mounts and all the parts fit. Larry needed help setting the timing, but other than that, he went through the proper steps to fill all the fluids and start the engine. It worked even better than he hoped. Mr. Hodges assured him that not even the graduates from the Vocational College could have done as well. Once again the rumor mill reported that Silvia would finish her class work from home, and Steve became something of a social pariah. Neither his former friends nor any woman classmate would have anything to do with him.

With fresh black paint sporting scarlet pin-striping, the Volvo was outstanding. Larry was invited to show it at the Easter Parade, and also in the Apple Blossom Parade. You know how difficult it is to stay focused on a process once the principle part is satisfied? He parked the Volvo in the back bay of the barn and covered it with a tarp. It might be a while before he saw it again. With little enthusiasm, Larry made sure all his tests were taken, and his books returned. He requested that his diploma be mailed to his home after a photocopy was included with his enlistment papers, because on the 22nd of May1961, he boarded a bus that would eventually get him to Fort Benning, Georgia. He was oblivious to the wedding ceremony that joined Silvia and Steve as husband and wife. She wanted a small private wedding before the baby was born.

Larry's new life in the U.S. Army was beginning.

Both Larry's dad and uncle had given him advice about the military service. His dad had said, "You will do fine as long as you listen to instructions." His uncle had added, "Don't try to be clever or cute, just do your best to follow your company commander's orders. Your Grandfather Daniel, and your uncle John David gave their lives believing in that."

There were three other recruits who boarded the Greyhound in Lewiston. They found available seats and settled in for a long ride. Larry had brought a Louis Lamoure novel to read, but the scenery was much more interesting. When they made their way through the mountains, he was spellbound. Highway 84 took them to Salt Lake City, where he saw the Mormon Temple Square. They didn't look all that different from the rest of folks. Four more recruits boarded, and one sat across the aisle from Larry. He tried to strike up a conversation, but realized the new lad was engaged in leaving home for the first time. Maybe they could talk later. They were in the mountains all the way to Denver, where they had a supper stop and changed drivers, along with adding five more recruits. Highway 70 took them east into flat farm country, which made it a bit easier to try to sleep. At best Larry napped through the night.

The bus arrived in Kansas City a little after seven a.m. but they were told it was now Central Daylight time and moved another hour ahead. Larry smiled at the notion of an added hour that was easy to endure. The passengers were told to take all their personal items with them when they went to breakfast, because they were changing to a fresh bus. Larry liked the sound of that because the toilet room was getting pretty ripe, and it gave him the exercise of listening to instructions.

A half hour later, he thought he would have his same seat on the new bus, but a young lady had already claimed it. He asked if the aisle seat was available and she invited him to take it, not aware that she was the one out of place. Larry was not sure, but it seemed to him that an additional five recruits boarded. Once again they headed east on highway 70.

"Are you headed for boot camp?" her quiet voice asked. "It seems like nearly half the people on board have that anxious face." Her smile was warm and honest. Larry admired her red hair and freckles, her blue eyes and lovely smile. She had the faint fragrance of wild strawberry.

"That's perceptive of you," Larry answered. "I didn't know we look like deer in the headlights. But it makes sense that the recruiters would schedule us to arrive in a group instead of trickling in." He waited for a moment, and then when she didn't say anything more, he asked, "Are you headed somewhere fun? I'll bet you're not going to boot camp."

"You are right about that," she said brightly. "I had to wait tables for a couple years to save up, but I'm enrolling in the Music Institute of Nashville. I want to compose songs." She paused for a moment and said, "I'm Sue Lambert."

"Wow," he whispered, "I've never met anyone who is going to be famous."

She chuckled quietly too. "How do you know that? I'll bet there are many people from your home town that are doing amazing things."

Larry shook his head, saying, "I don't know about that, and I know most of the folks in Clarkston. I can't think of one of them who has a new song in their soul. It seems to me they are coming downhill from nowhere."

Sue wrinkled her brow in thought. "That's a strange way to put it. What do you mean by, 'downhill from nowhere.'?"

"Think about it," Larry said. "If you are walking, running or riding a bike, when you go downhill you just coast. There's not much effort, and the only accomplishment is that you get to the bottom. But when you go uphill, there is effort, growth, and achievement. Maybe at the crest you discover that there is an even higher goal, where the vista will be even more breathtaking. Somewhere is always uphill, not down." It was the closest thing to a philosophical thought that Larry had enjoyed for a long time.

"My goodness," she said. "That sounds like a soul with a new song, if I ever heard one. Haven't you ever been in love, or had your heart broken?"

Larry thought of Silvia for just a moment. He smiled as he said, "I'm not sure I have. But that's not what I think about when I think of a soul with a song. I'll bet everyone on this bus has had their heart broken a time or two because they fell for the wrong person, were deceived, were at the wrong place at the wrong time. Those are the things ninety nine percent of songs are about, and they have very little to do with the soul. I'm thinking about the person who has a fresh melody because he helped a little kid get on the school bus, or gave directions to someone who was lost. He stopped to talk with a lonely old neighbor. You know, the accidental kindness that puts a smile on someone's face because a stranger cared; someone gave a flower to a hospital patient that no one else had visited. That's a deep melody that becomes a new song."

Sue took out a small notebook and wrote, "Coming downhill from nowhere. Somewhere is always uphill. When you coast you only get to the bottom." Finally she asked, "Are you a musician?" Her eyes searched his, as though it was an important question.

"I'm not sure what I am, besides a deer in the headlights. I guess the next few weeks will put me somewhere." He grinned and said, "And we know that somewhere is always uphill."

"That's a concept that sort of sticks with you, doesn't it?" she asked. "Do you mind if I use it in a new composition?" Once again she looked at him a little too intensely.

"I don't mind at all. In fact, I'm honored that anything we have said is worth remembering." He reached for his novel, thinking it would end the conversation,

"You didn't tell me your name," she said softly. "I'd like to stay in touch with you."

"That will be a challenge for the next sixteen weeks. I'm Larry Crown, and I really have no idea what my mailing address will be."

Sue was busy writing hers. "Here," she said folding the paper. "I'm pretty sure I'll be here for six months. If I haven't accomplished the first step of my dream, I may need to make a change." The paper smelled like wild strawberry.

"Just remember," Larry said with a grin, "somewhere is always uphill."

She pulled a book from her bag, and turned toward the window to read. Almost immediately she turned back and raised the armrest from between them, without saying a word. She turned back toward the window, but leaned back so she was resting against his shoulder.

Larry considered the gentle contact, felt her warmth. It was neither uncomfortable nor unwelcome. He checked his watch. They had chatted nearly three hours. Ten minutes later he felt her head rest more comfortably on his shoulder, and her body twitch. She was falling asleep.

The Greyhound bus was in St. Louis for a thirty minute food break as the fuel tank was refilled and a new driver came aboard along with three more recruits. Highway 24 would now carry them southeast to Nashville.

It was sunset as Sue hugged Larry farewell. "You promised to write me when you have a chance," she declared. "I'll be happy to see it. You have been a comforting companion today. I was a bit anxious about travelling alone. You made me feel safe. Thank you. I do believe there is a new song in my soul."

"I have enjoyed this day too. I really hope you have success in your song writing," Larry managed to say as she departed. Into the night he wondered if there was something more that should have been said, or if he would ever see her again. For quite a while he replayed their gentle conversations and he recalled the fragrance of wild strawberry.

Fort Benning Boot Camp

It was 5:20 a.m. Eastern Daylight time when the bus pulled into the Atlanta Greyhound depot. A Sergeant stood by the door as they filed off the bus, checking their names from a list. He had informed them that they had ten minutes to hit the head and grab a snack before they boarded the green U.S. Army bus. Whatever the morning was bringing, it had already begun. Larry whispered to himself, "listen and obey." It took the bus about ninety minutes to arrive at Fort Benning. Whatever Larry expected, this was much larger, vast! Men in green dungarees were marching, or walking to large brick buildings wherever he looked. "Breathe and listen," he told himself. "Just follow instructions." The bus turned at a large sign that read, "30th Army Garrison Reception Battalion." They went a ways further, made a couple more turns then stopped in front of a busy building with a crowd of men standing in line.

"You have twenty minutes to grab breakfast, ladies. Get a tray, take what food you will eat and return your tray and utensils to the scullery. Be back on this bus before 6:50 or you will start your intake process with a demerit, which I guarantee will be unpleasant for you." He opened the door and forty three overwhelmed young men surged off in search of food. Larry thought, "If it doesn't get any worse than this, I can handle it." Oh, it was going to get worse.

After breakfast the bus took them nearly a mile to another brick building with a sign, "Recruit Intake." Once again they shuffled off, but this was the last ride they would get for several weeks. From now on everything would be on foot. They were ushered into a large room with desks, and directed to fill out the necessary information requested. Larry was glad that he had brought photocopies of all the important documents. When the question of race came up, he marked "Native American." Since he had no allergies, medical or criminal history, he finished early and took the document to a process line. There, a file was made to hold all his photocopies and establish his direct deposit account. He was fingerprinted, and directed to the next room down the hall, where a dentist gave him a quick examination and sent him on. The barber had little to work with since Larry always wore a very short sport cut. But there was still enough to cause him anxiety when it was gone. He wouldn't need to worry about a hairdryer for a while. Then the morning turned serious.

He was directed to something of a locker room where he was told to disrobe. Even though he had anticipated the moment, there was the understanding that this was his separation from the old Larry. He had worn discard-able clothes, knowing that they were going to the Salvation Army. It would be a while before he needed civilian stuff anyway. Even Louis Lamoure went into the donation box. A doctor gave him a quick physical exam. Now that he was naked, a shower was next in line. Then a corpsman told him to close his eyes and hold his breath. A light dusting of insecticide powder was more an insult than a hazard. Larry was sure there were no lice on him. "Listen and obey" he reminded himself, as he used a towel to dry off. He wrapped it around his waist as he progressed to the next room.

Finally, he was issued clothes: three pair of green boxer shorts, socks and T-shirts, upon which he stenciled his name. A rain poncho, hat, two pair of dungaree green shirts and pants also received stencils. A pair of work boots, dress shoes and a set of dress tans completed his wardrobe. He received another towel, a green wool blanket, and a duffel bag to carry it all. He placed his wallet, with the ten five dollar bills he was allowed to bring, in one of the socks for security. A Corporal finally said, "Well, that takes care of the first step. Now go to building G33 and pick out a bunk, but do not unpack your duffel. Wait for your DI; he'll take over for the next ten weeks. Welcome to Fort Benning Company 91. Now go out the front door and turn left. Building G is about two blocks on your right hand side of the street, third floor, dorm 3. Good luck."

Larry headed for the front door, and three other fresh greens dropped in behind him, all carrying their duffle bags. They commented about the warmth of the morning and the uniqueness that from the four different corners of the country they had a common destination and purpose. One of them asked, "I wonder what the 91 means?" Larry answered, "I'll bet it means that ninety other companies have come through here so far this year. If that's the case there have been nearly ten thousand recruits in the last five months. I don't feel so alone." He chuckled, knowing that Fort Benning was the largest city he'd ever been in. He was anything but alone.

One of the others said, "Yeah, if they made it, we can too."

Another said, "No worries, Mates," in his best Australian imitation. It was easy to find G33. Larry scanned the large room and chose a bunk at the far end, thinking that it would be furthest from bathroom noise and smell. Two of his fresh companions came with him. He noticed several bunks had duffels on them. Perhaps they belonged to the group of smokers he had noticed near the front door. He also noticed five lockers that were already full of unpacked clothes. He found a copy of the Army Service Manuel on his bunk and decided to read a bit of it as he waited for the next step.

DI Custer

Men continued to gather for several minutes until a general surge of the outside people came in. The Corporal shouted "Attention!" And most recruits were wise enough to at least stand. A trim athletic man wearing a ton of stripes on his sleeve announced, "My name is Master Sergeant Bradley Custer. As your Drill Instructor, I'm going to be your momma for the next ten weeks. I promise you won't like it, starting with these five gentlemen." He pointed toward the full lockers. "Corporal Powell, would you please get their names. Gentlemen, you have one minute to repack your duffle, starting right now! If you fail to do that, you can retrieve your clothes from the Salvation Army and return home. I will not tolerate men who cannot listen." There was a mad scramble to complete a difficult task. When it was accomplished the DI said, "Gentlemen you have just earned the right to stay here another day. You will, however, be on latrine duty for the rest of this week, cleaning the toilets, sinks, and mopping the floor of the head before roll call at 8 a.m. sharp."

He walked up the side aisle of the dorm. "Now which one of you is Larry Crown?"

It was like a punch in the gut. With some trepidation, Larry raised his hand, saying, "Right here, Sir."

"Your information tells me you are Native American. How much?"

It was not a usual question, but one that he could easily answer. "Fifty percent, Sir."

"What tribe?" The question felt barbed, nearly hostile.

"Nez Perce from Idaho, sir." Larry was thinking as fast as he could, and decided this must be some sort of hazing humor. He relaxed.

"Have you or your tribe been in the Dakotas recently?"

Then Larry got it. The Drill Sergeant's name was Custer, like the Last Stand. "No Sir, we stay out of trouble." A general relief spread over the room as it became understood that this was not an actual confrontation.

"How is it," the Master Sergeant asked, "that a Nez Perce from Idaho has such an English name as 'Crown'?"

"Sir, my grandfather was Daniel Crow, he died at Bataan. My uncle was John David Crow, he died on Omaha Beach. They were Wind-talkers. My father added the 'n' to the family name to break the cycle. He thought it made us sound more proper."

The DI had slowly approached Larry. He was able to reach out and pat his shoulder, saying, "Good, I can sleep without worry that I might lose my scalp. I'm proud to serve with such a distinguished family." It had been a ploy by the DI to establish a connection with a new company, to show both muscle and humanity.

Larry said, "Thank you, Sir. I'll try to be very careful." He didn't dare laugh. He recalled his uncle's advice.

So began the journey of challenge and achievement for Larry. The Corporal demonstrated the proper placement of clothes and personal effects in the locker, how to fold the blanket so the stencil was easily identified. There was the inevitable inspection each morning to make sure these basics were learned and adhered to. They jogged to the armory where each recruit was assigned an old nine pound .30 caliber Springfield rifle. With it, they learned to do a synchronized 16 count manual, and it would be carried wherever they went for the next five weeks. The Springfield also came with the warning that if they should happen to drop it, the consequences would be most unpleasant. They learned basic marching configurations and movements. Then there were hours of tests. The Army wanted to know where best to use its personnel. Each recruit was given a notebook, filled with information. Larry learned to read ahead to understand the upcoming assignments, or schedule of inoculations. He understood that with this information, he could be better prepared than the average recruit who wanted to take a more accidental path. So each evening, after washing his clothes on the laundry table at the side of the building, he either wrote a letter home, or read his notebook or manual. Of course there was ample food every meal. Larry started pacing himself, realizing he was eating much more than he did at home.

His first run in occurred in the fifth week. They had just received their second round of inoculations and some were a little achy from them. The Corporal brought in a mail pouch just before evening chow. He was calling out the names of those fortunate enough to get mail. When he called out, "Crown," he sniffed the envelope and waved it in the air. A tall recruit by the name of Thomas grabbed the envelope and flaunted it in front of Larry, daring him to try to rescue it. Larry just shook his head, holding out his hand.

"Take it from me, or lose it, Tonto," Thomas jeered.

Larry shook his head, holding out his hand.

"Screw you, redskin." He tore the letter in half and threw the pieces toward Larry.

As he angrily picked up the pieces, Larry said, "Pay-back is going to be a bitch, Thomas."

The taller man would have charged, but the Corporal intervened. When the dust settled a bit, he said to Larry, "You did the right thing. We don't need to fight our own people." But Larry was already planning.

He used a little Scotch tape to reconstruct Sue's letter. He could almost hear her chuckle as she told him about a successful first attempt at sharing their song. "Don't you dare misunderstand, Larry. This is not written about you, but because of your thoughtful insight. I think I have a western hit. It's called, 'Somewhere's Callin' to Me.' The first verse goes: 'Now you went and done it; you got on my last nerve. You broke another promise, straight and narrow took a curve. I'm down at the bottom of nowhere, there's nowhere else to go, I'm tired of lame excuses, empty dreams with nothin' to show.' Then the refrain goes: 'Somewhere's callin' to me. I know it's all up hill, with plenty work, that's true. But somewhere's better than nowhere, as long as I am free from you.' Can't you just hear Patsy Cline singing that? Thanks for the idea in the first place." She told him a bit about her school and some of the other song writers, and asked questions about his progress. She signed it "Your devoted friend." Larry smiled broadly. It appeared he had forgotten the encounter with Thomas.

In the morning there was always a panic to get to roll call. As usual, Thomas was one of the last ones out of the dorm. He was hurrying down the stairs when he suddenly felt his rifle shoulder strap release. He tried to grab it, but only managed to knock it further down the stairs. There was a loud clatter as the barrel hit first, then it cart wheeled through the air and crashed onto the stock. Those nearby leaped out of the way. The horrified recruit saw the stock of his assigned rifle break into pieces. A crowd gathered to witness the wreck.

"Jesus H. Christ, Thomas," DI Custer bellowed as he came on the scene. "What kind of idiot are you? I ought to send you home to see if your momma can grow you a brain!" There were other comments about his manhood that Thomas didn't hear as he was scrambling to pick up the pieces. Finally the Master Sergeant said, "Can your little brain recall how to find the Armory? It's only a mile and a half from here. Instead of breakfast this morning, you carry every piece of that broken rifle over there and get a replacement. If you are not back by 0900, you will miss lunch as well. Now get out of my sight!" His eyes were searching the ring of by-standers for Crown. He had no idea how it had happened but he was fairly convinced that pay-back was in fact a bitch.

There were many in Company 91 who shared that suspicion. The larger lesson however, was that because of one silly prank, a man's military career may very well have been side-tracked. Thomas would now, at best, be on the DI's shit list, which was a permanent demerit. They understood that they were no longer in high school, that every decision here was serious. Most of them also knew that messing with Crown was a poor idea.

When the test scores came out Larry was very satisfied. He was in the top twenty, thirteenth to be exact. They went through fire fighting training, first aid, gas mask, and Rope Bridge building. But Larry's favorite for just plain thrills was the tower at the pool; it was like jumping off a three story building. Several of his peers had trouble with that, and a handful didn't know how to swim.

Marksmanship was also an enjoyable test. Right after lunch one afternoon they went to the indoor range where they were introduced to the 1911 .45 caliber sidearm. The Gunnery Sergeant demonstrated field stripping and cleaning the pistol. "You'll be able to do this in your sleep before you graduate," he forecast. Larry shot a qualifying round on his first attempt, and added another black on his second. When they went to the outdoor range, he did about the same with the M1 at a hundred yards. He was just average. But with the Browning 30.06, he was outstanding. At 100 yards, he went ten for ten on his first attempt. There were six others from Company 91 who did as well; Thomas was one of them. The Gunnery Sergeant asked if they would be willing to try qualifying for a marksman medal at 300 yards. They all agreed.

Since Larry had been the first to qualify; he was up first. He was aware the sights on the long gun were set for 100 yards and there was a breeze blowing from left to right. He asked the Gunnery Sergeant if he could have a provisional round to determine the range. It was granted.

Larry was just getting into the prone position when Thomas said, "Hey Crown, I'll bet you ten bucks that I beat your score." He still felt that somehow Larry had gotten the best of him several times in the past weeks, and was trying to rattle him.

Larry answered without turning around, "Come on Thomas, you know gambling is not allowed here. What do you want with more latrine duty?" Apparently rattling can go both ways.

"O.K. Tonto, how about loser takes the other's KP duty?" Once he had started, he felt he had to finish.

Larry held about six inches high and six inches left. "Provisional!" he called clearly.

"Ready on the firing line!" the command followed; "Fire one!"

The Browning barked. The spotter in the ditch in front of the target marked the hit just in the black at three o'clock. "Shooting five," Larry called clearly.

The Gunnery Sergeant called in reply, "Ready on the firing line. Fire five!"

Five rounds were fired at intervals that allowed the spotters to mark the hits, all in the black. Larry had held six inches high and about nine inches left. He accomplished a center grouping that could be covered with a playing card. None of the other marksmen had more than three in the black, and those were widely scattered. Larry was happy not to have the KP task for this week. It led to the final confrontation with Thomas.

The Company jogged the four miles back to their barracks. DI Custer had just told them they could have a few extra minutes before supper to clean up. He then said, "Dismissed," and with scarcely a pause. Larry heard him shout, "Crown, down!" Out of the corner of his eye, Larry saw Thomas's fist. A sucker punch was being thrown at him. He didn't have time to avoid it, but took a glancing blow on his eyebrow. He felt the impact, and was immediately woozy from the blow, but as he was spinning out of the way, his hand closed on Thomas' wrist. He continued to spin, pulling his attacker off balance, while his other flailing hand landed on the elbow and forced Thomas down toward the concrete street. The arm bar acted as a lever, increasing the force of the attacker's fall. Without the use of his right hand, he couldn't protect himself very well and landed face first on the pavement, spitting blood and teeth. Larry released his hold and staggered away, blood running down the side of his face from a deep cut, but a lesser injury than the one on the ground.

The Corporal was directed to accompany Larry, holding a small towel to the side of his face, to the infirmary for medical attention, while Mr. Thomas was taken to the stockade. He was no longer a member of Company 91. His Army future was in question. As DI Custer helped the unstable man stand, he said, "And to think that all of this has come from playing grab-ass with a girl's letter. How damned sad! You might have been a real credit to your family and country, son."

The last two weeks of basic training, called Military Occupation Specialists (MOS) by some, was hectic and focused. Drills were more intense, and classes had the urgency of final opportunities. Larry met with a placement advisor who presented him with a choice. Since Benning was a One Station Unit Training Center (OSUTC) he could take his Advanced Individual Training (AIT) on this base. His options were between the 194th Armored Brigade were he would be trained in Sniper warfare, or the 198 Infantry Brigade, where he would be trained in Logistics with the Third Squadron, 1st Cavalry Regiment. His experience with driving a flat bed hay truck, distinguished him as a top candidate for motor pool automotive training. He wondered if his shop teacher, Mr. Hodges had told them about his Volvo. He didn't wonder at all how his mom would feel if he was trained to carry a long gun and shoot people. He already had a strong hunch about that. He also thought Logistics would help him get a good paying job as a mechanic when he got out. He had thought about it enough to make a choice.

He sent his new address to both his mom and Sue. In the next mail-call he received a letter from Sue telling him about her new song, a country ballad. She liked it and hoped he would too. "Here are the lyrics: 'How could I do it? I let you go, without a kiss to let you know, How brave I think you are, how bold, to bring out what's best in me that I withhold. I should have called you back and told you, I want you in my life as more than a memory. How could I do it, when you mean so much more to me?'" The letter was signed, "Love, Sue." There was no explanation about the song, and Larry had the feeling this one may have been a bit more personal than the first one she sent.

Logistics Training

Graduation was a big deal for some in Company 91. Family members attended, but since it was all the way across country, Larry explained to his folks that this one was only a small graduation. It was not his major accomplishment, so they stayed home. He wondered if this might be the first accomplishment many of these soldiers had achieved. For him it was a morning off to pack his duffle and catch the base shuttle to Kelly Hill where he found the 1st Cavalry Garrison quarters. He presented his orders and was directed to a separate building and the office of 1st Lieutenant Luke Miles, the Motorized Company Commander and his chief assistant, Master Sergeant Manny Gardono. A Corporal gave him a notebook to read, saying, "You've only missed the first two chapters. There will be a dozen more AIT's joining in the next couple days, then we can get into serious work. Roll call is at 0800 in front of the building. You'll get more instructions then." He pointed out the barracks building and told Larry where he could find a bunk and another building where meals were served. It was all pretty relaxed.

The large dorm room was less than half filled with bunks, and most of them were empty. Once again he chose one away from traffic. He unpacked his duffle into the locker, and read the first two chapters. A handful of other trainees came in but made no effort to communicate with Larry, so he kept reading. In the back of the notebook he found a map of the Kelly Hill complex. It looked to him that a tank track circled around the entire hill and would make a terrific morning jog, if the weather wasn't too hot.

Dawn was just getting a good start when Larry opened his eyes, 0530 as usual. He quietly dressed, made a quick stop in the head and jogged into the morning. He was correct, it was a perfect distance to get the day going. When he returned to the dormitory, however, he noticed that his locker was ajar, and he could tell that someone had been through his stuff. There was nothing in there to take, except a few dollars in his sock, and that was still there. His alarm at being invaded was more the insult than anything. He hurried to shower before breakfast, but made a mental note to use the combination lock that had been provided.

The following three weeks was leisurely at worst. The classroom activities were a simple review of the notebook with a quiz on Friday. The rotation of trainees was divided into four squads, mainly for housekeeping and boundary watch. Each afternoon from 1600 one trainee had to walk the school boundary carrying an unloaded M1. His relief came at 2000, then a change again at midnight and at 0400. It was the watch's duty to awaken his replacement, so the whole thing was laughable, but a part of military training, none the less. Larry was in Delta Squad and drew watch about every other week. But he jogged every morning.

On Sunday morning beginning week four, Larry was about three quarters around his jog when he saw a man standing at the fork in the track. It was Master Sergeant Custer, in running apparel. Neither of them was wearing a cover, but Larry saluted anyway. The Master Sergeant smiled and shook his head. "That's not necessary, but it is good to see you, Crown. Are you getting along with the new session?"

"It's going pretty slow," Larry answered with a shrug. But I'm doing well."

"I wouldn't expect anything less," his former DI said. "You are an outstanding recruit. That's why I'm waiting for you this morning." Larry had not assumed their meeting was coincidental, but to hear that it had been planned put him on alert. "To tell you the truth, Crown, I need your eyes and ears at the Motor Pool. We have known for quite a while that something hinckey is going on, but we've never had any trusted intel. If you see or hear anything that seems shady, I want to hear about it. If you will place that rock over there," he pointed to the fork in the track, "on top of the one beside it, I will be here the next morning. Do I need to tell you to be cautious? This could be some really bad stuff, and I don't want you to get caught up in it. O.K.?"

Larry felt a wave of pride as he understood the DI's care. "I'll keep my eyes open, sir," was all he said.

"Perfect. Now pick up your pace so no one might know that you stopped for this conversation." Larry was already on his way.

The odor of corruption

During that fourth week, he established competence driving a box truck, forty passenger bus, and a truck and trailer. On Friday, Master Sergeant Gardono asked him if he was interested in earning some spending money. The twelve maintenance bays were opened to the soldiers on the base who needed work done on their car. "For an oil change, you'll get $10; for plugs and points, $10; and if you overhaul their carburetor it's another $10. The guys that want to do it usually earn fifty or sixty buck on Saturday alone. If you want to work Sunday, there's usually a tip on top of that."

Larry replied that he would very much like some extra spending money, and would work both Saturday and Sunday if he could. He was happy to receive a hundred and thirty five dollars, but not so happy to hear that Master Sergeant Gardono had pocketed two hundred seventy dollars from the same jobs. He was keeping the lion's share of what was being charged.

On Wednesday, Master Sergeant Gardono asked Larry if he was up to a special driving assignment in the evening, "I need someone to drive a bus into Columbus National Golf Course at nine, and then back. It'll only take an hour, then do the same thing again after midnight, for fifty bucks." Larry wondered how much he was charging for the service. "Corporal Todd will go along to help you find it."

"Sure, I'll do that for fifty, did you say for each trip?"

"Don't press your luck," the overweight Master Sergeant chuckled. "Twenty five an hour is great pay for an easy job."

At about 2030, Larry made his way into the maintenance building. A group of men he did not recognize were standing by the green bus, but began to stroll away from it as he began his checklist. He checked the water level, oil, and lights. He recorded the mileage on the trip log. By the time Corporal Todd arrived, Larry was set to go.

The directions were easy to follow. As the bus turned into the large stone entrance, Corporal Todd told him to turn left and go to the back of the clubhouse. "Now back down to the loading platform. Easy!" Larry stopped about four inches from the platform. "Good job,

Crown," the impressed young man said. "Now standby right there. I'll be back in a minute." He went back down the bus' aisle and opened the rear door. Immediately, two men appeared with a dolly, which they used to remove six frosty cardboard freezer boxes that had been placed on the two rear seats of the bus. Larry had to read it backwards in the rearview mirror, but he was sure the word printed on the side of the boxes was "steak".

As they entered the clubhouse doors, a group of young women stepped out, and began entering the bus from the rear. There was little conversation, more murmured wise cracks that caused some chuckling. Larry couldn't be sure, but thought he might have been the object of some of their humor. Corporal Todd closed the door and counted a dozen passengers. "O.K. Crown, take us home." It was true that twenty five dollars an hour was easy money. When they got back to Fort Benning, the Corporal explained to the gate guard that these were dance guests at the Officer's Club. They were waved right through. As the women exited, Larry thought several times that they were wearing far too much perfume. He was told to park the bus across the street in the big lot. He could stretch out on the seats and catch a wink or two because it would probably be a while before the dance was over.

In fact, it was 0230 when Corporal Todd returned to the bus to instruct Larry to warm it up and pick up the ladies where they were dropped off. As they boarded, he noticed the distinct smell of tobacco, booze and a musky body odor. It probably had not been dancing that these honeys had been doing. The trip back to Columbus was quiet. It was 0415 when the bus was parked back in the maintenance building, and the fuel tank topped off. Corporal Todd told him not to worry about any of his class schedules, since his service this night was of greater importance. An hour later, Larry was jogging around the hill. He had a rock to relocate.

Friday was a drizzly morning, but Master Sergeant Custer was there as Larry came around the brow of the hill. His pace was quicker because he had information to share. "Good morning, Sir," he said with little panting. He was in better shape than he had ever enjoyed.

"You called the meeting," the DI chuckled. "You must have seen something."

"Yes, sir. First I worked in the maintenance bay on Saturday and Sunday doing routine maintenance. Mr. Gardono charges thirty dollars for my service and pays me ten. But more important I think he is using the inventory off our shelves and charges them for it at regular prices, and he keeps the money. I haven't seen a receipt, but I heard him give a couple quotes. But the thing I believe you want to know about is that Wednesday night he had me help steal six boxes of frozen steaks, which were delivered to the National Country Club. I think it has been a regular outlet for stolen stuff. Then he had me deliver a dozen women to the Officer's Club, and I don't believe they were there for a dance. At 0230 I took them back to the Country Club. I don't know how many are in on it, but there were several loading the frozen food boxes, and Corporal Todd has been my boss.

"That's a fine job, son" the DI said quietly. "That's more information and quicker results than I hoped for. Now there are two things more. Here's my number at CID. If you get another assignment from Gardono, and can call me, we can arrest you and keep you safe. Then like a card castle I believe this bunch will fold on each other. If you still have the number of that sweet smelling lady that sent you the letter, keep it in the same pocket with mine. That way if you are ever caught trying to make a call to me, you can use it as cover. Second, if you are arrested, don't freak out. It will also be part of your new cover. We can move you to any number of places that need this same sort of cleansing. You are serving your country, son. I am just damned proud of you!" Master Sergeant Custer held out his hand to shake Larry's.

Saturdays and Sundays were routine maintenance days. Larry was especially good at tune ups. Plugs, points and a carburetor cleaning and adjustment made any car drive like new. Gardono had him scheduled as fast as he could go. It was darned profitable for at least one of them.

Something that broke the regimen was tucked in a letter from his mom. It was a newspaper article with a picture of a smiling young couple holding a baby bundle. The caption announced, "Mr. and Mrs. Steve Lucas welcomed a baby girl named Francine, born July 9th," The article explained that Mr. Lucas was planning to continue his education at Washington State University, and Mrs. Lucas was living with her parents-in-law until he graduated.

Two weeks went by, Monday and Tuesday were routine days, but then came Wednesday again. Master Sergeant Gardono called him into his office just after the first class session, and closed the door. He asked

Larry if he was capable of maneuvering an eighteen wheeler. Larry assured him that he had quite a bit of experience with a double axel.

"You don't have to drive it very far, just across the road to Lawson Air Port. The PX is receiving a large shipment that I want you to get. Pick it up about 1500, then bring it here to our test track. The southwest corner is in a depression that is pretty much out of sight. There are three pallets that we need to intercept. With a new Bill of Lading, they will never be missed. Do you have any trouble with that?" He scrutinized Larry's face.

"Sir, my task is to drive what I am told to drive, to where I am told to drive it. You are my Master Sergeant. I don't have any problems with that." But he realized that the three pallets had been sent by someone else who knew about the theft.

"I really hope I can keep you around here for a while. So many of these guys just want to see what they can get out of it for themselves. I'll make sure you get a slice this time." Larry thought he was hearing something from a B movie.

"I'll get the rig about 1330. Will that give me enough time?"

"That's a good plan. You won't lose any sleep over this one."

More than training

Larry tried to stay focused for the next two sessions of the morning. He tried to act as though his palms weren't sweating and his legs weren't shaking, but they were. On the way to lunch he stepped into another dorm to use their hall phone. Master Sergeant Custer answered almost immediately. After identifying himself, he said quickly, "There's a big rig robbery happening this afternoon at 1500 on the southwest corner of the truck test track. I'm driving the big International Harvester." He probably would have said more but the line went dead. Custer had hung up.

As Larry stepped out of the dorm, Corporal Todd said, "Hey Crown, that's not your quarters."

Thinking fast, Larry said, "I should have hit the head before walking to chow."

"Yeah, there's a phone in there too. Who did you call?"

Larry didn't need to try to act embarrassed, he squirmed a bit, reaching into his shirt pocket. "Please don't get me into trouble." He gave the Corporal a sweet smelling piece of paper. "She wasn't home, probably in school. I just wanted to tell her.." he paused as though embarrassed.

"For crying out loud! Gardono said you need a chaperone. I can see he was right. I'm going to be in your pocket for the next couple hours." Then giving back the paper, he added, "Is she as sweet as that smells?"

"Yup. She's cute and smart, and says she loves me. What the heck am I doing in boot camp?" They both laughed and Larry breathed a sigh of relief.

A fast lunch was followed by a slow lecture on tire pressure and rotation. At 1330 on the button Larry and his shadow were at the truck storage lot. When Larry started his check-list, Corporal Todd told him it was all good, he had checked it himself. "Let's get this huge hunk of dog crap on the road." Obviously he was in a hurry. It took longer to get out the service gate than to get over to the distribution warehouse at Lawson Air Port, and find an open bay for the truck. They watched twenty seven pallets of inventory for the PX loaded, then Corporal Todd signed for it and they were on their way back to their rendezvous. It was precisely 1500 when Larry pulled the truck onto the test track and circled to the southwest corner. There he found two small box trucks with men ready to change the load.

The first two pallets, cases of beer and boxes of liquor were apparently going to the same place. Without a fork lift, the pallets were taken apart and box by box were stacked inside the smaller trucks. Even the pallets and straps were removed. It was a well planned and coordinated exchange. Corporal Todd traded the Bill of Lading for an adjusted one, and told Larry to be on his way to the PX. "You did that just right, amigo. Get the truck back by 1700 and you get extra points on your Brownie Badge." If it was meant as a compliment, it fell very short. Larry had been expecting some sort of intervention, that didn't materialize, so he gladly climbed into the cab and fired up the diesel.

At the Base Exchange, he started to back into the first open bay he found on the loading dock, but a Corporal waved him off and directed him three slips further down the dock. "Is this your first time here?" he asked, but not unkindly. "That first bay is for perishables."

"Yeah, Corporal Todd is supposed to be my guide, but he got tied up." Larry was still trying to get control over his scattered emotions.

"I don't remember a Private ever bringing a truck in, let alone by himself. You did an excellent job. Do you have the Bill of Lading?" When Larry handed him the paper, his hands were still trembling. The Corporal chuckled, "You'll get used to it. Pretty soon these big boxes will be as easy to park as your car."

Larry nodded, but his hands weren't shaking because of this. He was still wondering about the heist. They counted twenty four pallets delivered. Everything was copasetic!

He didn't have much of an appetite for supper, couldn't manage to write a note to either his mom or Sue, and wasn't interested in studying, so he decided to take a little run, even though the evening was hot.

In the morning he ran again. When he returned to the barracks, he knew something was out of order. Corporal Todd did not show up for reveille. It was 0700 and most bunks were still filled. Larry clapped his hands and called out, "Wakey, wakey! Our Corporal is MIA, so if you want breakfast, you better be up and about." Some were stirring, and the hungry were hurrying.

At 0800 there was a general nervousness because the leadership was not present, neither Corporal Todd nor Master Sergeant Gardono. Finally, 1st Lieutenant Luke Miles, the Company Commander, appeared calling for the attendance by Squads. There was an absence in Bravo, and two others from Charlie. The nervousness became tangible as voices murmured in disbelief. The Lieutenant called, "Attention!" just as a green jeep with two M.P.s pulled to a stop.

"Who is Private Larry Crown?" one of them asked without a trace of politeness. Larry raised his hand and took a step forward. He was immediately handcuffed and placed in the back of the jeep. As they went after his duffle bag, the only thing that kept him from breaking into tears was that he remembered DI Custer saying, "If you are arrested, don't freak out. It will also be part of your new cover. We can move you to any number of places that need this same sort of cleansing. You are serving your country, son." But at the moment, Larry didn't feel like this was service. His peers were watching him being hauled away like a criminal.

Not a word was spoken as he was driven to building 19, Military Police Main. He was ushered into an interrogation room and the cuffs removed. Larry waited, uncertain what the next few minutes would hold. When DI Custer came in he had a wave of relief.

Wiesbaden as a Corporal

"Good morning, Mr. Crown. It is a busy day around here. We were able to arrest thirteen involved in the PX theft; you're number fourteen. The base news notes will simply announce that in an ongoing investigation fourteen enlisted men were arrested, and given lengthy prison sentences and dishonorable discharge from the service. No names or specifics will be given." Larry nodded, waiting for more information.

"Now about you," he smiled warmly. "You did a heck of a job! I couldn't be more proud of how well you managed that whole experience. Let's begin by agreeing your basic training is complete, Pfc. Crown." When Larry looked surprised, Mr. Custer added, "Oh, the Army has been known to be quite generous, as you will see. You have a choice today. Behind door number one is an assignment to Fort Lewis in Washington State, where you will once again be assigned to Motor Pool management. Door number two is a bit more adventuresome. Instead of surface transportation, you will have a sixteen hour flight to Wiesbaden Germany, where again you will be in motor pool maintenance. CID suspects that is a center for stolen American cars to be distributed across Germany. It is our hope that you can organize the sort of base routine maintenance for the general population that we had here. We need a list of the VIN numbers of the American cars, to compare with those stolen or destroyed in the states. It would be a clear career advancement if we can peel that problem too."

With a wide smile, Larry said, "I don't even need to think about that. I've been to Tacoma, but I've always wondered what Germany would be like."

"Are you positive that is your choice? You didn't consider it very long."

"I thought about how good it felt to put a stop to Corporal Todd and Mr. Gardono's tricks. If that could happen again, I'd feel like I am indeed a peace-time warrior."

Mr. Custer was quiet for just a moment before saying, "The only snag is I need you to be Staff Sergeant Jamal Robert's Corporal for

Wiesbaden. Do you think you can muster a bit more attitude in leadership? I hope you can, because I am having stripes placed on your shirts as we speak. When you get there, a Pfc. Terry Henderson will be assigned to you. Treat him carefully. He is my communication source, and was my roommate at West Point."

The hair on Larry's head tightened as he comprehended that his Master Sergeant was so much more than enlisted. On top of that information, he struggled to understand how a West Point graduate could become a noncommissioned officer. "I don't suppose I will need to salute him then?"

"If you do, we'll all be in the toilet," his DI said seriously. "I think our success here must not make us overconfident. This new challenge is international in scope. There are more and worse bad guys. You must be doubly cautious. Can you do that, Corporal?"

Larry thrilled to the sound of his new rank. "Yes sir, I'll give it my best effort."

"It will take all that and more," Mr. Custer said quietly. Then shifting moods, he said, "Standby here for a while longer. I'll have a car take you across to Lawson. You have a fresh set of tans in your duffle, with a cover. It would be a good idea to change before your flight. It won't be a full flight, but there are several more folks who will be restationed there." He held out his hand, saying, "Good luck, Mr. Crown. I'm praying this will have a victorious conclusion." Larry had never considered the notion that officers prayed.

The waiting room at Lawson was comfortable and to Larry's satisfaction, complete with a large tray of sandwiches. He changed into comfortable new clothes, and then helped himself to a couple Ham and Cheese, with a can of coke. A sergeant invited them to present their orders prior to boarding so he could complete the manifest. He also gave them a paper bag with another Ham and Cheese sandwich with a can of Ginger Ale and a Hershey chocolate bar. It would be supper. The sun was low in the western sky as they rumbled down the runway and lifted into a new episode.

A bit after 0800 they set down on the RAF Mildenhall Base to refuel and change the flight crew, then it was only another three hours to the Rhine Valley. By the time they landed, Larry had both reset his watch, and formulated the automotive ten point safety check that he would try to instigate. Inspecting the lights, brakes, lube and oil, filter, antifreeze, battery, belts, hoses, tires, and wipers, would give him ample opportunity to examine the VIN numbers.

Once again in the waiting room, another sergeant was checking their orders against the manifest and calling out their names. A lanky Pfc. approached saying casually, "Corporal Crown, I've got transportation to your quarters." He nonchalantly walked away, without regard for the Corporal's duffle bag. It was not at all what Larry expected.

In the Jeep, Larry asked, "Is Staff Sergeant Jamal Roberts still on duty?"

"Well, you see sir," the Pfc. nearly drawled, "You need to correct your clock. It's 5:45 here, and we are pretty much shut down for a summertime weekend."

"Is there any routine maintenance being done in the shop?" Larry was trying to learn some of the new parameters.

"No sir. Like I said, we're pretty much shut down for the weekend. In a couple months it will be the beginning of Oktoberfest. You probably lost a day with the dateline." There was an irritating hint of a smile.

Larry finally said, "I'll tell Master Sergeant Custer how graciously I was welcomed to Wiesbaden."

"Thank you sir. I've been trying to work myself back into his good graces after I kicked his ass." Now the grin was definitely irritating. Larry was convinced that they both understood the identity deception that was going on here; but it was significant to only one of them.

Pfc. Henderson drove to an older two story building tucked in a grove of trees, whose leaves were beginning to turn golden. He said again in that drawl voice, "This here is the NCO quarters for the ones who don't want to live off-base. I think there are three others here." He pointed to a building about a block further. "That's our mess hall. Breakfast is from 7 to 9; lunch is 11 to 1; and supper is from 5 to 7." Again Larry thought he was being intentionally irritating by not using military terminology. "I'll pick you up here Monday morning before 9." As he dropped Larry's duffle on the ground, he added, "You're in 14, at the end of the hall. Welcome to Wiesbaden." He drove away.

There was a momentary wave of panic as Larry considered how far from anything familiar he was. But then he thought about his "mission," to establish himself as a Corporal with attitude. He had two days to work on that.

Inside the comfortable building was a pleasant lobby, complete with a map of the base. He could identify a couple possible morning jogging routes. He would work on that too. Room 14 was a definite improvement over the dormitories he had been in. His room had a closet, a single bed, a table and chair, and an upholstered easy chair that promised to be a great place to read. This was the first good thing about this new location, and he was sure there were more. At the mess hall he asked about the location of the PX and learned it was only three buildings away, and open until 2100. He also learned that his American money was good on the base, but Deutsche Marks, called DM, were used off-base. Larry smiled thinking about the stash of cash he had accumulated working in the maintenance bays.

In the morning he found a favorable jogging route along a dirt road that followed a ditch. There was a faint path that joined the road back into the bone-yard of dead vehicles. It was an accumulated mess of old equipment. Larry wondered why it wasn't recycled as scrap metal, or sold to be reconditioned. He'd wager that a resourceful person could have a world of fun in there. After breakfast he wrote lengthy letters to both his mom and Sue trying to explain the sudden move to Germany, and trying to assure them there was no emergency. It still didn't make a lot of sense to him either.

Assertive leadership

Monday morning Pfc. Henderson's irritation continued; he picked Larry up for roll call five minutes after 9 o'clock! They were late! He knew there was no way a West Point graduate would be accidently irresponsible, so he consciously relaxed. The morning might have surprises.

They strolled into an office where four others were seated. Pfc. Henderson said, as they entered, "Our new Corporal arrived safe and sound. Meet Corporal Larry Crown." Then he turned to Staff Sergeant Roberts and said, "I've got a dental appointment." And he walked out.

"Henderson, get your ass back in here!" Larry barked. "I'm not sure what sort of country club you girls have going here, but it is going to see some changes as of today." The other three Pfc.'s got to their feet. Henderson gave the Corporal a deadly glare, but came back into the office. "You may have established a relaxed summertime attitude, but unless the U.S. Army has changed the rules, roll call is at 0800. If that is difficult for you to manage, take the heat." Larry was speaking quietly with intensity. "You may not be too impressed with a reduction of rank," now Henderson's glare was obvious, "so restriction to the base will be the result of your negligence. You will be dressed in issue dungarees, and know what your job is. I know what mine is. I was sent out here to kick your asses. It starts today."

"There are four oil bays, Glendale and Willic, get them cleaned out and inventory all tools appropriate there. Crosby there are four maintenance tables, you can spend the whole day cleaning them and getting an inventory of the tools. Henderson, after you change your dental appointment, you can sweep the entire facility. There are no questions because I made myself clear."

"Now if any of you are interested in making some extra money on weekends or evening maintenance, I'll begin scheduling work for us. With five of us, this could become a popular place. Staff Sergeant, here is an inventory list of material we need from Supply: 10/30 motor oil, oil filters, fan belts, hoses, headlights, and tail lights, that will be kept locked up here in the office. Receipts will be balanced monthly." He met the gaze of each man present, ending with and holding Henderson's. "Gentlemen, it is a new day. We are dismissed."

As the Pfc. trio left the office, Larry said to the Staff Sergeant, "We also need to do an inventory on available motor pool vehicles. I've only had a quick look around, but I don't see a hearse, or ambulance, even old ones. I don't see a tow truck, and I believe your town cars are AWOL too. Is there an accurate count of general purpose vehicles?"

"No, there has been no formal inventory in the last five or six years. My predecessor ran a very loose program. Folks just came over and checked out available vehicles as they had need. I really don't know where those vehicles have gone." He shook his head in honest defeat.

"I suppose," Larry continued, "there has been no systematic records of maintenance or replacement. What have you been doing with your annual budget?"

The embarrassed Staff Sergeant replied, "We've been under spending radically, which is why we have such a small staff, and few duties. Logistics is increasing its budget elsewhere by using us as a buffer."

"Jamal," Larry used his first name uncharacteristically, "things are going to get tense around here. I've been assigned to investigate a much larger issue than the motor pool. If you are in for the duration, I advise you to hang on, because it might get bumpy. It would be easier for you to seek a transfer stateside. How much do you trust the four Pfcs?"

"Glendale and Willic have only been here a couple months. There was a shake-up just about the time Henderson arrived. Crosby has been here about eighteen months, without taking advancement tests. I can't say I know any of them very well."

Larry thought for a minute then said, "I tacked up a couple announcements on the PX bulletin boards, offering a lube and oil change for twenty bucks. The phone number I gave them to call is this office. We'll see what happens." As the maintenance bay got a refreshing cleaning, Larry took a hike through the "bone-yard" of disposed vehicles.

Tuesday morning the 0800 roll-call was marred by Henderson's absence. Corporal Crown reported that he had discovered both the ambulance and the tow-truck in the stripped discarded vehicles. The odometer of each showed less than a thousand miles.

He also had three service appointments for official vehicles. Crosby, Glendale and Willic would each conduct a ten point safety check, and affect a routine lube and oil service. He also had three weekend appointments scheduled.

When Henderson finally entered the maintenance facility, Staff Sergeant Roberts informed him that one reprimand was recorded for missing roll-call, and his assignment for the day was to sweep the entire facility. By Friday morning Henderson had five reprimands and Corporal Crown recommended to Division Commander Major Thomas Howard that the Pfc. should either be incarcerated for thirty days and reduced one rank, or restationed. Larry also had appointments for routine maintenance for twenty two vehicles on Saturday. Both Glendale and Willic were delighted to anticipate seventy extra dollars, and had been prepared to capture VINs along with the other recorded service information. Crosby had a weekend planned off base.

An interesting metamorphosis took place on Saturday. The Corporal opened the facility before 0800. He was spirited in welcoming the appointments and encouraged the other two technicians as they helped work their way through the list. There were two vehicles that simply showed up without an appointment. Corporal Crown made them feel appreciated as well. That positive enthusiasm became contagious, and the three became a bonded team. When they were finished with the appointments, the three celebrated by planning a Sunday visit to the autumn public market in the city. Their bonus of eighty dollars each was more than they expected. Larry was grateful for the washer-dryer in his quarters. The work of the week was evident on his soiled greens. All in all, it had been an outstanding day.

On Sunday morning, Larry used a Jeep to haul ten cases of motor oil and filters to replace what they had used. He made sure clear documentation was evidence of their activities. He also mailed letters to his mom and Sue, and a report to DI Custer that could be read as a narrative of his first full week. It included the list of VIN they had recorded. He had no idea of the disposition of Pfc. Henderson's situation.

Shooting Star Market

A cluster of men in tans waited for the shuttle that would take them into the city center. Shooting Star Market was open from noon until 2100. When Larry heard the Germans speak of Schlossplatz, the annual festive event, he thought it sounded like speaking with a mouthful of spit. Along with a number of beer gardens, there was a host of local venders selling Christmas decorations and seasonal desserts. It was much more than the Flea Market at the Drive-in at home.

The shuttle driver was trying to make the short trip interesting by giving some local information. "The name of our city means 'meadow baths.' At one time there were 26 geothermal springs. About half of that number are still active. Also at one time there were many casinos operating here, but the Third Reich shut them all down. In '49 Spielbank a large modern casino was reopened. The oldest building is the old city hall which was built in 1610. Now that's old. During the war we lost about a quarter of the buildings to bomber raids. Said the other way around, we were lucky to have three quarters of our homes and buildings undamaged by the bombs."

"We have known a lot of change in this place. In 1929 a horse-racing track was turned into Erbenheim Airport as the development of flight was getting started. Eventually in 1932 the Luftwaffe Fighter Squadron 53 was based there. At the war's end the U.S. 1ˢᵗ Armored Division made it their headquarters. Then the Autobahn came through and divided a runway off, which is now a clandestine street drag strip for hot rods on Saturday nights. It's the same place with a lot of different action. Maybe next it will be changed back into a horse-racing track." He chuckled before saying, "Here we are at Schlossplatz, which means 'Palace Square.' The shuttle returns to the base on the half hour until 2130, which is the final run." The door opened and a captive crowd of thirsty men headed for the nearest beer garden.

By the time the first stein was finished, Larry knew that he needed to do more with the afternoon than get drunk. He excused himself saying that he needed to find some Christmas ornaments for his mom.

"I'll see you at 0800 in the morning," he said to his happy buddies, who were not so charitably driven.

The first booth he stopped to admire was that of a crystal craftsman. The delicate decorations were lovely to admire, but Larry pondered the long journey home, and doubted the probability of any treasure arriving unbroken. He stopped to look at some delightful beer steins, which he knew his dad would enjoy, but also knew that the same challenge would prevent their safe arrival. He switched his attention to a booth with furry soft hats that looked warm and comfortable. When he examined the price, however, he murmured, "My gosh, that's a whole month's pay."

He came to a booth that aroused his curiosity. It was called "Earth Warrior or Protector." A large stack of blue plastic garbage cans just like those all over the base was for sale. There were ample directions for their use as composters or downspout water capturers. Their low cost suggested they might be recycled from some other source. Larry decided to look a little deeper into that.

But first, a bakery booth captured his attention with a fruitcake cookie. Three for 1 DM was a bit more than he was planning to spend until he tasted the tangy sweet sample. He enjoyed the cookies much more than the big beer, and they were about the same cost. At the far end of the square he noticed an alleyway with only a few booths, and even fewer shuffling shoppers. Larry turned in to what must have been a painter's corner. The first one was a puzzle of form and color. As much as he tried, he had no idea what the random images might represent. The second one was a number of landscape paintings of meadows and mountain trails. They were pleasant but far from compelling. The third one was of nudes, sort of. Their proportions seemed grossly dramatized and awkward. Larry smiled, thinking that his notion that there is no such thing as an ugly body was not valid with these babes. He strolled on to the final booth where he found a lady in distress. A young woman sat dejected in the corner, and it seemed to him that she was weeping. "Verom?" he asked, running two fingers down his face.

She was wearing a deep blue full skirt with a light blue blouse and a pink scarf over her shoulders. Her eyes were almost as blue as her skirt. When she studied his face, she reflected, "I believe you should have said, 'Varum,' which is the German word for 'why'. Verom deals with mathematics I believe," she replied in very clear English. Her countenance brightened and she sat more upright. "In any language, however, a kindness is appreciated. Thank you for asking. I am so frustrated. I have been sitting here since the market opened and you are the fourth person to stop, and the very first to speak to me." She sort of shook herself, and asked, "May I show you some of my father's paintings? For those who understand the Cubist style they are provocative and insightful. He studied with Herr Paul Cézanne."

Larry looked at the six hanging works of art. The colors were muted and the shapes difficult to identify. He shifted from foot to foot uncomfortably, and the young woman began to cry again.

"I do not expect an American serviceman to be interested in these old paintings. Furthermore what would you do with them, unless you are a collector or curator? I believe one day they will be respected as an important step in art history." A tear traced down her cheek. "But I so sincerely hoped I could help my father. He was an instructor at the university"

Larry asked, "Is your mother employed?"

Her head shook as she took a deep breath. "I was just a very young child. The Russians raged against civilians as well as the military. She was in Hannover teaching music when the they struck without warning. The university building she was in collapsed." A sob escaped. "Obviously the war is never very far behind us, is it?"

"I'm sorry," Larry murmured. "What sort of help does your father need? Is it just the two of you?" He was wondering if there was any practical help he could offer.

"It is his breathing. He must have expensive inhalers every day. His pension will pay to see the doctor, but not the pharmacist. And yes, it is just the two of us." She peered directly into his eyes.

Larry shrugged slightly. "I only have 40 DM with me. Would that help?"

"That would cover his inhaler for more than a week," she answered hopefully. "Will you take all six, then?"

Larry didn't know how to answer her question. "I was offering the money," he hesitated, "as an assistance."

"For a serviceman, you are especially kind, or mistaken in what I am offering. I am desperate to help my father, but not desperate enough to beg, nor become involved in other complications. Thank you for your concern." Her eyes never left his face.

"Then, may I purchase your paintings for 40 DM?"

"Yes you may," she answered quietly.

"If you are in this same stall next Sunday, may I purchase six more if I bring 50 DM?"

The beginning of a smile turned up the corners of her mouth and a twinkle in her eye underscored the truth when she said, "Yes you may; with gratitude."

"Does your father have many pictures to sell?" Larry asked with a similar lightness.

"Dozens," she answered with a chuckle.

"Perhaps one day soon you may have enough confidence in me to allow me to come to your home for the paintings. I believe soon the Shooting Star Market will be over."

"Perhaps that would be a wise convenience," she said.

As Larry handed her the Deutsche Marks, he said, "By the way, my name is Larry Crown."

"Larry I am honored to meet you. I am Estella Laven, and my father is Heinrik." She held out her hand, saying, "I hope I see you again next Sunday. Their handshake was gentle, but both of them were aware of the strength of the other. With her free hand she presented the six paintings in a cardboard carrier with strong handles.

A purpose for prosperity

He returned to base in time to fill a tray with supper. Then in his room, he looked closely at the paintings, still having difficulty in recognizing shapes or forms. He did, however, find a card on the back of each work, identifying the date and place it was painted, and the name the painter had given it. That was helpful. He realized that he was looking at a reflection of the anguish of war, through the eyes of one who had survived it. The six works took on a deeper and more significant meaning. By the time the lights were turned off, he had become familiar with each one, and grateful for his accidental discovery.

There was a more normal rhythm beginning in the motor pool. Roll-call was a time of assignments and by this second week, there was a growing list of vehicles that needed service. Staff Sergeant Roberts guessed it was because folks were just waiting, and tired of doing the service jobs by themselves. There were enough appointments to keep the Pfc. trio busy, or at least occupied.

On Wednesday Larry received a request from a 2nd Lieutenant to do a minor tune up on his Plymouth Belvedere slant six after hours. He would pay for the work. Larry responded that if the vehicle was in the motor pool by 1600, he could have new plugs and points, a carburetor tune and a lube and oil change by 2000. When Lt. Charlie Ruger came for his car, he was glad to pay $10 for parts, and $20 for labor. He told Larry that he also had a big block Dodge that could use some of the same attention, if he could bring it in Thursday evening.

When the black Dodge rolled in, Larry recognized immediately that it was not a family car. The built in roll bar and safety harness said "street racer." He also noticed that it had been repowered with a Ford 360 V8. He recorded VIN and motor serial identification numbers as he was going about his chores. When Lt. Ruger came back to pick up his car, Larry pointed out that he had given the carburetor a bit more juice. It had been running pretty thin. "I'll bet when those two other barrels kick in this old boy gets up and dances!" He was thanked for his service with a $10 bonus. As he was cleaning up, a warm smile stayed on Larry's face because in two evenings he had earned enough for six more paintings.

Friday, when Waste Disposal came around to remove the cans of waste oil, and leave six new ones for next week, some of the puzzle pieces began to fit together, Larry remembered the stack of blue cans in the market. He was pretty sure they were the same cans that had removed garbage and grease from the galley, as well as the motor pool's dirty oil. Someone was making a business from the stolen cans. Once he had thought about the ease these containers had going through the gate inspection, he wondered what else might be going out inside them.

Saturday morning there were two cars waiting for Larry to open the facility. He had scheduled twenty six for the day, and eight for Sunday morning, and if last week was any evidence, they might have a couple more trickle in. Larry had developed a check-list for their own benefit. When the oil and filter was refilled, and all the plugs replaced, the pit person would call-out, "Check-list!" The one nearest would begin, "Radiator?" "Check!" "Washer?" "Check!" "Oil fill?" "Check!" "Belts?" "Check!" "Hoses?" "Check!" "Battery?" "Check!" "Lights?" "Check" "Brake lights?" "Check!" "Wipers?" "Check!" "Tools?" "All present and accounted for!" "You're good to go!"

It was an effective check-list, and entertaining for the folks waiting for their vehicle. By the end of the day, they had serviced thirty one cars, and had VIN numbers for all of them.

Sunday was a cold drizzly day. The three hurried to finish the list of appointments, plus the four who had shown up without one. Monetarily speaking, the trio thought this was the best of all assignments, with a little work, then a lot of beer garden. At the PX Larry purchased a tan winter raincoat and an umbrella for his Plaza Square visit, hoping that Estella would be in her booth.

In fact, she was waiting for him, protected from the rain by a gray raincoat. "You remembered," she said cheerily. "I was afraid you might change your mind about the paintings." She held out her handshake for a greeting.

He opened a paper sack containing three fruitcake cookies. "How could I forget you when these tasty cookies are so nearby?" He offered her one then enjoyed one himself as they stood in the shelter of a canvas roof. "How is your father today?" He was genuinely interested in both Lavens.

Her eyes were happy as she replied, "He's resting comfortably. He wants me to express our gratitude for your generosity." She finished her cookie with a smile.

Larry wanted to chat with her, about anything, so he asked, "Estella, are you in High School?"

"Our education structure is a little different" she answered a bit guardedly. "I'm just finishing Form 14, which means I can begin at the University in the fall. As a dependent of faculty, I will be tuition-free. I don't think I could attend otherwise." She hoped that answered his question so they could speak about the paintings.

"Tell me…" he thought he detected a hesitance on her part, "about the paintings you have brought for me." He watched her relax and knew it was the correct question.

"These were painted in the years before the stormy wartime. I believe you will see a lightness and joy in these. I should have told you that father has placed an explanation card on the back of each work."

"I found them," Larry said brightly. "Their names helped me understand the mood and surrounding story they contain." He was happy to sound a bit informed.

Estella was quiet as she studied his face. "Larry Crown, you are unlike any Army person I have met. They all seemed to have only one or two things on their mind. You seem calm to me." She thought for just a moment. "Yes, less possessive. Is that the right word for it?"

"I think I know what you mean. Aggressive people seem to forget that we are guests in your country. It's easy to think, because there are so many of us and we are armed, that we can take what we please. I hope that is never the case with me." He was quiet as they listened to the soft rain on the canvas overhead, and the run-off splashing on the stone street.

Now it seemed to Larry that Estella wasn't in a hurry for their time together to end because she said, "I believe there is one more cookie in your sack. May we share it?" He was certain she would have a musical laugh and hoped that he might hear it soon.

"Yes, indeed," he chuckled. Offering her the sack, he suggested, "You divide it, and I will choose which half is the larger."

When he made his choice, she said playfully, "You played a trick on me by taking the lesser. Thank you. I adore these Yuletide cakes, and get to enjoy them so rarely." She savored the last bite.

Larry knew it would become awkward for them both if he tried to stretch the time more, so he took out his wallet. "Do I recall you promised six paintings for 50 DM?"

"And do you recall that I said I would very much appreciate your generosity? Especially since there has not been one other shopper here today. This means that my father will have another restful week, able to breathe freely." She reached behind the sheltering fold of canvas to produce another cardboard carrier filled with paintings. As she handed it to Larry she said softly, "I do not want to presume, so tell me about next Sunday."

"Will your father still be in need of an inhaler, and will he still have some paintings to sell?

"Yes to both questions," she answered with a voice soft and warm.

"Then it will be my genuine pleasure," Larry said matching her tone, "to continue my collection of Cubist paintings, unless the price is frightfully increased."

She knew he was being playful, so she attempted to match him. "Sadly, we find the cost of delivery unmanageable." She offered him a slip of paper with her address. "We live about three kilometers northwest from here, in the Nordenstadt Borough just on the way to Frankfurt. I have written easy driving directions." Then not sure how much more kidding would be appreciated, Estella continued, "I have come to trust you completely Larry Crown, and look forward to next Sunday greatly."

"I do as well," he softly replied. "Six paintings for 50 DM?"

She offered her handshake, but found herself wishing for an embrace. Inwardly she smiled; it was probably the result of the fruit-cake cookies.

Love or loneliness?

All the way back to the base, Larry replayed their conversation, the look of her pretty face and warmth of her hand. It was ridiculous to be this attracted to a girl he had seen twice for what, a half hour? Then he asked himself how many other girls had he chatted with in the past five months? None! No wonder he was so charmed to be in her presence. She was attractive, and he was attracted. "It must have been the fruit-cake cookies," he said out loud. He enjoyed an early dinner with time to do his laundry, and write letters to his mom and Sue. Curiously he had not received any mail from Sue since leaving Benning. He wrote another report to DI Custer, making sure he included the VIN numbers from even the most current lube work. He also shared with him his suspicion about the blue plastic garbage containers.

Larry was awake at 0530 intent upon a morning run. It was dark and rainy outside, and his intention was rapidly evaporating. Instead, he decided to examine the paintings he had acquired. He opened one at a time, trying to see the painter's motivation. Then he read the card that accompanied each one written in Heinrik's own hand. The longer he looked at each one, the more fascinating it became. Larry realized that by the time he was ready for breakfast, he was invigorated and feeling a positive flow of energy. He wondered if the paintings were having an effect on him or if he was having a flashback to fruitcake cookies.

Roll-call was something of a challenge. Staff Sergeant Roberts was surprised at the volume of activity that had been accomplished during the week, especially in the off-duty time. Glendale and Willic were in poor shape to do any physical labor. They were pretty hung over, and Crosby appeared to have come out second in a brawl. His face was swollen and a light shade of green. When he walked it was with an obvious pain in his ribs, and the knuckles of both hands were bruised and torn

Corporal Crown ordered Crosby to go to the infirmary for medical attention. He told Glendale and Willic to go to the PX and fill up on black coffee. "Be back here sober at 1000, or be written up. I'll try to cover for you until then." He was sure there were no maintenance appointments before then anyway. The three wobbled out on their assigned duties.

When they were alone, Larry asked the Staff Sergeant if it would be possible to request additional staff from Captain Howard, the Logistic commander. "Pfc. Henderson is obviously not coming back. If we could have two or three replacements, we could operate this place like a motor pool. I'm amazed at how much work we have generated in just ten days. I think many have just been waiting for us to get this ship turned around."

"Are you taking appointments for off-duty work?" The Staff Sergeant was just looking for information.

"Crosby doesn't seem to want extra money, but the other two are pumped with the notion that they can add another fifty bucks for a day in the grease. I think that is how they were able to get enough beer to get sick. And as for me, I am grateful to have a little extra money to purchase some souvenirs for my mom. My paycheck is still going back in a direct deposit to the states."

The Staff Sergeant nodded in understanding. "That sort of explains a few things for me. I've thought you behave more like an officer than an enlisted grunt. I have suspected that you might have been sent here undercover to unravel the problems." He had a friendly open expression. "Whatever works, I'm happy with what has been started, and quite frankly I was a little afraid of Henderson. I'm glad you got rid of him."

"Yeah, he was a puzzle to me, too," Larry said with a smile. "Say, have you noticed all the blue waste cans that leave the base and never come back? I think some have food scraps, some grease from the cookers, and of course there are the used oil ones from our bays. I wonder where they go to be disposed, and why they are not reused."

The Staff Sergeant replied quietly, "I think there are a lot of questionable things that go on around here. It seems no one wants to look very closely at it though."

The Corporal said, "If you would write down a few of the things you are nervous about, I can forward it to my DI from boot camp. He's a Master Sergeant from CID. I'll bet he would like to look into it." Then thinking of a more current situation, he asked, "When can we get the study books for Pfc. and Corporal rank advancement?

I'm thinking if I avoid strong drink, I can stay ahead of Glendale and Willic. Crosby is another puzzle that I'd like to know a little more about." Another busy week was underway, and under control. Just the way we like it!

The week passed uneventfully, averaging just under twenty vehicles a day for routine lubrication. Larry had requests for three off-duty tune-ups. The only surprise occurred at 1500 Friday afternoon. Larry heard Staff Sergeant call, "Attention on deck!" The four men who were cleaning the bays stood still. They were receiving a surprise inspection from Captain Howard, Logistic Commander.

"At ease, Corporal," the Captain said, motioning them to climb out of the bays. Then still looking at Larry, he asked, "How many vehicles have you serviced this week, Corporal?"

"Ninety one, sir, and three off-duty tune ups," Larry was careful to maintain eye contact with the commanding officer.

"Just the four of you have accomplished that?" the Captain asked as he inspected the four oil bays,

"Yes, sir," was the only necessary answer.

"Have you inspected the fire extinguishers?" the Captain asked.

"There are six in the facility, sir; all filled with current inspection tags."

The Captain pulled out a couple tool drawers to find the tools properly cleaned and arranged neatly. "Do you have a trauma first aid kit available?"

"Yes, Sir; there are three; one on each side of the work stations, and one in the office." Larry opened a metal cabinet to show a white container with a red cross.

Turning toward Staff Sergeant Roberts, the Captain said, "This is an excellent surprise inspection, Sergeant. Your work spaces are squared away with no debris evident. Commendations will be recorded for this facility. If I send you three more men, will your output increase?"

"If you send me three more like Corporal Crown, I guarantee it, Sir." He gave a rigid salute, which was casually returned by the Captain.

"As you were, men," the Captain said lightly. "And have a good rest this weekend."

The Sergeant had a wide smile as he said, "Thank you, Sir." He was aware that this first surprise inspection would look good on his record. He was also aware that the credit had to go to his new Corporal.

Serious success

Before 1600, a Major from the Armored Division brought his Chevy Camaro in for an off-duty tune up. Larry agreed to do the work, grateful that he was earning 100 DM, before the weekend. It was also a large block V8 with lots of attitude, with oversized back tires, and little concern for luxury or comfort. The Major was complaining that the engine was running rough and requested a diagnosis. In the process of replacing the plugs and points, Larry discovered a crack in the distributor cap and a short in a spark plug wire. He managed to solder a repair to the wire and strengthen the cap temporarily. He explained to the Major that this facility was not an auto supply store, but he was confident the temporary fix would help smooth the engine until he could more properly care for the repair. He received a $20 gratuity for his diagnosis, and added the VIN and serial number to his growing list.

On Sunday afternoon he missed the house the first time he drove by it. He had been mumbling about the streaky windshield wipers on the Jeep, and promised that he could do something about that, but not just now. He turned around and went back down the long block looking for the house. No wonder it was difficult to find, it was a cottage set back off the street behind overgrown shrubs. When he finally walked up to it, he sensed the neglect that Mr. Laven's illness had allowed. He rang the bell and heard running feet coming to the door.

"You found us," Estella fairly sang. "I was afraid that my instructions…" Before she finished her sentence she gave him a warm embrace, even though there were raindrops on his coat. "Come in please," she invited.

Larry entered a dimly lit room that had sparse furniture and considerable clutter. A thin man sat in an overstuffed chair. He made effort to rise, and had the musky smell of sickness, finally he sat back down, too weak to stand.

"Papa," Estella said quietly, "this is the American soldier I have told you about. He has come to visit you." She spoke in German.

When she interpreted those words for Larry, he thought that was not exactly true. He had not come only to visit but to purchase six more paintings. The visit was bonus. As he held out his hand, he said, "And I didn't come empty-handed." He gently held her father's fragile hand, then he offered a paper sack to Estella. "I made a stop at the market on the way here." When she opened it she found fruitcake cookies. "There are two for each of us, unless you insist on eating one of mine as well." He finally heard her laughter, and he was right. It was like music.

She moved some papers from the sofa and invited Larry to sit down. "I was just preparing a pot of mint tea. May I offer you a cup?" Larry had to remind himself that his emotions were easily stimulated by this lovely lady, and propriety was an absolute must if he expected to be invited back. Her father said, "Es ist serhe gute."

"That would be very nice," Larry answered her. "My mother enjoys mint tea in the evening."

"Papa thinks the cookies are very good," Estella interpreted. Then in a more reflective tone she added, "I also enjoy a cup." She said softly as though reminiscent of her own mother, "especially on a chilly autumn evening." She served them each another cookie with their tea. "You are so very thoughtful to bring these delicacies." They were both feeling the awkwardness of the moment,

Larry finally said, "I've had time to study last week's paintings. You are right, they are brighter and more full of life. Was your mother's name Helena? The softness and green freshness of that one felt like new growth and freedom. The flowing shapes suggest a merging together. I'm thinking there was a lot of love in it."

Estella looked at him for a long moment. "It feels like just a moment ago I said to you that I am surprised at your kindness. I remember that it was a week ago, and yet you still surprise me by your sensitivity. Many have looked at that painting and saw nothing. You didn't know her and yet you can find my mother's affection in it. I will tell Papa how successful he was."

"I am surprised myself at how these paintings affect me. Usually I like to run in the mornings. But on a rainy day, I have found as much new energy and refreshment from studying your father's work. These truly are marvelous." Larry hadn't thought about sharing that with anyone else.

She was afraid he was about to take out his wallet and bring their time together to a conclusion, so she asked, "What part of the United States are you from?" She hoped she wasn't too obvious.

"The state of Washington is in the northwest corner of the country, bound on the north by Canada, and the west by the Pacific Ocean."

That sounds remote and beautiful," Estella breathed a sigh.

"The eastern half of the state is rolling hills and farm land. That's where I lived, in the town of Clarkston." He told her a bit about his home, then concluded by saying playfully, "Now I live in Wiesbaden Germany."

"Do you have a large family there?" she kept the conversation going.

"My father and mother live in the house my grandfather built sixty years ago. I have a sister who is twelve years older than me, and a brother who is nine years older. I think I might have been a surprise baby when they thought those days were over." She snickered at his humor.

"And how long will you be here?" she asked, but not so playfully. She realized her question implied both an interest in new information, and awareness of an ending. She did not welcome that latter thought.

"Well, I'll be in the Army at least two and a half more years. It could be right here." He didn't welcome the conversation of endings either, so he took out his wallet. "You did say six for 50 DM, didn't you?"

"Yes I did," she smiled, "with much gratitude. We are confident that Papa will rest well for another week. The doctor has advised him that this condition is not temporary, but will become progressively more demanding. Soon he will need oxygen. I'm not sure what we will do then." When she shook her head, her curls accentuated the movement.

"Didn't you say that you have dozens of paintings?" Larry asked optimistically. "I've shipped a box home for safekeeping, and mom tells me there is lots of empty space in my bedroom for more."

"But I don't want to abuse your generosity," she answered earnestly.

"What are good friends for," he remained bright, "I want to help however I am able." He gave her a slip of paper with the telephone number of his desk in the Motor Pool. "Just in case you need to contact me during the week," he said with a friendly grin.

She placed her hand on his chest, saying, "This is the third week you have been our savior. I don't know what else to say besides 'thank you.'" She allowed her hand to remain there, warm and pleasant.

"You are most welcome," he said. "I am already anticipating next week. May I return for more paintings next Sunday afternoon?" He offered her the 50 DM.

"Please, please do. I will look forward to that too." She turned to find the bundle of paintings in a cardboard carrier. Her hip brushed his leg and he was aware again of her slim but muscular body.

"What is your favorite cookie, if I should happen to visit a bakery?"

"Everything is so good," she giggled at the thought. "Have you ever tasted a chocolate éclair? It has a creamy center and a rich chocolate coating. I suppose that would be my most favorite, if I had a choice."

Larry started to turn toward the door, saying, "auf wiedersehen." Mr. Laven raised his hand in a brief farewell.

Estella wrapped her arms around him and stopped him. Against his chest, she whispered, "Good bye, just until next Sunday." There were tears in her eyes.

All the way back to the base, Larry was thinking of words to a new country song, "I've got a feelin' I'm feelin' a feelin' like I've never felt before." As pleasant as it was to reflect on her warm embrace, her trim athletic body, Larry pondered if this was another time when he would wind up over his head with intense feelings that he couldn't manage. He concluded that all he could do was be forewarned and cautious.

Compassion or just passion?

December days were so short it was still dark when the base was bathed in the recorded order, "Ah-ten-shun!" and a bugle played the flag raising. Walkers stopped and turned toward the flag center. Cars and trucks stopped, all who could, saluted the flag. It may have been Larry's favorite part of the day. Wiesbaden was considerably smaller than Fort Benning. Perhaps the importance might have been because for these brief moments, they were all united in a patriotic action. They were reminded what they were doing there, and why.

At roll-call Staff Sergeant Roberts introduced three new Pfc.s assigned to the Motor Pool: Anderson, Ortega, and Powell. They had little experience, so they would shadow for a week, as training. Corporal Crown informed them that they had a pretty full complement of appointments. "For the rest of the winter," he instructed, "we will replace all windshield wiper blades. If anyone asks about it, simply tell them it is our new safety campaign. Who can fault safety, right?" He then explained the opportunity of off-duty work for extra cash. "If anyone is interested, let me know." So began another routine six and a half days of labor, and thirty minutes of leisure with Estella.

By Christmas Eve Larry had sent three more boxes of paintings to be stored in his bedroom. He also sent a box of German souvenir presents for his family to enjoy. He asked the cook if it would be possible to have some containers of the dinner that he could share with a civilian invalid and his daughter. The cook explained he would fix a care package only if Larry promised to return the empty containers.

When Larry carried the box of dinner into the Laven's cottage, Estella was quite surprised. "You told me you would provide us some food, but this is marvelous." In the kitchen, they prepared plates with turkey, mashed potatoes and gravy, green beans, cranberry salad, and yeast rolls. The container of apple crisp made her giggle with joy. He had even purchased a bottle of Riesling to make it celebrative.

It was not an easy chore to help her father to the table, now that the oxygen bottles were his constant companions. But with a simple Christmas decoration for ambiance, all three of them had tears of gratitude. Larry asked Estella if it was their custom to share a grace prayer. When she answered, "It is a special part of the feast," he asked if she would say it. "Only if we hold hands," she replied. Larry hoped it would be a long prayer.

Eventually plates were emptied, happy Christmas memories shared, left-over food, enough for two days, placed in the refrigerator, and containers washed. Larry had stretched his visit as long as it appropriately could. Now he was already anticipating next week. "May I provide another dinner for the Happy New Year?"

"I would very much like that. My father wonders if you are courting me. I told him you are interested in the paintings, and we are just friends. But he says I do not look at you as a friend, but with affectionate eyes."

"Your father is an artist," Larry said quietly. "He sees what others may not."

Estella came across the narrow distance between them. Wrapping her arms gently around his shoulders, she kissed him ever so sweetly, lingering in the enjoyment. "I think so too," she finally said.

Larry finally backed away, a bit. "Estella, I must not take advantage of your generosity either. I must not complicate our friendship." He took out his wallet, which was a signal for departure. "Did we agree on 6 for 60 DM?"

In November, Larry had taken a three day diesel training course in Stuttgart. As that information became known to those who needed a diesel injector tune-up, evenings and weekends became more specialized for him, and more lucrative. Almost every evening he was in the service bay, and weekends he could schedule four appointments and still have Sunday afternoon free to visit with Estella. From his point of view it was all about her. From the Army's point of view he was a Corporal intent on advancement. An envelope under the drawer in his room had grown fat on his off-duty activities. Aside from his own PX needs, and the paintings, he had accumulated 780 DM, and hadn't touched his direct deposit account in the States.

On New Year's Eve, the cook grinned when Larry came in with a small box. Obviously he was visiting the invalid artist again. "Are you taking painting lessons?" he asked jokingly.

"Crap no!" Larry answered. "I'm after the painter's daughter." There was plenty of laughter in the galley. But Larry remembered that last kiss. It so reminded him of Silvia, and he remembered the heartache that came from that. The food containers had a generous portion of Lasagna, garlic bread, and Brownies. All he needed to make it a festive evening was a bottle of Rhine Red wine. He was grateful that no one had questioned the Jeep "road tests" he conducted each Sunday afternoon, or New Year's Eve.

A light rain had hung around all day. Larry was grateful for the covered porch as he rang the doorbell. He could hear her footsteps, and the door opened to a dazzling smile. Estella pulled him to her and kissed him again in a way that was far more than welcoming. She took the box as he took off his raincoat. Larry noticed that Mr. Laven's chair was empty.

"Father has caught a cold," she answered his inquiry. "He developed a cough that has tired him. He is in bed, asleep." Larry thought that information was given for more than one reason. The table was set for only two, and candle light made a romantic atmosphere. She kissed him again as they were serving the food onto two dishes.

As they enjoyed their meal, Larry tried to direct the conversation in her direction. She told him a bit about her studies; there were few trips to the countryside, but she had seen two castles. She loved gymnastics, but was getting too busty, which was information that he didn't think he needed. She had dated a few boys from the school, but they were still growing up. All the while she was talking, she was also sipping. When Larry raised the question of six paintings, she told him there were few of the ordinary size left. Beside her father's chair there were four smaller, and two larger ones that he would enjoy. But she urged him not to think about that because it usually meant he was preparing to leave.

As they cleared the dishes there was more kissing, and Estella was obviously affected by both arousal, and Rhine Red. She was a bit unsteady as she pressed against Larry in a way that was meant to arouse him as well. She finished her glass without noticing that he had not even finished his first glass. She invited him into her bedroom, and he offered a counter proposal that they sit on the sofa.

"Don' you think I'm pretty?' she asked as she leaned into him. "I fine you very fine." She started to chuckle, slurring, "I think I said fine two times." She kissed him again wetly. She raised her feet onto the sofa, stretching out, then turning so her face could be against his lap. This was either a fantasy, or a colossal disaster about to happen. "I think you are beautiful," he answered, stroking her hair and neck. "I think about you all the time." She was moving rhythmically against him. "But we must not get too carried away." He slid out from under her and rolled her onto her back, her head on the pillow. Gently he removed her shoes and stroked her feet. A comforter was folded on the back of the sofa; he slid it over her and kissed her gently. "Happy New Year, my sweet friend. May 1962 be an even better year for you." Estella made an effort to wrap her arm around him, but it ended when she seemed to slide into sleep.

Larry smiled a strong satisfaction. He certainly could have ended this evening in a much different way, one far less noble. He had taken the high road, and was very pleased, if somewhat frustrated by it. He placed 60 DM on the table, and the paintings in the Jeep, along with the box of empty food containers.

Trouble

He was still in deep sleep when a heavy knock on his door rolled Larry out into an emergency. He opened his door to an M.P. who established his name, then asked him to come along to the hospital emergency room. "Staff Sergeant Roberts was found in an alley downtown. He was severely beaten, and wants to talk with you before they ship him to Bethesda," the serious young man said.

The quiet trip to the German hospital was opportunity for the M.P. to tell Larry that Sgt. Robert's unconscious body had been found near his car, which was still at the crime scene. "Apparently there were several attackers. It looks like they used baseball bats on him. He has several very serious broken bones."

When Larry looked into his room, he was shocked to see splints on both legs, wide cloth wraps around his ribs and a large bandage over his left eye. Sgt. Roberts had bandages on both hands from defensive wounds and his right arm was in a sling. There wasn't much left undamaged on him. "Sergeant Roberts," he said softly, "It's Corporal Crown."

The unbandaged eye opened, and his mouth murmured something. Larry realized teeth were missing making speaking difficult. He leaned in close to the patient; "What help can I be to you, Sgt. Roberts?" He leaned even closer to hear the answer.

"Fank oo," he made out. Interpreting as best he could the Sergeant then explained that he was following the bluc barrel waste truck; that's where they trapped him in the alley. His keys were there on the side table. He wanted Larry to have the Crown Victoria. After a long pause, he told Larry that the Motor Pool hearse was traded for the Ford. Lieutenant Colonel Brighten from 1st Armored Division brings cars in the transports of tanks from the states. There was someone who would pay a lot more for the hearse than the Ford. Larry knew that it was painful for Jamal to speak, but it was of major importance. "In the file drawers is a file named 'To Do.' It's the pink slip, and my winnings from Saturday street racing. Crosby is in it too. You can have it all, if you get the guys that got me." Larry wasn't sure if the Sergeant was moaning or weeping. It was pretty much the same. He took the keys, and asked the M.P. to take him to the crime scene.

At noon he called his mom and dad. It would be eleven o'clock New Year's Eve in Clarkston. He loved hearing their voices, and told them a bit about Germany. He finally explained about the paintings, which he believed would one day be worth his retirement. That little fib would probably protect them anyway.

It took him most of the afternoon to write a difficult letter to Master Sergeant Custer. It was, after all, a hear-say accusation about some very illegal activities involving a top officer. He explained that Sergeant Roberts had been beaten but not robbed, because he was following the blue barrel truck. It was a deep dark mystery. He finally asked the whereabouts of Mr. Henderson. He was needed to pass along communications. It felt too casual to send pertinent information in such a casual manner as these letters.

Roll-call was just finished with assignments made for the day when the phone rang. Larry answered "Motor Pool," thinking it would be someone seeking an off-duty appointment. "This is Captain Howard's office. He has cleared his calendar for a 1000 meeting in building 8 with Corporal Larry Crown. Please advise him to be prompt." The phone went dead, apparently hung up when they had conveyed their message.

Larry knew there was nothing major to be worried about, so his interest was sharpened, within a couple minutes the phone rang again, and again he assumed it was about off-duty work. It was Estella.

"This is the first time I have tried the number and it works!" She must have been nervous because she was telling him obvious information. "I missed you yesterday," she said softly. "I suppose after such a childish mess, you might not want to come back."

"That is far from the truth. I was afraid you might not want to see me again after our libations," he answered playfully.

"Larry I had to take Papa to the clinic this morning," she said sadly. "He will be there more than a week the doctor tells me. It is an opportunity for me." Larry's mind was racing to understand what she might be after. "My Romance Poetry instructor is taking a group to Paris Wednesday. I'm embarrassed to call you for help, again. The trip costs 300 DM, which I do not have. Would you consider purchasing the final dozen of Papa's paintings for 300? They are larger ones, and I believe the best of all."

His heart felt heavy, for suddenly this delightful and affectionate young woman seemed just like all the other avaricious people looking for an easy score. However, he also felt something very wonderful in her too, so he agreed. "Of course I want to help you. Will you be home from school by 3:30?. I could stop by then."

"Oh, you are my savior again! Yes, I will be home and waiting to see you." She was the light and bubbly Estella again.

"But I must hurry back to the base," Larry added. "I have many obligations to care for this evening."

"To see you and hold you again is all I am looking for."

Larry wished she hadn't said that because it was obviously untrue. She wanted the money.

Sergeant Crown

Everything was running smoothly at 0945, so Larry asked Glendale to answer the phone and get a call back number while he went to Captain Howard's office at Logistic Center. Arriving on time, he was ushered into the Captain's office.

"At ease, Corporal. I won't take much of your busy morning. I just have a couple questions to ask you." Again Larry was trying to anticipate what this might relate to. "Tell me, son, was it your idea to start the ten point service check-list?"

"Yes, sir, to promote efficiency."

"And was it your idea to install wiper blades on all the base vehicles?" The tone of the question was not very threatening, but a little.

"Yes, sir. It is the first step in a base-wide safety emphasis. Lights and brakes will be inspected next."

"And all of that originated with you?"

"Yes, sir. I did get Staff Sergeant Robert's permission before we began, though."

"Yes, I see." The Captain was still as though weighing an idea. "Tell me Corporal, do you think you can keep the Motor Pool operating this smoothly without Mr. Robert's leadership?"

"Yes, sir, we are up and running by the book this morning."

"What I'm asking is, can you take charge of the Motor Pool?"

Larry hardly hesitated before saying, "Yes sir, I believe I can."

"I believe you can too, Sergeant. Consider this a field promotion and add another stripe on your sleeve. If you do as well as I'm hoping you can for the next nine months we will add yet another stripe. I'm hoping I can give you incentive to make this a career posting."

Larry snapped a salute, saying, "Thank you, sir."

Back in the Motor Pool, he searched through the file cabinet until he found "To Do." There were 36 100 DM bills in it! He transferred three of them into his wallet, ready for the afternoon. The Pfc. team of six was perking right along. He smiled as he thought about taking his shirts to the PX for new stripes. "Damn! I'm Sergeant!"

Before he left the base to visit Estella, he stopped at the Air Freight Office to explore the possibility of crating the large paintings. He was told that it would be a bit expensive, but an easy chore. He also stopped at the PX for two chocolate éclairs.

The guard at the gate asked, "Early liberty Corporal?"

"No, sir, off-base business."

"Isn't this Sergeant Robert's Crown Vic?"

"Yes, sir. He's in the hospital. That's my off-base business." It wasn't true, but the guard passed him through without more questions.

As he walked up to the cottage door, he was conflicted. Part of him hoped that Estella would greet him with the passion he had recently received. The responsible part of him, however, hoped to see the demure Estella. It was the latter one that opened the door and shyly invited him in with a tender embrace.

"I recall that you like chocolate éclairs," he said offering her the paper sack.

"Yes, they are my very favorite," she answered with delight. "Come into the kitchen and we will enjoy them now." It was as if she had never thrown herself at him, never smothered him with kisses.

Around pastry bites, she told him of her excitement in the plans for Paris. There would be so much to see and learn, and the joy of being with her classmates.

"How many are going?" Larry asked with some interest.

"One other girl and one boy," she said. "We will be a cozy group."

The pastry was gone and there was no further reason to stay. Larry asked, "Twelve paintings for 300 DM?" He had noticed the stack of paintings standing against her father's chair. When he asked about the health of her Papa, she said simply that he was no better, maybe a little worse. This was not the same caring, tender, gracious woman he had known for the past four months. He took the first armload of six that fit flat in the trunk of the Ford, then six that stood behind the front seats. He gave her the 300 DM and she gave him an ever-so-tiny embrace. Without a mention of gratitude she closed the door. Larry had a bit of a sour taste in his mouth and thought to himself, "I feel another country song coming on." He would have been plain angry if he had known the truth, that it was only Estella and the instructor going to Paris.

What would Sue write about this? "The station's empty, you got left behind, too young to choose, to make up your mind. I'm sorry for you, but not enough to wait, for you to grow up, it's just too damned late. The train pulled out without you, it's a cryin' shame. There's no one to help you, no one to blame. The station's empty, you got left behind." Or something like that.

Surprise inspection

For two weeks Larry did nothing but work, eat and sleep. He was in the facility every morning to turn on the lights and open the door. Then it was appointments until 1600. After that the appointments paid. He usually turned out the lights by 2000. A lot of money accumulated in fourteen days. The trouble was there was no point to it any more. He wasn't acquiring paintings or getting close to a sweeter friend. But he had lots of time to think.

In his weekly letter to Mr. Custer, he suggested an inroad to the Saturday night street racers. If supply could send him a Chevy 426 V8 with a four barrel carburetor, and a spring loaded four speed, he could rebuild the old tow truck. Its body and frame were like new. With dual rear wheels he would have more traction than any hot rod. Without trying it, he only had the hunch, but he was pretty sure it would blow away anything else on the street. At worse, it would recondition an essential vehicle back into the inventory. He also sent VIN and serial numbers for ninety three American cars.

It was the last Wednesday in January, and the rain had finally stopped for a bit. Larry was desperate for a run, so in the early dawn darkness he set out on his familiar path. He had almost forgotten the route. Halfway round he found a man standing in the path, waiting for him. As he came to a stop he recognized Master Sergeant Custer.

"Good morning, sir. Are you out for an exercise on German soil?" Larry didn't know what to say, so he tried to be humorous.

"Good morning, Sergeant. I am damned proud of you. You are every bit the man I hoped you would be."

It was more praise than Larry was prepared to hear, but extremely welcomed. He stood still waiting.

"You've done more than an entire squad of trained investigators could have managed to do," the Master Sergeant praised. "Stand by this morning for a surprise inspection in the Motor Pool from Captain Howard, and a couple other officers. I will be in the mix of record takers. Do you have any records of the work you have done in the past five months?" The Master Sergeant studied his face.

"Yes, sir, I have kept complete records of whose vehicles that were worked on off-duty, as well as routine maintenance." Larry was glad to be able to answer in a positive tone.

"But do you have VIN and serial numbers?" the Master Sergeant pressed.

"Yes sir. By the numbers, sir," Larry answered. He really liked Mr. Custer and hoped like hell that he was righteous. It would be a shame to bust such a good man.

"Then be ready, amigo. I have a subpoena for the Crown Victoria and its pink slip. You know that I hold you completely outside this situation. It will either be Sergeant Roberts or Lieutenant Colonel Brighten from 1st Armored that takes the fall for a great deal of felony charges. If it's Brighten, we might get him to roll over on his accomplices."

Larry wondered what else they might talk about here in the darkness.

"Hey, how's it going with you and the sweet smelling song writer?"

Larry could have said, "For crying out loud! We're standing in the darkness anticipating a surprise inspection and you want to talk about a has-been flame?" But of course he didn't. He answered, "I haven't heard from her since Benning, sir. I'm afraid I didn't make the cut." He chuckled to ease his discomfort.

"That's too bad, Mr. Crown. Her loss! But good things are going to happen for you in the near future. Remember to trust that promise. You are probably not going to be in Germany much longer. CID sees you as a hero. You are going to be a great service to your country. Now carry on! I'll see you in about three clicks. Remember, we don't know each other." They ran into the darkness, in opposite directions.

Just before 0900 Larry saw the entourage enter the Motor Pool facility. He stepped to the door of the office and called in a loud voice, "Attention on deck!" Those in the lube pits climbed out and all six stood rigidly at attention, as did Sergeant Crown. As the group drew nearer, he said, "Good morning, sir, all present and on duty." He saluted briskly.

"At ease, Sergeant. We are here to inspect your books and take into evidence Sergeant Roberts' automobile and pink slip." To the other six, he said, "As you were, gentlemen."

"I understand, sir, please come into the office." He knew where the files were, but made it appear that he was unprepared. "Here is the pink slip for the Crown Victoria. What other files are you interested in examining?" When they told him, he produced a fat file of hand-written pages.

"Sergeant, are these your records? Did you write these from the work you have done either during regular hours or off-duty?" Captain Howard asked.

"Yes, sir. These are my pages with names and dates. This place was run pretty casually and I wanted to leave a more traceable foot-print."

"Do you mind if I take these with me today?"

"I do not mind at all, sir. I wrote them hoping they would be seen and appreciated." Larry didn't seem to be intimidated by all the brass in the office.

"I'll make sure these get back to you, son. I'm impressed that you took it upon yourself to be so organized." As one of the other officers scanned the desk-top calendar of appointments, Larry's gaze caught Mr. Custer's, who nodded ever so slightly.

The Captain asked, "Do you have a hydraulic dolly?"

"Yes sir," Larry answered, not knowing what might follow.

"If you can have a couple strong backs to help you, there's a crated engine in the truck at your loading dock. I believe you requested a rebuild for the Motor Pool tow truck."

"Thank you, sir. It will be another step in making this place five by five." He called Crosby, Glendale and Willic to lend a hand.

"I like your attitude, Sergeant, and what you have accomplished in a short time." He looked at the other officers. "Anyone else have questions for the Sergeant?" Once again Larry caught Mr. Custer's nod of approval. "Then if we have no other business," he looked directly at the Sergeant, "will you bring the Crown Victoria through so we can load it on the truck. It is evidence in an upcoming shit-storm here on the base."

Before Larry had an opportunity to fall in love with the Ford, it was gone. "Funny," he thought," that's just like the women in my life."

Tugger

He did, however, have a new love in his life. With Willie's help, he used a Jeep to pull the tow truck carcass into the back corner of the Motor Pool. With the team of six caring for routine appointments, Larry was free to work most of the day on his trophy rebuild. Only off-duty appointments took him away from it. January was consumed moving the firewall to make room for the larger engine, and making new motor mounts. February accomplished new suspension and drive shaft, plus a header exhaust system. Finally by the end of March the engine was carefully fixed in position, and the cooling system attached, along with all the electrical. When the engine started it was like rolling thunder. Larry got goose-bumps it was so loud when revved up. The six gathered in applause for Larry's accomplishment.

"Hey, Crosby," Larry called, "Let's take this tugger out for a test flight. Do you know someplace we can safely do that?" He was sure that if the Pfc. had street racing experience, he would direct him to the abandoned airfield.

"Yeah, I know a place that rarely has a police presence. It's not far."

Larry was careful to respect the speed restrictions on the way. But once that ribbon of empty concrete was in front of them he asked Crosby if he was ready for the trial. With a big grin he nodded approval. "Three, two, one," Larry pressed the accelerator hard. There was a bit of burning rubber, but like an unstoppable power, the truck leapt forward. Crosby murmured, "Damn!" Larry was pretty sure he was travelling about 120 MPH at the quarter mile mark, because the speedometer was on the post. When he eased off the gas, both men were laughing joyfully.

"O.K. Mr. Drag-man, do you think that was enough sprint to be competitive on Saturday night?" Larry's gaze was steady with no hint of judgment.

"Crap, yes!" Crosby chuckled. "This is a Mother Tugger! My Chevy wins about half the time, and I know this was way faster than mine." Then he added, "And it looks so deceiving, like a old piece of crap."

"Crosby, I never asked about the beating you took when I first got here. Did it have anything to do with street racing?" Larry's gaze was steady.

"Yeah," the Pfc. answered softly, "I had two good runs one evening. The rules of the street are you get paid if you win three in a row. The Staff Sergeant for 1ˢᵗ Lieutenant Shiply made sure I didn't get a pay day. Now I understand that he controls the winners. There are always a couple who make it seem like we all could possibly win, but we won't. It's rigged."

"Is Shiply Culinary Command by any chance?" Larry was beginning to join the dots.

"Yeah he is. How did you know?"

"Just a lucky guess. It seems to me there are some squirrely things that go on in the mess hall. I just want to be cautious. It's good to know who I can trust." Larry asked if Crosby wanted another test run. It turned out better than the first. They decided it would be a good idea to keep the Tugger under wraps on Saturday nights, until whatever storm was coming cleared out the hazards.

On May 5ᵗʰ Larry called home to celebrate his 20ᵗʰ birthday. The most recent letter from his mom had mentioned that his dad was having some health issues. It was just good to hear their voices.

By the end of the month both Glendale and Crosby finished the test and were advanced to Corporal. Crosby was given the responsibility to run roll-call. It was the first time Larry felt at ease with the way the Motor Pool was operating, and there was good evidence that Captain Howard's appreciation was noted, for he asked Larry if he and one other from the Motor pool would attend a five day diesel training opportunity at the Mercedes-Benz plant in Stuttgart. It would mean a two hundred mile Autobahn test of the Tugger, where there was no speed limits.

They were acting like high school kids. Watching the rear-view mirrors, they would see a much faster car closing from behind them. Larry checked the speedometer. He was going seventy miles an hour, on just two barrels of the carburetor. Then as the car pulled alongside the junky looking tow truck, he would press down the throttle and feel the other two barrels fire power to the wheels and the car was left behind in a puzzle. Corporal Crosby chuckled as he said, "I'll bet he thinks something broke on his car and he's slowing down." Larry noticed that the speedometer was posted at 120. He slowed down again to a reasonable speed, and received a questioning look as the auto finally caught up with them and passed by.

The five days passed very quickly with interesting sessions on the advantages of diesel engines, their operation and maintenance. There was perhaps more interest from the hosts who were fascinated by the Tugger. Larry was asked several times if he would take folks on a test run on their track. He never turned down an opportunity, especially when they refilled his gas tank. But when the evenings turned to rich food, strong drink and playful women from the city, he was less interested. He had enough trouble without seeking more. Apparently Crosby didn't have troubles at home for he very much enjoyed the available hospitality.

The storm of justice began to descend on Wiesbaden by the middle of June. Five officers were arrested first, with charges of grand theft, racketeering, dereliction of duty, assault, and conduct unbecoming. Then fourteen enlisted men faced the same offenses. Two deserted rather than face the lengthy imprisonment their crimes would bring. It was also their attempt to enjoy the sizable cache of money their criminal activity had accumulated. It didn't work. When they were arrested they were given even more lengthy prison sentences. The purging came as a surprise to many, a relief to a few, and a huge satisfaction to Sergeant Roberts in his convalescence. Corporal Crosby inherited the opportunity to conduct Saturday night street races, which would result in considerable income for him, and a future career path. It also meant that the Tugger could play occasionally, if not for competition, at least for exhibition.

A time to Grieve

A beautiful summer morning was interrupted by a call from Captain Howard's office. The Red Cross contacted him with the request to send Sgt. Larry Crown home. His father was gravely ill, not expected to live. Larry was instructed to report to the air terminal for a flight to Clark Air Base on Luzon, Philippines. From there he would be flown by air freight to McCord Air Base in Washington, and have a car available from the motor pool for his use on furlough. Larry was surprised how smoothly the plan worked, and how much anxiety he was feeling about its reason.

It was almost 1900 when he pulled the green Ford into his driveway. Nothing had changed and yet everything had changed. His brother's car was the same, as was his sister Jan's. But he was not the same young man who was last here fourteen months ago. He hurried to the kitchen door.

They greeted him as something of a hero home from battle, hugging, kissing, and weeping generously. Finally his mother told him, "Your father had a stroke, a big one. He's been on life support for three days, and we need to make a decision how much longer. The doctors say there is no hope. His heart is still beating, but maybe it's the machine that is keeping everything working. There is no response of any sort." She was lost in more weeping. Michael, Larry's brother offered to drive him to the Lewiston General Hospital, but Larry said he was very familiar with the location of the hospital. They all went in the green Ford.

Larry hated hospitals. They were filled with the smell of chemicals and suffering. A doctor was talking to a nurse in the ICU when the family arrived. He led them into a sterile room with a body of the man Larry remembered as his father. The tubes and wires connected to him, however, became an unwelcomed memory. The doctor explained the extent of the stroke as major. No one said anything so Larry asked, "What prognosis does he have to survive?"

"His survival is doubtful," the doctor said quietly, "and if he does, there is every reason to believe that he will be unable to care for himself, ever again."

A tear traced down Larry's cheek. "Dad would not call that living. It would be hell for him to be an invalid. He would resent that." There was a pause as he considered a more painful question. "Are his organs still viable for transplant?"

"Yes," the doctor said gravely. "The damage was to his brain. All other organs are working properly."

Just then a chaplain entered the ICU and offered to pray with the family.

Larry said, "You can pray for his comfort and our courage as we do the proper thing. He must die with dignity and offer hope to others who are on waiting lists." The rest of the family was surprised by Larry's insight and leadership. They knew he was right, but had been afraid to say it. The chaplain prayed and the doctor said he would get the forms needed to turn off the machine and harvest useable organs.

Michael spoke to the still form of his father, reaffirming love and appreciation for years of family strength. Jan wept as she tried to do the same thing with words of an affectionate and grateful daughter. Larry gave him thanks again for the lessons they had shared, the laughter and stories. He kissed his father's cold cheek. Larry's mom may have had the hardest time. She was not prepared for this to be her last moments with him, but she knew that ready or not, it was. She vowed the love they had always shared would be a treasure forever, and kissed him again. Then the family stood still, lost in their own thoughts and grief.

The doctor came back in with some papers. The air in the room seemed heavy and still. As Larry's mom signed them, Larry thanked the doctor for making it possible for him to be present with the whole family at this moment.

"Thank you, Sergeant, for having the strength to do this proper and very difficult thing. I'm proud to be with you tonight." The doctor was having trouble controlling his voice. When the nurse came back into the room, there was a pause and then the doctor nodded. She switched off a rocker switch and the machine was still. A silent minute crept by. Finally Michael said, "Dad died three days ago. I'm glad he didn't have to know about this."

The drive back to Clarkston was quiet. Michael was impressed when Larry shared that his day actually started on Luzon Island in the Philippines, on the other side of the international dateline. When his mom asked how long he would be home, Larry answered, "It took me two days to get here and will take three for me to get home. Will dad's funeral be in the next five days?"

"We'll make sure it will," she answered. "Your dad said he wanted a short quick funeral."

Back in the kitchen his mom brought out a warm apple crisp cake with ice cream. There was also a fresh pot of coffee, which Larry found helpful. The flight had been tiring, but not as much as this past hour. Coffee might help.

"Mom, thanks for holding on to those boxes I sent. I couldn't figure out what else to do with them." Larry explained a tiny bit about how he came to purchase them. When asked if he was still seeing Estella, he sadly answered, "No, I think she was either more interested in my money, or the guy she went to Paris with. In either case, her dad doesn't have any more paintings to sell. I don't know a thing about art, and at first I just thought these were weird. But the longer I studied them, the more I appreciated his work. I think these will be worth a pretty penny some day."

He tried to think what a responsible person would do. Then he offered, "If you want, I can get a storage unit in Lewiston to get those five boxes and the crate out of your way. There are about a hundred ordinary size paintings in the boxes, and fourteen big ones in the crate. His work was done before the war when the world was beautiful, during the war when it was dark and broken, and then after the war when Wiesbaden was recovering and hopeful. I'm surprised that even if I don't recognize the subject of the painting, I get the mood or feeling it is telling."

His mom was quick to say, "No, don't move them. You told me to put them in your bedroom, but I like them in my sewing room. They're out of the way in the corner, and remind me every day of you. I want to keep them here."

Michael said, "Speaking of pretty pennies, would you be willing to sell me the Volvo? What would you take for it?"

"I don't know. I like that car a lot. I've got over two thousand in it, so maybe that's out of your range."

Michael said, "I'd pay you twenty five hundred, if you'll take payments of a hundred a month."

"Yeah, I could do that. You make twenty five payments and then I'll sell you the car. You have a bad habit of dumping cars, remember?

I want it to be your car, not mine that you wreck." Then he told them about his rebuild of the Tugger and doing 200 kilometers an hour on the Autobahn. For just a heartbeat he wondered about the Motor Pool and how they were getting along without him.

Michael was again surprised by the maturity of his little brother. Larry had been right; he had never had a car, or a lady friend for that matter, more than a year without some big wreck. Maybe it was time for him to grow up too, after all he was twenty nine and still single.

His mom asked, "Is there anyone special you want to see while you're home, son?"

Before Larry could answer, Jan said, "Hey, I heard that Steve Lucas and Silvia are busting up. She's pregnant again and he declares that this one is not his either. I heard she's getting a fat settlement from the family."

Larry said, "No, mom, there's no one but you guys that I want to spend time with. But I'll help you clear out some of dad's things, if it's not too soon." That started both his mom and Jan to begin weeping again. He realized he was tired to the bone and needed a good night's rest. There were hugs around and the promise to begin the day on the right foot.

At 0500 Larry opened his eyes and struggled for a moment to recall where he was. After a bathroom stop, he pulled on cut-offs, a tank top and some running shoes that felt delightfully normal. He took off on a six mile run through familiar neighborhoods, and was back before 0630. He had showered before his mom got up. The coffee was made when she came into the kitchen.

"I forgot what an athlete you are," she said in greeting. He was grateful to give her a warm hug. It had been over a year since he had that morning privilege.

As they enjoyed a cup of coffee, she asked, "It seemed to me that Estella was a special lady to you. What happened? Why is she just water under the bridge now?"

He considered his answer. "She was probably the nearest I've ever been to 'in love'. For about three months I worked hard for six and a half days a week just to spend a few minutes with her in her father's home. On New Year's Eve, she got a bit tipsy and a lot amorous. I both liked it, and big time didn't. I was finally disturbed by her behavior. The following week was when she put the nail in the tire by asking me for $600 for the last 12 of his paintings. Her dad was in the hospital and she didn't show any concern, except for the money. I'm glad there was never intimacy beyond some kissing. It would have seemed like prostitution to me. I am satisfied that I took the high ground and have a clear conscience. But darn I was attracted to her. I think I am ready to meet some special lady who wants to be loved well."

His mom had a warm smile as she mused, "I wish Michael could be this grown up. He goes through girlfriends like playthings. There is a lady out there somewhere right now, who is hoping that you will find her, will become part of her story, will father her children, and make me a Grandmother at last." Her smile had lost its brightness and was more melancholy.

"I will tell you that it is easy to fall in love with Germany though," he said to change the subject. "The cities are clean and old; there are real palaces and castles. The food is rich and the beer is prevalent and cold. I have been charmed so far. But I have also been part of a CID investigation. That's Criminal Investigation Division. We just arrested a couple dozen important people who have been like racketeers. I think a serious relationship with a lady might just get in the way, and that's sad. I want what you and dad had, a long happy marriage with kids." Once again he made his mom cry, damn it!

"I'm sorry to be so weepy. I haven't been able to get the scene out of my mind when that nurse turned off the machine." She wiped the tears from her eyes and blew her nose.

"You know it helped me a lot when Michael said that dad had died three days ago. Last night was a time of closure for us, especially for me." That made her nod with understanding. "What I'd like best is if you have some chores you'd like me to do, like mow the lawn."

"Well, Mister, since you offered, I can put together a laundry list." That brightened them both. Larry was busy until she called him in for lunch. It wasn't a surprise that was just the time that Michael showed up saying, "Is lunch ready?"

They were eating Ham and Cheese sandwiches on dark Rye bread, washing them down with Rainier Beer. Larry tried to describe the Shooting Star Market and Palace Square. It was hard for them to envision the splendor, but easy to see how impressed Larry was by it. He described his Motor Pool as a huge facility with glass windows on three sides. "There are four lube pits and four work stations. We can have eight vehicles at a time being serviced. I have six enlisted men working with and for me." He rattled on about the base.

Finally Michael got a word in, "My boss gave me the rest of the week off to take care of things. This morning I stopped at the bank and raided my savings account. Did you mean it when you said you'd sell me the Volvo?"

Actually, Larry hadn't meant it for sure, but now in the glare of the moment, why not. "Sure, if you have the cash, I have the title."

Michael laid an envelope on the table, saying, "I have been thinking a lot since last night. Some of the things you said stung. But I realized you are right, about most of it. Larry, I'm jealous of the man you've become. You seem a lot bigger, older, wiser than when you left. I feel like I'm the little brother now." He took a deep breath before admitting, "I want the Volvo to remind me what a dedicated man can accomplish, what focus and hard work can achieve, and I promise to take care of it. I want to follow in your footsteps." His mom was weeping again.

"Then let's finish these brewskies and go get it off the blocks. It might take a bit to kick the tires and light the fire, but I put it away carefully, and we'll have her running in a jiffy. Then with a Bill of Sale, we can go to the State Farm Insurance office near the school. That's where I got the title and license last year." His afternoon was planned just right.

Jan joined them for supper. Their mom had made a big pot roast and a lemon meringue pie. When there were only empty plates left on the table, they began telling favorite stories and their mom brought out a photo album. That stimulated more stories. When a picture of a successful deer hunt was featured, Michael asked if he could use dad's guns for the hunting season.

"Of course," she said, "just make sure you clean them when you're done."

Two at the table understood that to mean when he brought them back. One of them just heard the "clean them" part.

His mom asked Larry "Is there anything of dad's you would like to keep or to use?"

"Thank you. I'm so mobile right now, I don't know what I would do with it. But I'm sure you will think of some treasures. If you can just put them in the dresser in my bedroom, there will come a day when we can look through them together. Maybe when I know what to do with the paintings." The rest of the evening was spent remembering dad's favorites: Favorite place to eat out, Favorite fishing hole (By the way, he wanted to be cremated and his ashes scattered above the Big Rock Hole), his favorite hunting area, his favorite friends. They laughed a lot and wept a bit.

Before retiring for the night, Larry said, "As much as I'd like to stay for more time with you all, I must leave Thursday, immediately after the funeral. It's a five hour drive to McCord, then a three day flight back to Wiesbaden. I may be a bit late when I get back. Fortunately I have earned a couple get-out-of-jail-free cards, so I won't be in big trouble."

Wednesday was pretty much a repeat of Tuesday, except when Michael came to lunch he reported that the Volvo was a magic carpet. He had taken Sharon out to coffee this morning and she thought it was the most unique car she had ever been in. She agreed to go out for dinner in Lewiston. He was almost whispering when he said, "I will not waste this special opportunity. Thank you, brother."

"Just remember, Michael," Larry cautioned, "the car doesn't make the man, but the man can make the car so much more interesting." They both chuckled.

Larry brought a bucket of Kentucky Fried Chicken for supper, then with Jan, they talked into the evening. Larry assured them that his future was unclear, but extremely promising. "Speaking of promises," he said, "I want to give you a phone call every Sunday at six o'clock in the evening. That will be 0700 Monday morning for me." He gave her a one hundred dollar bill, saying, "I'll call collect. Please tell me when I should replenish my stash."

By 1230 Thursday Larry was packed and ready to go. Wearing his dress tans, he escorted his mom into the Rolling Hills Funeral Home. They were on time to greet the family and friends who came to say "goodbye" to Walter Crown, beloved husband and father. Larry recognized many of those who attended; a few were strangers who had known and respected his dad. He had called the transportation center at McCord to determine availability of an eastbound flight. If he could be there by 2000, he was advised, there was room on an Air Freight to Thule Air Base Greenland. It would be close, but it was his best choice.

Larry heard little of the words of tribute to his dad. He was distracted by odd memories and worries that invited his attention.

However, as the speaker was nearing the end of his talk, he told a story that captured Larry's attention. "There is an old story," the speaker said, "that requires your imagination. It is a story about a conversation between a Voice and an unborn baby. The Voice asks quietly, 'Babe, are you ready?' And the baby answers, 'Ready for what?' 'To be born of course,' the Voice replies. 'What does that mean?' the baby asks. 'It means you will leave this place; be on your own, where you can grow, explore, learn, and experience the wonder of a great mystery.' 'Did you say, leave this place?' The baby asks. 'I don't want to leave this place! I am warm and safe, well fed, and when mom sings, my whole world is filled with music. No! I don't want to be born.'

"But of course, we know that he was born on August 24th, 1911 in Post Falls, Idaho. His first experience was that of tender hands ministering to his needs and loving arms welcoming him into this world. He grew, he learned, he explored. He met a lady named Irma while attending school in Spokane. They married and gave life and love to Michael, Janice, and Lawrence. He worked, played, shared his wisdom, until one day, quite unexpected, the Voice said, 'Babe, are you ready?' The babe, now a man, answered, 'for what?' 'To be born into a much greater mystery, of course.' the Voice whispered. The babe answered, 'What does that mean?' 'You will leave this place and be completely free in a life of the spirit.' Once again the babe answered as before, 'No, I don't want to leave this place. I have work yet to finish, conversations with my grandchildren, yet to be born. No, I don't want to leave this place.' But we know that he did, on Friday July 19th.

"I have one more question today," the speaker said gently "It has to do with what we know of the nature of a God who has revealed to us pure and perfect love. Doesn't our faith tell us that once again that babe experienced tender hands ministering to his needs and loving arms welcoming him into a profound mystery?"

The room was still until the speaker spoke words of committal, shared a prayer, and finally gave a benediction. Larry escorted his mom out, and then gave her a hug and a kiss.

"Mom, I am so sorry to leave like this," he said sincerely. "I'm grateful for the hours of conversations we've shared. Now I have just enough time to catch a flight to Thule Greenland tonight. I promise to stay in touch." The green Ford was the first one out of the parking lot. It was heading west, rapidly.

Back to Routine

He had twenty minutes after returning the car to Motor Pool and loping across to the flight center. A much needed bathroom break and a cup of coffee were his only conveniences before his name was called and he was escorted to a waiting cargo plane. Inside, his seat held a paper sack with a Ham and Cheese sandwich, an apple and a can of ginger ale. All the comforts of home were provided even though there were no other passengers on board. Right on time the C-141 lumbered into the evening sky, with the setting sun behind them. It would be a ten hour flight to Thule Air Base in Greenland for fuel, and then another ten hours into Wiesbaden. Their path was very nearly over the top of the globe, he had been told. His jump seat couldn't recline, so Larry stretched out on the metal floor. His blanket under him and a couple foul weather jackets he found in a hanging locker on him, kept him warm enough. A partially inflated Mae West life jacket was his pillow. When he finally walked through the Wiesbaden base gate, it was 1830 Sunday evening. He was tired and hungry. Fortunately the mess hall was still open and his room was within walking distance.

At roll-call the six welcomed him back and shared words of condolences. There were also playful accusations that Crosby was running the place into the ground. Larry thought it was as good to be back as he had anticipated. They had enough work to stay occupied both during regular hours and off-duty.

August passed routinely. But on the second Tuesday of September, Larry received an order to attend a meeting in the office of Captain Howard. Since everything was proper in the Motor Pool and he hadn't been off-base for six weeks, he was pretty sure this would just be another informational report. It turned out to be considerably more.

"Good morning, Sergeant Crown," the Captain greeted. "Please have a seat and be comfortable." When they were both seated, he went on. "I was sorry to hear the nature of your recent emergency furlough. Do I understand that your father passed away?"

"Yes, sir."

"I'm sorry for you and your family. That must have been a difficult time."

"Thank you, sir. I have a brother and sister who are close to mom and can take care of her."

The Captain nodded his understanding. "Master Sergeant Custer told me that he was your DI in basic and saw something very special in you. In the aftermath of the arrests here on the base and your role in helping with that, I see that he was right, and I'm happy to commend you. Another meritorious ribbon has been added to your bar."

"Let me start our conversation by asking if you have given thought to your military career? Do you think you will re-enlist when this tour is over?" He was still, obviously expecting an answer.

"I have not, sir. My notion today is that I will not re-enlist."

"I'm curious to know why you feel that way. Are there not enough incentives to make army life attractive to you?"

"Are we having a conversation, sir? May I speak freely?" When the Captain encouraged him, Larry continued, "I love Germany, but as far as incentives go, the army hasn't shown me much. For the past ten months I have worked an average of 75 hours a week. Granted, much of that was optional off-duty work, but it was still in the Motor Pool. I work, sleep and live in the Motor Pool."

"But hasn't the army compensated you for those hours?"

"Well, sir, to tell you the truth, I have yet to cash an army check. I signed up for direct deposit and have been doing O.K. on the extra money I have earned in off-duty maintenance. I'm pretty sure the incentive I am looking for is a real life, with a home and perhaps a wife and some kids. There is little compatibility between a normal life and a combat-ready army."

"Are you telling me that you have not taken any money out of your direct deposit account in fifteen months?" There was a look of surprise on the Captain's face.

"That's correct, sir. And I have about five thousand discretionary DMs in my room now."

"The reason I am asking these questions, son, is I have been invited to appear before the Senate Ways and Means Committee to talk about the strength of our Armed Forces. They are building the next four year budget which includes our projected cost of another war, this one in Vietnam. They want to know how stable our enlisted force is."

"I don't envy you, sir," Larry said with a sad smile. "I've seen the same pictures you have of young men burning their draft cards. If we have to throw them in prison for the crime of avoiding the draft, I'd say we are pretty shaky." He was quiet for a moment. "If you are asking a greasy mechanic from the motor pool what he thinks about the army, I'll tell you that things this big, like a huge barge, take a long time and a lot of room to turn around. I think part of the problem is that the army uses past answers for future questions. We tried to fight Korea the way we won WWII. The Russians finally decided to quit funding the Chinese army, so we won, kind of. Now we want to fight in the jungles like we did in the mountains because the Chinese are funding the North Vietnamese action. We don't fight from horseback anymore and I think soon we won't truck our troops to the battlefield. We'll use massive planes to bomb the enemy Commanders and Generals instead of the enlisted ranks into submission. Then helicopters will bring in ground troops to clean up and control the battle. I think the day of the gas engine is limited; diesel will be such a practical replacement."

A smile had bloomed on Captain Howard's face. He had asked for an opinion, and boy didn't he get one. "You've never tapped into your pay?" he asked incredulously.

"Not a nickel, Sir."

"Then it wouldn't be too important to you if I offered a pay raise or a higher rank?"

The Sergeant replied, "Of course I would welcome a raise, a stronger pension, but for the most part, rank to me means more responsibility and opportunity to learn." Then grinning, he added, "But at the end of the day doesn't it all come down to who salutes first, and who has to go speak to the politicians?"

Captain Howard thanked him for his time and vowed they would talk again soon. "You are like an enlisted Will Rogers, Sergeant. I haven't had a conversation in the Officer's Club that could match this."

Staff Sergeant Crown

By the first of October test scores were in, and Larry was made Staff Sergeant. By the 15th of February he had orders to report to Long Binh Post, 33 kilometers from Saigon, Vietnam. The sprawling facility was the United States Army base, Logistics Center, and major command headquarters for US Army Vietnam. He was in charge of one third of the motor pool, which was divided into Maintain, Repair, and Replace service vehicles. His orders were to fly to Clark Air Base and then a second flight into Bien Hoa Air Base, which had a population three times larger than Wiesbaden.

The heat walking across the tarmac was uncomfortable for Larry, even in February. He knew his tans would be sweated through by the time he got into the terminal. As he opened the door a cool draft welcomed him and a corporal holding a placard with "SS Crown" was even more welcomed.

"Let me get your duffle, Sergeant," he said respectfully. "I've got a Jeep right outside." He drove to an enormous facility that seemed to stretch in every direction. The Jeep stopped in front of the Officer's Quarters. "My instructions were to bring you here to room 114. I don't ask why, just when, and how. Let me help you with that, sir."

Larry checked his watch and asked "I know I have crossed four time zones? Is it 1535?"

"Yes, sir, it is. I'm supposed to give you a half hour to freshen up and then deliver you to the Major's office at 1600 hours."

"Isn't it Sunday? I'm surprised offices are open today."

"Yes, sir. Me too. But I am learning that there are still a few things that I don't need to know, just need to do." He guided Larry to a very nice apartment that looked away from the base. It was considerably nicer than what he expected. After a few minutes the Corporal returned to guide the newcomer on a tour of the main base. Finally, the Jeep stopped in front of a building with a sign, "Logistics Central."

The Corporal said, "The Major's office is just to the right as you go in. Welcome to Long Binh Post, sir."

The next Corporal was just as polite and Larry's suspicion began to rise when he was told, "The Major is expecting you, sir. Go right in."

Larry knocked lightly on the officer's door and heard, "Come in, Staff Sergeant." When Larry opened the door he couldn't believe his eyes. Major T. Robert Henderson was Pfc. Henderson, now in much different clothes.

Chuckling, the officer said, "I'll give you a moment to get refocused, Mr. Crown. I understand this must be hard for you to grasp. Some of the time the uniform helps make the man into something more useful. I assure you these bars are authentic. By the way both Captain Howard and our mutual friend Mr. Custer have talked my ear off about what a splendid enlisted man you are. I hope so. I need a good one for several reasons. That's why I asked for you specifically."

"Sir, I apologize for any disrespect I may have had for you at our last meeting. I was unaware of…"

"You did precisely what I wanted you to do. You reacted like a superior noncom. I just had to fight down the grin. No harm, no foul." Major Henderson was still for a moment, thinking. "Sergeant Crown, we are sitting in a very dangerous place and time. Vietnam is about a thousand miles of tropical coastline with poor security and no dependable control. The French tried to colonize it a hundred years ago and they have finally admitted it can't be done. With the end of the war, like Berlin and Korea, this place was divided; everything north of the 16th parallel was assigned to communist China's control, and everything south under allied control, that is, us. The war department is concerned that what they call "the domino effect," might occur. They fear if either Laos, Cambodia, or Vietnam falls into communist control, a cascading of power will cause a shift. China will have an enormous advantage over all foreign powers. I'm not sure what our little effort here can do about it." He studied Larry's calm attentiveness.

"I was impressed with how quickly you turned around The Motor Pool at Wiesbaden. This one is bigger and I'm afraid the morale problems are deeper. I wanted to meet you before you meet them. Can you be very hard ass with them in the morning? I need you to be very tough, not polite. There are six or eight who must be controlled, maybe removed. They have no respect for discipline or instructions. Staff Sergeant Frank Sweet is looking forward to your arrival. He is going back to Benning to finish his career. I have already received permission from 181ˢᵗ Infantry up at the Da Nang Air Base who need six overworked Pfc.s to be swapped out with six or eight who have some fight in them. Tomorrow morning I want you to take names and Tuesday morning I want you to send them here for transfer. Just get me their names and I'll take care of the rest. That should get the attention of your crew and build your reputation."

"There are two other situations that might be connected. We have a hydrocodone problem on this Post. It started about six months ago and has gotten nearly epidemic. We also have a very militant group of 1ˢᵗ and Second Lieutenants who are highly aggressive, and I think dangerous. I want you to keep your eyes and ears open. I can't order you to investigate, that's my job. But I would very much appreciate your help.

"You are billeted in the officer's quarters for a much different reason. It was no mistake, I assure you. But I am going to let my wife Barb tell you about it later. Once again, this is not an order, and it is definitely beyond military boundaries. If you choose not to help her, we will discretely move you to NCO quarters. Do you have any questions now?" Larry shook his head saying "No sir, I'll try to do it by the numbers." The Major held up his hand, saying, "Remember, we don't know each other to make this work."

"For your orientation, the NCO mess hall is the fourth building east of here and a six mile running path is out the west end of your quarters. This is a cool and dry part of the year to use it. I'm very glad to see you again, Staff Sergeant Crown."

Larry stood, and snapped a salute, saying, "Thank you, sir."

It was just getting light when Larry found the path. By the time he returned, he was sweaty and grateful for a cool shower. He had learned last night that the mess hall had designated zones. The two tables furthest from the noisy serving line were set aside for Staff Sergeants. There was just one other at his table, which made introductions easy.

At 0750, he walked into the Motor Pool building designated for Maintenance. He introduced himself to SS Sweet, who introduced him to Corporal Kenny Lewis. "How punctual are you, Corporal?" Larry asked pleasantly.

"We're not too tight about that, sir. Folks have a habit of showing up a little later."

"Well, Lewis," Larry said with an icy voice, "bring a notebook to roll call in three minutes to take names. We are about to tighten this place up."

At 0800 Lewis called a half group to attention. SS Sweet introduced the new Staff Sergeant, who immediately asked the group to stand at the opposite end of the facility, away from the door. He recognized the Corporal who had met him at the air field. Another one was also organizing his squad to stand together. "This way I will be able to see who is interested in remaining at this facility, and who would just as soon fight communists in the jungle." Those words changed the ordinary Monday morning atmosphere to one dramatically more important.

They stood at attention for four minutes before two more walked in. "Corporal Lewis, write the names of those men for me." In a much more demanding voice he barked, "You two stand at attention near the wall." They continued to stand at attention in a silent maintenance bay; two more straggled in five minutes later and were added to the wall-standers. There were questioning looks, but all were silent. Four more came in after six more minutes and were added. Finally at 0822 two more came in casually. They were surprised to see a new configuration to roll-call. Larry had them stand at attention with those at the wall.

"I'm surprised, gentlemen, that knowing a new Staff Sergeant was to be introduced today, you have such a piss poor way of showing up for roll-call. I traveled from Germany and made it here on time. Take a look around you. There are a number of Pfc.s that are slithering around in the jungle trying not to get their ass shot off who would love to be able to stand comfortably and safely where you stand today." He saw some disrespectful murmuring and joking in the wall people. Immediately he walked over to them, dividing off the tardy first two from the rest. Larry said, "Gentlemen, don't bother to come to roll-call in the morning. Pack your duffle immediately. At 0800 report to the Logistics Central. We'll see what other entertainment we can provide you in Da Nang. You eight are dismissed to get your shit together."

The reality of what he was saying soaked in slowly.

"You can't do this to us," one of them barked.

"Corporal, will you call the M.P. for a pick up." Larry walked up to the speaker and said, "I'll even give you the first shot, tough guy.

Then we'll see what I can do. You had better make it good 'cause you won't be going to Da Nang with your buddies, but the infirmary."

The speaker was immediately aware of the Staff Sergeant's size and athletic build. It wouldn't be much of a contest, he was sure. There was no positive solution for this situation, so wisely he raised his hands in submission.

"Sit your ass down and wait," he commanded. To the other seven, he said, "Get out of my sight. If you are late in the morning it will be the stockade, then Da Nang. Do you understand?" He wasn't speaking loudly, but ice cold contempt. "If you get back here, it might be in a body bag." He turned toward the remaining men still at attention. "Roll call is at 0800. If you want to have a really shitty year, be two minutes late." Without another word, he walked into the office.

Quietly the Corporal said, "We have four trucks coming in this morning and six cars. Being short handed, we'll need to hump along. Dismissed." The stunned sixteen men remaining hurried about their business.

The two Staff Sergeants looked at each other for a long silence. Finally Sweet said, "That was brutal. They didn't see it coming."

Larry answered, "I hate to think I have just put eight men in harm's way. I hope they have adequate training. But I know I am bringing in six men who will have a grateful attitude and be the foundation of change for all the others here." As they waited for the M.P.s, Sergeant Sweet tried to orient Larry to what was working well in the Motor Pool, and what was not. When Larry asked him if there was anyone who could supply him with a painkiller stronger than an aspirin, the Sergeant shook his head. Then he answered quietly, "You might ask Staff Sergeant Keith Ohm from Replacement Motor Pool. I think he needs some now and then."

Before lunch Larry found the Post News office. He requested an announcement that beginning immediately personal autos could receive routine maintenance in the Motor Pool during off-duty hours for the payment of parts and labor. He gave the Motor pool phone number to make an appointment.

Tuesday morning roll-call was prompt, with a twinge of anxiety. His first day had been rough on the men of Maintenance. Some wondered if that attitude would continue. At 0800, "All present and on duty," Corporal Lewis reported. He had a bit of the twinge as well.

"Good morning, gentlemen," Staff Sergeant Crown began. "We had a bouncy landing yesterday. There is no reason to believe that should continue as long as you stay on time, and on top of your assignments. There are going to be some changes, as you know. I hope some of them are good. We have a light schedule today, only two trucks and seven Jeeps. If you have those wrapped up by 1200, we can knock off for the rest of the day. Make sure your work stations are squared away, and all tools cleaned and properly stored. One thing more; if any of you are interested in working on civilian cars after duty hours, give your name to Corporal Lewis. I'll make a roster." He intentionally left out the part where they would be well compensated for their work. They were unaware of the Huey helicopter that lifted off at 0845, with a passenger list of eight.

At 1630 the Huey was back from Da Nang, now with six passengers aboard. Corporal Jim Hughes, who had so graciously welcomed SS Crown, was asked to show them to their new quarters and get them squared away.

Roll-call began at 0800 with Corporal Lewis introducing: "Pfc. Bill Thomas, from Georgia, Pfc. Howard Stahl from Virginia, Pfc. Guy Brown from California, Pfc. Patrick Adams from Boston, Pfc. Shane Johnson from North Dakota, and Pfc. Paul Porter, from Oregon."

SS Crown welcomed the new replacements, saying, "Corporal Hughes has given you a tour of the important parts of the base and warned you that our roll-call is at 0800. There are few other rules than that. I do, however, have an opportunity for you if you'd like to earn some discretionary cash. We take appointments for after duty-hours work. Saturday morning is usually a busy time when a fellow can pick up an extra $50. That could pay for all the beer you could drink on the weekend. Let Mr. Lewis know if you would be interested." All six raised their hands to be on the list.

Another hand was raised from the ranks. When SS Crown asked, "Yes, what is it?" the young man said, "You didn't tell us there would be extra money, only extra work. I'd like to be on the list, sir."

"Mr. Lewis, put that man's name on the waiting list. If we generate the interest I believe we are going to get, we will use him."

"But that's not fair," one of the men in the back row said.

The Staff Sergeant walked around to him and asked directly into his face, "What in God's name gave you the thought that any of this is fair? Jesus, you are not on the playground anymore. This isn't the Mouse Club. Fair means we all do our duty. We stand tall, and obey commands. I'm not here to hold your hand. If you don't like it, lip off once more. Changes will happen for you, I guaran-damn-tee it." The room held their breath for they had seen how swift that change could happen.

SS Crown returned to the front and said, "We have another light day, nine Jeeps. Corporals Hughes, Lewis and Scott will determine if our work is complete by 1200. I'd like another short day and I'll bet you would too. Let's get to it. Dismissed."

Friday afternoon, a metallic dark blue Pontiac came in for a lube and tune up. Larry was finished with it by 1800 as promised. A Mercedes-Benz was waiting for him at 1830 and was lubed and injectors adjusted by 2130, as promised. He hoped this was the point of the spear of change that the Motor Pool would enjoy.

Saturday morning he had appointments for six Lubes. The new Pfc.s agreed they all would like to work as a learning team. Larry demonstrated the process to them, and introduced the ten point safety check. They were finished by 1000, and had earned enough for three pitchers of beer, each! This was a good day!

As Larry was closing the service bay, he noticed a black town car at the service dock of the Replacement facility next door. A couple of officers were watching him, which seemed unusual enough for him to make a mental note of their presence and the plate number of the Lincoln, especially on a Saturday morning.

Bereavement

It had been a fine start for Larry. The part of the puzzle he still couldn't figure out was his room in the Officer's Quarters. There seemed to be no one in the facilities next to his. Getting used to having his laundry done for him and folded on the clean sheet every Friday, however, was habit forming. He was just thinking seriously about going to bed when a soft knock on his door startled him. He looked about to make sure the room was tidy.

He opened the door to a very lovely lady who was smiling at him as though they knew one another. "Sergeant, you can invite me in for a glass of wine," she said softly.

Larry was very confused, but he was pretty sure he didn't have any wine to share. "I'm sorry, Ma'am, I'm afraid there must be some…" He didn't get to finish the sentence as she pushed around him saying, "I'm Barb Henderson. I believe you know my husband. He works here on the base."

"One of us must be very confused," Larry started to say again. Once again she cut him off by asking, "Sergeant Crown, don't you want to know why you were given the up-graded room?" Larry closed the door after her.

"You look a bit confused, Sergeant. May I call you Larry, it would be much easier. My husband says you catch on pretty quickly, so let me begin by asking again for a glass of wine." When Larry shook his head saying, "Ma'am there is no wine in this room," she said in an exasperated way, "For goodness sakes, I'll get it myself." She walked to the small frig built into the counter. "I just filled this." She brought out a bottle of white wine." May I pour one for you?"

He shook his head, saying, "No thank you ma'am."

"I'm beginning to think either my husband is wrong about you, or you just don't know how to talk to girls. Which is it, Larry?" A captivating smile curled her lips as she took a sip.

Finally Larry said with a bit more spunk, "I do not believe he is wrong, I just need to choose the girl myself, ma'am."

"There we go," she said brightly. "Now we have a start. Do you have a mom, or sister at home?" Her manner was light and nearly playful.

"Yes ma'am, I have one of each," Larry said trying to understand where this was going.

"Larry, do you like girls? Bob told me you were hanging around with a Wiesbaden girl for four months, seeing her every week, and never got her into bed. Is that true?" She acted as though it was unbelievable.

"That is true, ma'am." Then he told her the short form of how he had met her, and why he saw her each week.

"You know, Larry, most guys would have gone for something a lot warmer and softer than those paintings." Her voice was softer and less playful.

"That could have happened, but it wasn't in my program, ma'am." He said the words softly also, but they were strong. "I really wanted to help them."

"O.K. now, I think we are over the initial jitters, and I like you. I think I am going to invite you into a very bizarre part of army activity. We are now in the wing of the Officer's Quarters designated as "Bereavement." This is where families, and by that I mean wives, of officers who have been shot down or captured, are moved when there has been no contact from their man for ten days. It may seem callous, but the army needs to move them out of the front line, so to speak, and shelter them in a safer environment. They can stay here for three months. Then, if there is still no definitive contact about their husband they must return to the states." She waited for any questions, and took a sip of wine. "Right now there are four wives in Bereavement."

"O.K. here's where you come in. Are you ready to hear it?"

Larry nodded, saying, "Yes, Ma'am."

Barb continued, "The women who come here are in distress. Some are overwhelmed with anxiety, some are angry, and others are so depressed they think about hurting themselves. They need a hall monitor, a safe place in a very large strange one. They have access to the chaplain, and to a counselor of course. Larry, I am asking you to be a shelter in their storm. Please do not misunderstand; I am definitely not asking you to be a gigolo or some boy toy. Many men would see this as a target rich environment for a lot of free sex. That would destroy the intent of Bereavement. Most just need someone to talk with, maybe to share a glass of wine and assure them that they are safe. You may let them hug you; you may rub their feet, listen to them, and let them sleep on your couch, but only once. If you take one to bed with you, your part of the program is over. Is that all clear enough to you?"

"Yes ma'am, I understand. I'll treat them with the respect I give my sister."

"If you can do that, Sergeant, you will have my respect and admiration," Barb said softly. "Few men could be so disciplined. You will have a Specialist designation added to your rank and an additional 30% to your monthly pay." Then remembering a fact from another conversation, she asked, "Is it true that you are not touching your monthly paycheck?"

"Yes, ma'am, I'm getting along without it. This past week I've earned $50 by doing off-duty maintenance work on officer's cars. That's enough to take care of my expenses and a little left over."

"Larry you make me think of the Buddhist Monks who walk the roads here, seeking help for those in need. They don't take for themselves. It is altruistically beautiful." Then thinking of something else she added, "Your little frig will be automatically stocked with provisions for you to offer hospitality. I don't think you will abuse the generosity. Finally, the group of women will have a spokesperson. Right now it is Rita Carver. She has been here a month, so she has another eight weeks of eligibility. Then she will name her successor. It is not your responsibility to manage their time here, only the condition of their heart to the best of your ability. The password they will use to meet you is the same one I used to begin our conversation. 'Sergeant, you can invite me in for a glass of wine.' Now does all of this make sense to you, Larry? Do you have any questions?" She took the last sip from her glass.

"May I ask them if they would like me to stay in touch with them after they leave Long Binh?"

"You may not", Barb said immediately. "That suggests you are in control. They need to feel a sense of privacy. But if you wish I can have some business cards printed with your contact information. That would show them that you sincerely care for them, yet leaves them in control if they want to be contacted. Does that make sense?"

"You know it does make sense," he answered. "This is like the first humane thing I have seen from the army in an inhumane time. I really don't know if I am strong enough to stand with these ladies, but I'll try. I don't think temptation will be my problem, but the depth of their hurt." He thought for a moment, then said, "No wonder I get such a fine living space."

Barb laughed a genuine chuckle. "I feel like you're my little brother, which is the perfect proof that you are the one for the job. Thank you for the wine and thank you for demonstrating my husband's ability to see quality in his men." She gave him a warm embrace and left. He pondered the scope of what he had just agreed to do, and be.

A new track

Larry's inner alarm clock woke him at 0515 even if it was Sunday. It was time to run before the morning got hot. At the far side of his loop, he came upon a very old airstrip, one that had obviously been unused for a long while, yet one that also had potential for street racing. He thought about the possibilities on his way back in, and while he was showering. Walking to the mess hall, he thought of something else. He needed some sort of transportation to avoid sweat soaked clothes.

He was earlier than most other partakers of the brunch. Once again there was only one other Staff Sergeant at the table. When Larry introduced himself, the other said, "Yeah I heard you are a bad ass, dumped eight out for missing roll-call. Usually that's a slap on the hands not Da Nang. My Name is Keith Ohm, Motor Pool Replacement.

Larry said a bit off-hand, "Yeah, I might have gone a bit overboard on them, but I wanted to grab their attention. On top of that, I have been suffering like a son of a bitch. Flying here from Wiesbaden I got some sort of a sinus thing. I've tried aspirin. They can't touch it. It's lasted all week. I feel like I'm having a period. I need something stronger, maybe a cheap drunk." They ate in silence. But when SS Ohm was finished he leaned close to Larry and laid a couple pills beside his tray.

"Try these. If they work, I know where you can get more, 10 for $20. You can pay me later." Larry made it look like he popped the pills and washed them down with some orange juice. SS Ohm walked away, and Larry folded evidence in his napkin.

The rest of the morning was spent letter writing. The first one went to Captain Henderson in an effort to keep contact with him under wraps. He invited the Captain to meet him on the jogging path any morning at his convenience. Larry had information the Captain might value. Then he wrote a letter to Major Roberts asking for the status of the Crown Vic used as evidence. He asked, "Now that the court action is finished, might it be released?" Finally he wrote to his mom, even though he would continue to keep his promise to call her. He tried to explain what a Bereavement Specialist might do, and how he came to be recruited to do it.

At this latitude there were about equal hours of light and darkness in each day. It was twilight when he walked to dinner and total darkness when he walked back to his billet after calling home. She must have been watching for him because Larry had scarcely closed the door when he heard a soft knock. He opened the door to a darling woman dressed in a blue and white tennis skirt and blouse. She wore tennis shoes and a very sad expression. "Sergeant Crown, you can invite me in for a glass of wine. My name is Rita."

He opened the door wider and invited, "Please come in, Rita, or would you prefer me to call you Mrs. Carver?" That was enough for the tears to flow as she reached for him. There was a long silent embrace while her body convulsed with sobs. He waited patiently, gently cradling her and trying to ignore the warmth of her strong body. Finally he asked softly, "May I pour you a glass of wine, or fruit juice, or something stronger?"

Rita took a deep breath, gathering her composure. "Yes thank you, do you have a bit of apple juice?" Her face was nearly pleading.

"That's what I wanted, too", Larry said honestly. He was struck by the challenge of the situation. He had been told of how vulnerable these women would be. Now he was feeling it full force. She was most desirable, and in need of his compassion. Carefully he poured them small glasses and they sat on the sofa. "How long have you been in Vietnam?" Larry asked after a bit.

"We arrived just before November. Don was flying recon out of Pleiku. It had seemed like a pretty boring job for a month, looking for any troop movement or possible camps. Then just after New Year's, he started the same grid search. On January 6th there was no radio contact of trouble. He just didn't return. Huyes flew over the territory several times, but anything under the jungle canopy is completely out of sight." She took a tiny sip. "I have tried to keep my faith and hope for any good news. I would welcome even hearing that he has been captured, is a prisoner. At least I would know he is alive. Not knowing is hell." Another tear traced down her face.

They sat quietly until Larry asked, "Do you have family in the states, someone you can talk with?"

"Sure," she replied without changing her expression. "I have my parents, and Don's. I have a sister and several friends we met in Officer's Training, and flight school." She took another deep breath and continued, "There are also the chaplain and professionals that would try to help." She sat quietly for a couple minutes, and then she turned her back toward him and leaned back against him. Larry wrapped his arms around her, being very careful to hold her shoulders gently. She was warm and soft with a very pleasant fragrance. He reminded himself that this was a test of his dependability. He could earn her trust only if he held strong to the high-ground. To help him be stronger, he thought of Barb Henderson saying that he was like a Monk, caring for others. They rested in the stillness of the evening for a long moment.

A fresh sob shook her. "I just don't know how I can handle all this," she whispered. "It's like the biggest darkest enemy." Another silent sob rattled her small frame.

"I can remember the most difficult task I had to do on the farm," he told her. "It was the summer before my senior year and I had a job mowing, baling and delivering a farmer's alfalfa, four big fields. If I had concentrated on the whole job, I would have been overwhelmed. I was told to do just one row at a time. One row at a time, to lift those heavy bales onto the truck-bed. One row at a time got the job done." He gave her shoulder a little squeeze.

He spoke softly into her hair, "Our task is to maintain our faith that he is going to be rescued tomorrow. One day at a time is all we need to do. Can you visualize his smile?" Her head nodded positively. "Can you hear his voice greeting you again and telling you he loves you?" Her head nodded again. After another lengthy silence Larry said, "Rita, you are a terrific wife. I look forward to meeting Don and hear him tell you how proud he is to be married to you."

There was yet one more lengthy silence, and then Larry released her and gently helped her sit up. A little over a half hour had gently drifted by. He stood up and offered to help her stand. She came to him to give him a tiny kiss on the cheek.

"Oh Lord, Larry, this has been such a good interlude for me. You are just what I need to make it. You are gentle, strong, and even though you have never been married, you seem to know what to say. I trust you completely."

Rita looked into his dark eyes, saying, "You must know that Barb asked me to be the guinea pig, to see if such a young man could stay focused and not get carried away. I'm very happy to say that you stayed on task. You have so exceeded what I expected. You're like a young friend. I'll tell the others they can trust you, too. I hope I can come back."

"I'll keep the apple juice chilled," he said as he opened the door for her. "It has been my privilege to meet you, Rita. We can manage this, one day at a time." She gave him a gentle embrace, and left.

That's how it began. The women must have agreed who would visit next, for Larry never worried about a schedule. February turned into March and Gwen moved into Bereavement.

Major Henderson followed the information Larry had given him. After arresting Staff Sergeant Ohm, there had been a lengthy interrogation that had revealed a network of distributors. The town car at the Replacement loading dock was the connection to the narcotics transfer. The car helped identify four 2nd Lieutenants, who were distributing to both the base, and stateside. There were also seven arrests of NCOs who were dealing the hydrocodone for them. The main PX in Cholon was identified as their source, and placed on probation. March became April and Rita returned to Virginia. Susanne took her place, and now there were five, again.

The Motor Pool was running smoothly, with appointments both off-duty evenings and Saturdays. Larry usually took the 1600 appointments so his evenings could be open for Bereavement, but he continued to send Mr. Custer a growing list of VIN and engine serial numbers. Corporal Hughes had assumed responsibility for running the Saturday night street races, even though there were only about a half dozen cars that were regulars. It was all pretty calm and predictable.

Charger

The letter that Larry received from Captain Roberts changed that a bit: "Sergeant Crown, I am sorry to say that the Ford taken as evidence was disposed through proper channels." That meant nothing to Larry, except someone else wanted the Crown Vic. He read on. "I can tell you, however, that a vehicle taken from Lieutenant Colonel Brighton's garage has been cluttering the evidence room. We are happy to dispose it to you, since most of the engine and the pink slip title is in the accompanying crate coming to you aboard a C-133; ETA Long Binh 5 May along with a shipment of Jeeps. You will be contacted." Larry read it again to be sure he understood that he might have a new challenge as well as a 21st birthday present. In fact it was a Dodge Charger, with a 427 V8 and more goodies than he could count at first. Work, work, play a little, Bereavement, his life had a regularity that many might think was boring, work, work, play a little, Bereavement. Larry found it so fascinating, he re-enlisted when his tour was completed.

May turned into June; Sue left and two replaced her, now there were six. The Dodge made its appearance at the Saturday night street fun. There was no one that could run with it. Larry agreed that he would only do "exhibition" runs, until Lieutenant Whitney made a serious offer. He was a junior officer from the 90th Replacement Battalion located in nearby Bien Hoa, the arrival point for most enlisted men who were being sent "up country." Some were calling this Long Binh Junction, or LBJ for short, just like the president. When Mr. Whitney heard the roar of the Dodge and saw how it dominated, he offered Larry four thousand dollars for it, more than the car cost new. Work, work, play a little, Bereavement. Finally, Larry knew he really didn't want to spend more time on the powerful car, so he traded the pink slip for a money order, paper for paper.

On August 2, 1964, the U.S.S. Maddox was on a communication exercise near the Gulf of Tonkin. Three North Vietnamese Torpedo boats maneuvered to within 2000 yards of the destroyer. The skipper saw that as a flagrant act of aggression and opened fire with 3 inch and 5 inch shells; 180 rounds were fired and an F8 Crusader strafed the torpedo boats. The larger result of the action, more than the damage to the ships and the death of four North Vietnamese sailors was that Congress passed the Gulf of Tonkin Resolution, which gave the president justification for deploying U.S. troops and the commencement of open warfare against North Vietnam. Soon the Bereavement would have sixteen wives who waited. The possibility of individual attention was now a thing of the past.

Furlough

Mr. Henderson was ordered to a new post in Virginia with the new rank of Lieutenant Colonel. His final order before leaving Long Binh was sending Staff Sergeant Crown on a two week furlough. It had been two years since his father's death, and time for him to see his mother. Larry found an empty eastbound air freight that was going to Travis Air Base in California. From there it was an easy hop to McCord Air base in Washington.

When Larry drove the Motor Pool Ford into the driveway he was struck with the memories. Nothing had changed! It was the same place, the same feelings he had as a high school student. A wave of nostalgia flooded over him, causing him to wait before going in the house. Sadly, when he finally did go in, he found his mother weeping. She had misunderstood the green car and the delayed exit from it. She thought she was getting bad news. It only took him a moment to dry her tears and change them to smiles. "I'll be home for a week, unless I run out of chores to do," he told her. She hugged him as desperately as the ladies of Bereavement.

Supper, as he expected, was a production. His mom made sure that Jan was there, with her steady fellow. He had two children who lived with their mother, but their relationship seemed serious. And surprise, surprise, Michael had popped the question to Sharon and they had summer wedding plans. The table was loaded with good food and a happy family.

There was plenty of conversation. They wanted to know about Vietnam, and what he thought was going to happen there with a big troop build-up. Finally Jan got around to the gossip part, of who was getting married and who was getting unmarried. "I heard that Silvia Shepherd has divorced the hippy Jerry Spooner, and is already going out with an insurance guy from Pullman named Harvey Waltz, who is ten years older than her. She's got kids and so does he. It sounds like a soap opera." Larry assured them that the army was a poor place to meet a prospective wife. Michael said the Volvo was still an eye-catcher. He was taking special care of it.

In the morning after a refreshing run, Larry asked his mom if she wanted to go into Lewiston with him. "I've been real excited to see that Plymouth Barracuda. I'd like to see if Winslow Dodge has one in stock." It was something they could do that would get her out of the house. "Hey mom, are you still driving dad's pickup? That thing was a hunk of junk when I learned to drive."

"But it reminds me of him," she answered lamely.

As it turned out there was a soft yellow Barracuda with tan leather seats. There was a lot of haggling for over an hour. But finally when the salesman lowered the price because there was no trade-in, and lowered it again because he was going to pay in cash, and finally lowered it again with a serviceman's discount, Larry bought it, paying considerably less than he had gotten from the sale of the big Dodge. He told his mom that since she was not authorized to drive the Motor Pool Ford, she would have to drive the "Cuda" home.

Over a cup of coffee back in the kitchen, Larry explained that he didn't have a car and it seemed unnatural. "But since I will be kicking around all over the world for the next twelve or thirteen years, may I leave it here? I hope you will feel that it is our car, and will feel free to drive it instead of the pickup. My one provision is that under no condition may Michael drive it." She nodded in understanding and thanked him for the gorgeous car. He had satisfied the purpose of his leave. The rest was just rest.

Back in the Long Binh Motor Pool, Larry watched the year-long influx of a major personnel change. Almost all of U.S. Army Vietnam HQ Command (USARV), 1st Logistical Command, and many other Army units dispersed in Saigon were moved to Long Binh Post to resolve centralization, security, and troop billeting issues. Long Binh Post was a sprawling logistics facility and becoming the largest U.S. Army base in Vietnam. When the Officer's quarters were needed by real officers, the wives were moved stateside and Larry was moved to NCO quarters. The days of Bereavement were changed forever.

He was sad over that for several reasons. He had become very fond of those wounded ladies. It was something like falling in love with a whole bunch at once. But it also meant that he had to surrender his Specialist designation. When he asked Major Polk, the new Motor Pool Command, he was asked if he had stood before a Court Marshal. "No sir," was Larry's honest reply.

"The only way rank or ratings may be reduced is by Court Marshal, Sergeant Crown. You are trained and approved as a Specialist 3. There may be a future need for that ability and you will be ready. Let it stand." Larry didn't agree with that, but it did make the lesser quarters more acceptable. It also paid for his weekly laundry bill.

War is deadly

The war hit home on February 7, 1967 when the Viet Cong managed to attack the Long Binh ammunition storage with mortar fire, destroying 15,000 high explosive 155 mm artillery projectiles. Windows in the Motor Pool were shattered a mile away.

Larry was promoted to Master Sergeant in May of '68, when he re-upped for the second time. He was assigned the duty of overseeing the provisioning of coffins. Apparently no other officer would take the task. Empty coffins were ordered, flown in from the states, and then warehoused. Each day Hueys flew in with body bags from upcountry. Larry's detail of seven Corporals would transfer the body bags containing the remains of one of America's finest into a coffin, store it in a cooler until a plane was prepared to fly eastbound with a full compliment. They would then transfer the coffins to the aircraft that would fly to Guam, then Honolulu, then on to Travis Air Base California. It was not laborious work, but incredibly tiring because in each bag was someone's son. Someone at home was waiting for this man to walk through the door, or share a beer. This might be someone's father.

In 1968 the failed Tet Offensive, which intended to overthrow the South Vietnamese government, marked a shift in the war. Military reports claimed significant U.S. progress, which was illusionary, demonstrated by the rising number of fatalities, soon to be over 58,220. As corrosive still was the fading support at home, which began to undermine U.S. initiative.

Clark Air Base, Philippines

The eleven months on coffin detail did something to Larry. As soft and compassionate as the Bereavement had shaped him, this task, done in the increasing atmosphere of negative criticism, made him cold and cynical. In May of 1969, he was finally transferred and was put in charge of the Motor Pool at Clark Air Base, Luzon Philippines. He knew how to run an efficient Maintenance and Repair facility. The only addition he made to the existing plan was off-duty routine maintenance, which was a welcomed source of additional income for him and several others.

On June 23rd, Staff Sergeant Todd Henry stood at attention in the office of Lieutenant Colonel Steven Talbert, the Clark AFB Commander. "Yes this is a serious charge Sergeant. Dereliction of duty can carry a reduction of rank or worse. Did you actually countermand a direct order?"

"That makes it sound so serious sir. He has this ten point safety check that he instructed the men to do during maintenance. They are shouting back and forth, and it is laughable. I told them to stop it, that's all. That wasn't countermanding his orders, exactly."

"Were his instructions clear, Sergeant?"

"Yes, sir, but…"

"Were his instructions difficult to follow? Or were they counter to any other procedure the men were trained to do?"

"Well no, sir, but…"

"Are the men in any way endangered by doing it, Sergeant?"

"No, sir, but it makes them sound like a bunch of kids. It's bad for morale, sir"

"Yes, I can understand why he wrote you up. You don't like Master Sergeant Crown, do you?"

"Sir, he is like a buck in rut. He has a mean streak, I'm telling you. He restricted four of our men to their barracks simply for missing roll call."

"Sergeant, you are standing here today because you have failed to recognize military discipline. I can tell you that he has calmed down if he only restricted them. At Long Binh he had them transferred to Da Nang for the same thing. He must respect your status, Staff Sergeant; he could have had you tossed in the stockade. It is regrettable that you have failed to respect his status. I will warn you that if you fail to follow his orders, you will be found derelict of duty. He was in Vietnam almost five years. The last year there he had the very worst assignment imaginable. What you identify as a mean streak is a rock-hard understanding of his mission." The Commander was quiet as he pondered the disposition of the charge.

"I must do something about this charge that respects his status as well as protecting yours, this time. I am restricting you to the base for one week and placing this in your service record. Your punishment is to complete the third chapter of the basic training manual on chain of command. As your commander, I am warning you to tread easy around the Master Sergeant. Next time you will not get off this lightly, I assure you. He takes his assignment seriously, as should you. You are dismissed."

Seventeen months later, Lieutenant Colonel Steven Talbert was transferred to Fort Lee in Virginia. One of his final decisions was to transfer Master Sergeant Crown to the Motor Pool command at Fort Leavenworth Kansas. He felt that nine years away from the U.S. deserved a break. Larry couldn't have agreed more. The Lieutenant Colonel also thought that an easy posting might make it more probable that the Master Sergeant would reenlist next May and become a career soldier.

Back in the USofA

October air was sweeter, the chill in a morning run was more invigorating. The leaves were turning golden, and war was a long ways away. How could it have been any better? Larry requested a Christmas furlough. It had been ten years since he had celebrated the holidays with his mom. The snow began the week before he was scheduled to leave. After three days, the streets were choked and the trucks and buses were all using chains. The mood in the Motor Pool was shifting into emergency mode.

At first Larry decided to run two ten hour shifts of plow drivers. As the snow continued and the temperature dropped even colder, he joined in the rotation of drivers as they tried to keep the main road open 24/7. The Department of Defense's only maximum security prison, and the Midwest Joint Correctional Facility, which were part of Fort Leavenworth, had to have free access. Sherman Army Airfield was finally closed when the snow could no longer be removed. Larry had a very white and exhausting Christmas. Thankfully, with the New Year a warm rain came from the south, and Larry was convinced he could finally get on with his furlough. With no available Army air freighters to hop, he could board a Greyhound bus that would change drivers in Utah, and he would switch buses in Boise. It would still be all good.

He took a shuttle into the bus depot in Kansas City. The westbound express was lightly filled as it rolled out in the early morning. Larry dozed and watched the flat terrain pass by. Soon they had turned west in Nebraska. Lunch was in North Platte and dinner in Laramie, Wyoming. They were right on time, even though it was snowing. He thought there might even be a bit of sleep before Utah. The further west they went, however, the harder the snow was coming down. Finally Larry chose to forget about napping and kept his eyes on a road that was looking like a candidate for chains.

He wasn't sure what he saw, but Larry was suddenly alert. There was danger ahead. Then he saw it again, a faint reflection of a red light. "Driver, slow down!" he called. "There's danger ahead!"

Without waiting for any response he shouted, "Shift down!" Then he commanded, "Hit your flashers to warn the truck behind us!" He wasn't sure that any of it was registering with the driver. "Shift down again, damn it!" his voice demanded. They were coming to a curve and the brow of a hill. "Tap your brakes, you're going too fast!" Larry firmly cautioned. Suddenly before them was a scene of chaos, confusion, and scattered vehicles. The road was completely plugged with more than a dozen fender-benders. There were already emergency vehicles on site, an ambulance and a police car. A highway tow truck was hooked to an eighteen wheeler, and a smaller half ton tow truck was pulling a car out of the ditch. "Oh shit!" the bus driver erupted. But because of Larry's warning, he had slowed enough not to join the mess, and so too had the string of traffic behind him.

The bus crawled to a stop not far from the little tow truck and Larry asked to be let out. He almost ran to the police car, demanding that the officer get some flares out on the road, especially uphill where it was a blind spot. Folks coming from the west would be able to see the lights for a couple miles.

He turned toward the little tow truck realizing that another mistake was happening. He whistled and tried to get the old guy's attention. "Lower your boom!" he shouted. He repeated it twice as he tried to get his attention. "Your boom is too…" the rest of it was lost as the car, lifted too acutely, slid off the side of the ditch and jerked the hook free from the frame. Everything reacted to the release like a slingshot. The car thumped down and the tow truck sprang up. None of that was important, but the hook and pulley on the cable slammed into the old operator like a whiplash. He folded over and fell in the ditch. Larry was only vaguely aware that a woman leapt from the truck, screaming or crying. They both ran to assist the old man. Larry got there first and saw arterial bleeding from his thigh. She was pounding on Larry's back, urging him to do something.

Remembering his training, Larry pulled off his necktie and fashioned a tourniquet. Using a nearby stick, he twisted the tie tightly and told the man to hold onto the stick while Larry tried to ease him out of the ditch. All the time the hysterical woman stayed at his back, babbling. Someone in the bystanders flashed a picture, and then another. The medical technician from the ambulance rushed over to help. He bent down to listen carefully to the old man, then he ran for the nearby policeman. Larry finally turned around and caught the woman's hands. Gently he rubbed them and told her that the man would be O.K. His gentleness finally helped her settle down and simply hold his hands in return. With the help of the technician and the police officer, the three got the old fellow on the gurney and into the ambulance. The EMT stopped long enough to say to Larry, "He told me to tell the Master Sergeant that he appreciates all you tried to do and says that he will be eternally grateful if you take care of Crystal."

"Is Crystal his truck?" Larry asked in confusion. "I suppose he wants me to get these folks out of the ditch." He asked the bus driver to pull his duffle out of the baggage hold. As covered by mud and blood as he was, the clean set of tans would be most appreciated later.

The driver who hadn't completely recovered from the panic stop, said, "I would have made a mess if you hadn't warned us. I still don't know how you saw it coming." He gave Larry a coupon for the rest of the trip.

"I paid attention to the road," Larry growled. "Have a good trip."

He lowered the mast on the little truck, waded into the muddy ditch to re-hook the tow wire, and simply tugged the car out. He used the traction of the truck instead of the winch. He had the other two out as easily. Those cars were a bit scraped and muddy, but perfectly able to continue on their own. All three offered him a fifty dollar bill each and wished the old fellow a speedy recovery.

The remaining police officer came over to express gratitude for taking charge when it was needed. "I'll stop in to tell Reverend Sharp that you're bringing Crystal home. He might have a woman from the town stop in to help."

Larry asked, "Do the folks care that much about his truck?"

The officer chuckled, understanding the confusion. "It's not the truck they care about, Sergeant, but Crystal, his daughter. She's really impaired and may need some help settling down after seeing her dad so banged up. I'll tell them you are coming along; it's "Pop's Towing" in Reliance, about 12 miles west of here. Thanks again. I'm proud of all you did here this evening." He reached over to shake Larry's hand.

Crystal

It was then that Larry finally looked at the young woman. She had long straight black hair and almond shaped eyes the same color, that seemed to hold their gaze. She had high cheekbones and full lips. The attractive lady was very slim, even in her heavy sweater. Cleaned up a bit, he thought, she would be eye-catching. Her expression was serious, probably because of her worry over the care of the old man. Larry looked around and saw nothing more that would keep them from leaving. He signaled her to get in the truck and she immediately took her place. As Larry slid in, she reached out her hand, palm down. Larry thought she wanted a bit more rubbing, but when he started she pulled her hand away, then repeated her palm down. Larry wondered a moment, then offered his palm up. She nodded, and grasped his hand. With her free hand she touched her chest, and then his. She released his hand and sat back, looking straight ahead. The highway tow truck was still maneuvering the big rig back onto the road.

It only took a few minutes before he saw a cluster of lights ahead through the snow. One of them was on a building with a white sign, "Pop's Towing". Lights were on and Larry could see folks moving around inside. He pulled the truck beside the building and entered a huge mystery. The first one to shake his hand was wearing a clerical collar.

"Good evening, Sergeant," he understood the sleeve stripes. "I'm Pastor Joseph Sharp of the High Plains Parish, and this is Dory Fisk a neighbor. Thank you for helping strangers this evening." Larry noticed the young woman was busy with the hand of Dory, who looked up and nodded. The pastor continued, "I'll bet you need to get out of those wet clothes. You can use the bedroom behind the kitchen to change."

When he came out with fresh tans, Dory said to him, "She tells me that you tried to save him, that you are very brave and strong." A tear was coursing down her cheek. "She tells me there is a policeman on his way here with very sad news, and something very important." Like a scene in a play when no one has a line to say, the four stood still, waiting. Perhaps three minutes passed before the bright headlights lit the room momentarily.

The Highway Patrol officer from the accident came in. Looking at Larry he said, "I'm sorry to be the bearer of bad news. Mr. Crandall was too injured to make it to the hospital." The girl gave a soft moan. "Your help was excellent, but apparently the pulley also hit him in the abdomen. I think his liver bled out, internally. He was alive long enough to make a statement and give me a signed document for you, that says simply, 'power of attorney'. I suppose you should ask a lawyer what that means." Then looking at the pastor, he said, "Joe, he told me to have you give them his blessing. That's all he said. Does that make sense to you?" The girl was looking down at the floor.

"It's something of a puzzle, Marty, but we'll try to figure it out. It has been a long night for you. I hope you can get some rest." The pastor shook his hand.

When he was gone, Larry said, "I am so … confused. I seem to be the only one in the room who doesn't know what's going on. How did she know that officer was coming? And how did she know it would be sad news. I thought I had stopped the bleeding enough for him to make it."

"Sergeant, it is way too complicated to explain tonight. Let me start by saying that Crystal has a deep way of understanding. She usually knows what I am going to say before I do. If she holds her hand palm up, she is listening to you. If she makes you hold your palm up, she wants to tell you something. It will seem weird at first, but if you give it a try, you will see that you understand what she is writing in your hand."

"Please don't reject this as baloney" he went on. "It took me a while, then one day I could understand her clearly. The story I heard is that her mom was Shoshone, from the Washakie tribe up north of here. Someone convinced her that her daughter had a bad spirit. She left that little girl on Pop Crandall's porch more than twenty years ago. He couldn't turn her over to authorities, so he raised her as best he could. It may have been something he taught her to listen to the silence. She never went to school, yet she can read and write just fine." The girl was touching the hand of the woman.

"Sergeant, Crystal wants you to know how deeply she appreciates what you did this evening, and hopes you will not choose to leave."

A shiver raised the hair on the back of his neck, because he had just been thinking about getting out of this spooky place. "She knows that you have been sad because of the dead men you tried to help. She knows your heart can be happy again." There was a bit more exchange between the two women. "She apologizes for smelling offensive to you. She thought all men stink, until you smell so nice, like soap."

Larry shook his head with a wry smile. That had been his thought too, exactly.

The pastor advised, "Perhaps we should get some rest too. Sergeant, I am telling you this only to build some credibility between us. We are not a bunch of nuts. I was a Chaplain in the Army; my rank was Captain. I was with MacArthur when he returned to Manila. I have seen the terrible side of war, and the lovely side of peace. I hope you can find the same thing, but first some sleep in the back bedroom. I'm guessing the sheets haven't been changed for a while, but the blankets will keep you warm. I'll return in the morning and we can figure out the next step together. I'll pray for wisdom."

Dora said, "I'll bring some sweet rolls if you can find the coffee pot."

I hear you!

Then it was just the two of them, looking carefully into each other's eyes. Hers were deep and dark, like looking into a vast night sky. She thought his looked dark and guarded, like someone who had been betrayed. She held out her hand, palm up. He placed his over hers obediently. She softly held his hand and then with her free hand she touched her chest and then his. She turned his hand over and did a little squiggle with her fingertip.

"Yes, good night," Larry answered, "But I'm not your man." Oh shit! He understood that! "I hear you!" he muttered in confusion. Crystal hummed as she went into her little bedroom, leaving Larry to explore his thoughts, and the rooms at the back.

Day 2

It was still dark when he opened his eyes to the new day. For just a moment he struggled to determine if this was real or a dream he was having. It was real alright, real confusing. The bathroom was primitive, but usable. Then he shaved and showered in very cool water. He pulled on his work khakis. The kitchen was still the cluster mess it had been last night. It was a good place to begin, after he lit the wood heater, and set the coffee pot on the stove. He was on his second cup and the kitchen was pretty squared away when she came out of her room.

Crystal was wearing a T-shirt, just a T-shirt! With long trim legs, a flat tummy and deep neck-line, she was a vision of attraction. She held out her hand palm down. He obediently placed his hand under hers and her finger made that tiny contact.

"Yes," he answered, "Good morning. You're welcome. You look very beautiful, too. Would you like coffee or tea? I don't know what else is available." He poured hot water in the teapot. There was more communication and he answered, "I think you said it is nice to have someone else do the work." She shook her head and touched his palm. "Oh, you said someone sweet do the work." She nodded. They were communicating and this was just the beginning of the day. Larry thought, "I'd better be careful with my imagination. I could get carried away with such a darling woman."

Crystal held out her hand palm up. When he placed his on top, she held him softly then very deliberately touched her chest, then his.

He thought it would be a good idea for her to get clothes on before folks came and made the wrong assumption. Immediately Crystal went into her bedroom to dress.

Dory came first, with a warm platter of cinnamon rolls. Then Pastor Sharp arrived, and with him was another senior lady. "This is Susanne Thomas. If we get the other three, you will know the entire congregation." There was good morning laughter. Larry noticed that Crystal's face did not reflect the humor. But then her eyes met his and he knew she was quite delighted with the morning, even though a difficult topic had to be discussed.

Pastor Joe said, "Susanne was just a girl when Pop came here. He had inherited some money and wanted to start a town. He was going to call it, 'Top-of-the-world,' because we are very near the continental divide. Someone else had the idea of Reliance. He and the town have struggled for fifty years," the pastor said.

"How much land did he buy?" Larry asked.

"Oh I think he has thirty acres or more. That's ten times too much for a service station that never really became one, and ten times not enough for a farm that didn't either. At this altitude not much grows anyway but cattle."

Larry caught Crystal looking at the sweet rolls and suggested that folks could have some coffee or tea with them. Again he found her looking at him with that steady gaze.

Eventually the small talk gave way to the important stuff they needed to face. The pastor started it by saying, "Larry, when you got on that bus, you had no idea what the day was going to bring. Now it appears you have a considerable responsibility that you did not invite. Pop made his statement to the police officer for a reason. I don't know what he had in mind, but I'll sure try to help you see it clearer. You know, Pop was enlisted in '17, when the war ended. He said he never even got out of boot-camp. He was a lucky one I guess."

He went on by saying, "Pop may have been desperate, or very insightful when he gave that power of attorney to you. None of us, but you, can make the decisions that need to be made in the next few hours or days. First of all, there is a body in the hospital that needs our care. I think that is the place to start."

"Pastor, I think you are right, after I stop at an attorney's office to make sure I can do anything legally. I'm assuming Crystal won't need to go through that."

"I don't think Pop ever legally adopted Crystal," Susanne said softly. "When it comes to legal stuff, I think that little last minute scrap of paper is going to be very special."

Larry said, "There's probably a car around here. I'll drive into Rock Springs and get stuff started. Who wants to go with me?" Crystal's hand moved ever so slightly.

"I'll go along as a witness," Pastor Sharp said.

"By the way," Larry asked Dory, "what does it mean when Crystal holds one hand and touches my chest with the other?"

"I think that was Pop's way of kissing her. I haven't seen her do that with anyone else."

Larry found a seven year old Chevy Nomad station wagon in the shed. He remembered to throw his mud and blood covered tans in the back for a cleaners. The three eased into a slippery morning.

The attorney was skeptical until Pastor Sharp gave him Marty, the highway patrol officer's name, who gave the name of the EMT, who verified the deposition. For $25 the attorney filed a power of attorney in Larry Crown's name. The second bank they tried affirmed that Paul Crandall had a checking and savings account. There was a $1200 balance in the checking, and $33,800. in savings. Larry withdrew $3000 from savings. The next stop was a funeral home where cremation arrangements were made and paid. The trio made their way to the hospital to pay for any expenses. Only Pastor Sharp viewed the body. There were a few personal items to be retrieved. Finally before lunch Larry stopped at a men's store to get a warm shirt, jacket and working boots. His dress shoes were not intended for walking in slushy snow, and he remembered to drop off his uniform at a cleaners.

The sandwiches had been ordered when Pastor Sharp said, "Larry, I can see the good organization you have put into the morning. At the risk of sounding critical, did you think of Crystal's wishes before you arranged for the cremation? She might have wished a more traditional burial."

"I know I am occasionally callous", the sergeant replied, "but this is not one of those times. She told me what she thought should be done. I was just following her wishes."

"Now I am skeptical," the pastor whispered. Looking at her, pastor Sharp asked, "Is that true? Did he do what you intended?" He held out his hand for her light touch reply. Then he stared at Larry. "Sergeant," he finally said, "I apologize. You have been here less than twelve hours and you seem to be able to communicate with Crystal as well as any of us, maybe better. I'm sorry to be so dim-witted."

Larry answered him quietly, "I don't know how it works, but I sort of hear her voice in my head. I even know the beautiful sound of it. I'm glad I understood her." Before they returned to Reliance, Larry fueled the station wagon and stopped at a grocery store. You can take the sergeant out of the motor pool, but you can't….. It was snowing heavily on their way home.

A deeper mystery

He was watching the snow fall outside the front window. The road was so covered there were no fresh tire tracks. Perhaps the highway had been closed somewhere east of them. "Larry, can you hear me?" the thought was in his head. He turned and looked at Crystal seated across the room.

"Yes, I can hear you," he thought.

"How is this possible do you think?" Her words were never spoken.

"I have heard songs of people who have simpatico. Perhaps that's us. I don't know how it works."

"Do you mind if we talk like this," she thought politely. "For a very long time I have hoped someone would come along who could hear me as I can hear them."

"No, I don't mind at all. I'm not quite used to the idea, but it seems sort of fun," he replied silently.

"Pop knew that you are a good man. You tried to help him, and you calmed my fears," she thought softly. "But it is very strange to have a man take over in Pop's place. I don't know how to act."

"I understand how strange that is for you. It must feel like I'm an intruder. I would leave if I could, but..." He knew there was no place to go in the snow-bound world, and besides, she needed someone's assistance.

"Please don't think that. Can we agree that this is strange for us both, although I believe I like it more than you do. There is no resentment in my heart," her words were soft, more like a prayer.

Larry thought, "There is not so much resentment, but frustration in my heart. I am a man who is comfortable leading, in control, and this is neither."

"Perhaps we can get to know one another," she thought. "Will you tell me about your family?"

He thought of his mom, the death of his dad, his sister Jan, and brother Michael. He thought of his room, and their plain but happy home. The wonderfully amazing thing is that she saw it all.

She asked him about school.

He thought about summer vacation, work in the hay fields, the football season and ultimately Silvia.

She saw it all and understood his confusion and pain.

She asked him about the Army.

He thought about boot camp and the conflict, training school and being an aid in an investigation, of Wiesbaden and Estella, Long Binh, and Clark. A tear trailed down her cheek as she felt the enormous challenge of a cooler warehouse full of coffins.

She saw it all and understood how a happy young man can be twisted by the years of service into a strong rational warrior, who can leap into the dark and snow to save a strange old man in the ditch.

She asked him about love.

He thought for a moment before coming up with the memories of Bereavement, the beautiful, fragile, lonely women he had tried to help.

"Were they attractive to you?" she thought.

"Yes, very," he answered.

"Did they want you to touch them?" she wondered.

"Perhaps; they were all very lonely," he responded.

"But you did not take them into your bed?" she questioned.

"No, it was not me they longed for. They needed their husbands. I would have been artificial, and a hurtful distraction." Larry thought.

I don't understand," her thought was agitated. "Love is confusing and very complicated."

"Yes, love is all that and still it can be quiet, calm and beautiful." He wished they could change their thoughts to something else.

"Will you kiss me?" she thought clearly, "Not like Pops did, but as you wish to. I have never had that sort of kiss." Larry sat quite still for over a minute. "Please," her thought was unmistakable, and undeniable in its pleading.

He moved across the room to her, and gently lowered his face to hers. He kissed her softly, but with growing passion, and heard her think, "Don't stop! I want more."

Larry stood up, thinking, "That is the danger of love. At first it is inviting, then insatiable. It confuses the proper order of our life. Can you imagine a carpenter building a house roof first? The foundation must be shaped and good framing made before all the rest. We must continue to work on the foundation".

"Occasionally may I have a reminder of what a fine roof I will have someday?" she thought playfully. Her mind was still for a bit, then she thought, "This seems like teasing, to let me see without enjoying the rest."

"Yes, teasing is a good word for it when someone I have known for such a short time wants me to kiss her and arouse her, and more!" Larry walked to the window and studied the snowfall in the afternoon gloom.

Several minutes passed, as silent as the drifts he watched. "Tell me about your earliest memories," Larry thought finally.

"Thank you. I was afraid we weren't talking again. I have no memories of my mother and only a vague collection of Pop's frustrations trying to have a business here. He made very little money and spent most of his inheritance just keeping this place open. The highway people wanted to build a road to Superior, which is only about seven miles away, and this would be the junction to the highway for them. But Pop wanted too much for this property, perhaps hoping for a way out. I think the idea died. My adolescence was a long fantasy of being in the arms of someone who could carry me away. It has been terrible to live in a world of silence where I hear other people's thoughts. You know the odd part is that while I can hear them, non-Indians can't hear me. You must have a good part of tribal heritage for you are the first who can hear me." She was quiet for a long while, then said, "I think Pop knew that he was fatally injured. I heard him thank you for coming to his aid, and I heard the desperation as he wondered what would become of me." Her tone changed, "Do you know, this is the longest, most serious conversation I have ever enjoyed. I'm starting to think about the roof again."

Larry was amazed at how open and free she was, and how natural this form of communication had become in just a few hours. "Then let's think about something else, like the decision I have to make about the Army. My enlistment is over the end of April. I could sign up for another three years. I have eleven more years until retirement when I could receive a pretty nice pension for the rest of my life. That is a safe and secure picture. But I feel like I am selling the rest of my best years for a handful of money. I have saved my pay for nine years. There's over a hundred thousand dollars to start some business or go to school or, I don't know what," He took a deep breath, glad for finally saying it, or thinking it, out loud.

"That feels good to you, doesn't it?" Crystal thought. "You've been dragging around that decision for months, yet in your heart, you have already made up your mind."

"O.K." Larry thought, "That's not fair to think about my feelings, about the thoughts I've been hesitant to think about. Wow that was twisted."

"May I have another kiss?" Her thought was soft and quite inviting. "Please."

"It is what I desire more than another breath," Larry thought. "Would you still want it, though, if you knew it would start a fire? And that little fire would grow larger and larger until it consumed the house, and we would never see each other again?"

"What an absurd idea! That couldn't happen!" Her thought was aggressive and irritated.

"It happens all the time with people who have what they call 'one night stands.' They find someone who will make love with them without making a foundation. There is momentary fire, and they are gone in the morning." Larry had a momentary memory of both Silvia and Estella.

Crystal suddenly understood what he was saying. Larry was attracted to her, considerably, but was cautious because poorly managed, it could destroy their future. "I understand, Larry," she thought. "I still want a kiss, but not more.... right now." After an unresponsive minute or two, she thought gently, "Please."

Working together they made a passable spaghetti dinner from the groceries Larry had purchased. He also presented Crystal with a container of Shampoo, a bar of soap, and a tube of pleasant smelling lotion.

"I might not understand how to use these," Crystal thought playfully. "Maybe you should shower with me, to show me."

"Yes, Bubble Head," he thought in defense, "And maybe I should drive into Rock Springs to the Best Western Motel where I would get some peace and quiet."

"No one has ever called me a Bubble Head." There was a long pause and a tear brimmed in her eyes, "And I have never chased away someone who is as dear to me as you are becoming. I will tone down the teasing." She went into her room for the night, leaving him to do the dishes.

"It serves me right" he thought with his hands in the sink. "I could have made my point after we had cleaned up the table."

"Yes, you could have, Bubble Head." He heard her thought clearly, "I would have happily helped. Good night. I think I'm falling in love with you." The house was silent surrounded by drifting snow.

Day 3

Once again he woke in the cold dark house, but he was no longer confused. He knew where he was, if not why. He shaved, showered and dressed, eager to get the heater going, and for the smell of perking coffee. "Good morning, my Prince," he heard distinctly.

"Good morning, Lovely Lady. The tea water will be ready when you come out." His thoughts were so easy, and so clear.

"Must I be dressed, or may I come out like this?" she thought.

"I don't know. What are you wearing?" he asked silently.

"Just what I always wear to sleep, nothing."

"Hey Bubble Head, are you trying to start the morning with an argument?"

"You make a lot of noise," she thought, "but I'm pretty sure you would like what you'd see." Her tone was soft and very flirty.

"I'm sure I would, but then I'd need to throw you out into the snow to put out the fire." His tone was also much softer than it could have been.

"Yes sir, Mister Master Sergeant. I'm almost dressed right now." She came out wearing her T-shirt.

Larry walked over to her and delivered a gentle morning kiss, thinking, "You look beautiful whatever you have on." After a pause he asked, "Would you like some French Toast for breakfast?" Again he was delighted in effortless communication.

"How is it that you can think about food when you have just kissed me?" she thought.

Verbally, Larry answered, "Because I am more interested in building our future than setting fire to our morning." Then he thought, "Let me show you a fun way to fix breakfast."

When there were only empty dishes left on the table, Larry thought, "When we're snowed in there is not much to do, is there?"

Crystal raised her foot to the seat of her chair, consequently exposing a great deal of bare leg, and more.

Immediately Larry got up, gathering the plates. He tried not to think angrily, but the tone was there, "For goodness sakes, she is making this very difficult. I'm trying to help a dead man, and she is acting like a teenager!" He picked up the dishes and she went into her room. An hour passed with him standing at the window watching the snow continue to collect.

The phone rang. As Larry picked it up saying, "Pop's Towing", he was ready to tell the caller that they were closed. Instead, he heard a woman's voice ask, "Is this by any chance Master Sergeant Larry Crown?" Larry hesitated, wondering who in the world would know how to find him. "Yes it is, ma'am. How can I help you?"

"Sergeant Crown my name is Leslie Carr. I'm a reporter for the Rock Springs Times. I'm so relieved to find you. We have been back tracking from information we got from the Greyhound bus driver. May I have a moment of your time?"

"I'm snowed in and happy to be of service."

"Do I understand correctly, sir, that you were on a westbound bus that came upon a multi vehicle accident, east of Reliance? That when there was an incident with the tow truck, you leapt into the muddy ditch to pull Paul Crandall to safety and administer first aid?"

"Yes, ma'am. He had received a nasty injury on his thigh and had arterial bleeding. I used my necktie to fashion a tourniquet. The Highway Patrolman and an EMT helped get him in the ambulance." He didn't add more of the account.

So she asked, "Did you remain on the scene as your bus continued on its way so you could pull three cars back on the road and return Mr. Crandall's tow truck and ward to his home?"

"That is all accurate to my recollection, ma'am. I finished the job he had begun."

"Is it also true that in the ambulance, Mr. Crandall gave a deposition and signed a document that gave you power of attorney on his estate, and that before they could get him to the hospital Mr. Crandall died of his injuries?"

Larry answered more guardedly, "Ma'am, I'm not sure how much of that is public information. Perhaps you should be in touch with Pastor Joseph Sharp of the High Plains Parish. I've only been here thirty six hours. He has been a great help in showing me where the light switches are and the coffee pot."

"Oh Sergeant, you have been busy with much more than coffee pots. Did you make arrangements for Mr. Crandall's cremation?"

When Larry assured her that he had, she asked, "And what disposition have you made for the ward? What are your plans for the future of the property?"

"That pretty much takes all the time I have for this interview, Ms. Carr. You are beginning to sound like a rag tabloid to me. Have a good day." He hung up the phone. In less than ten seconds it rang again. On the fourth ring, he picked it up saying, "Pop's Towing."

"Please forgive me, Master Sergeant," Ms. Carr's voice was soft and contrite. "I apologize, sir. I did not intend to offend you. This story is so full of human interest, I may have gotten swept away. We received a copy of a photo taken at the scene of the accident. It clearly shows you helping Mr. Crandall, both smeared with mud and blood. Our editor would like to use the photo. On the Associated Press, however, it may go beyond our region. May we have your permission to print it? This call is being recorded."

"Yes, you may print the picture," Larry said with a bit of a growl. "If it gets to Clarkston, Washington, my mom might understand why I didn't make it home on furlough. Have a good day, ma'am." He hung up the phone and walked back to the window to watch the snow continue to fall.

"May I talk with you?" the voice was soft in his head. "I'm so very sorry." She stayed in her room.

"Of course we may talk," he answered, and she could feel his authentic relief in hearing her voice. "I'm grateful for the snow keeping us close together."

"I'm so selfish that's all I have been thinking about, being close with you. I didn't think about how you must feel, trying to save Pop, trying to help me, coming into a strange place with a burden you didn't ask for." A quiet sob caused her to pause. "Am I a ward? What is that, some sort of stain on me? You've been here less than two days and I feel like you are the dearest part of my life." He could tell that she was weeping.

"A ward is not a stain, it's a legal description for someone dear who has no other title, not a sister, or child or wife. It is not bad, it's just not very specific." He paused for a long moment, then thought, "Come out of your room and I will kiss you." Her door opened immediately. She was wearing her over-sized sweater. After a couple cups of coffee and a couple more tender kisses, he reminded her about the bar of soap, shampoo, and body lotion he had purchased for her. "I may be silly for helping you become more desirable than you already are. We'll get control over these raging feelings."

"Are they my feelings only, or are you feeling a yearning too?" she asked silently.

"Sweet Lady, I am a very healthy normal man. I want everything you want, but with a degree of control. I just hope we can build the foundation and frame first," his thought sighed. "I hope that one day in the future you will have a daughter who wants to give her body to a man she scarcely knows. You will be able to tell her from your own experience the satisfaction of not giving in to desire only."

Crystal rose from the table and went into the bathroom to cleanse herself.

When she was finished Larry helped dry her long hair and complimented her on such a pleasant fragrance.

"Does it excite you, arouse you?" she wondered.

"It makes me appreciate you and I understand that you want to be admired."

After a lunch of sandwiches and chicken soup, Larry called his mom. He tried to explain the situation. Finally he laughed when his mom considered that perhaps the fates had chosen him to spend enough time with a lovely lady that he might actually get serious. That made Crystal break into a grin. He told her that he loved her and would call again when he had more real information. "It's still snowing like crazy", he said before their call ended.

"Your mother loves you very much," Crystal thought. "She knows that you are the responsible child, and the generous one. She's a wise lady; I like her very much."

"How can you say that?" Larry's thoughts asked. "Could you hear her voice as I heard it?"

She nodded. "If the thought is in your mind, it is in mine as well."

"Crystal, where did you get such a full vocabulary? Pop wasn't very well spoken" Larry wondered.

"Pastor Sharp has given me many of his words, as has Dory. She was a teacher. I think I received a lot from them." Crystal seemed relaxed and content. "I believe you have given me many new words too."

"If you could do anything you wanted, what would it… Crystal, focus! What sort of a career would you have if you could choose any?"

"That's easy. I'd like to be your wife and the mother of our children. Beyond that, I'd like to be an artist painting wildlife, like birds, bears and especially wolves. I love the idea of wolves. You know, they mate for life." Her thought was almost a giggle.

Larry smiled, "As do Swans and Eagles, among others," he thought.

The afternoon slid by. They enjoyed the last of yesterday's spaghetti for dinner. They tried to play some card games, but found it frustrating. They both knew what cards the other had. They spent more time laughing than anything else.

Day four was Sunday, but they didn't know it until Pastor Sharp snow-shoed over to deliver an elk casserole made by Miss Dory. He told them there had been a number of phone calls about the Army Sergeant who had sacrificed his furlough. "You're something of a folk hero, Larry. Much of our nation is seeing demonstrations against the military. You stand out as a model for patriotism and service." Larry watched the expressions on Crystal's face. Occasionally he would think a response that only she could "hear."

"The DOT says they are about to reopen this north highway," the pastor reported. "The big plow will probably be here tomorrow. Then we'll be able to shovel the driveway and get back to town. Have you made any decisions about the future?"

"Oh please tell him you will stay, Larry, please," Crystal's thought was pleading.

"I'll tell you, Pastor Joe, this has been a challenge. The police officer told me that Crystal was impaired, which I soon learned was bogus. She hasn't many social graces, but she is intelligent and a kick to be around. At first I felt painted into a corner, but we've pretty much worked through that. We've grown very fond of one another, however, especially when she started her special way of speaking right into my head." Larry took a deep breath. "I'll tell you the truth; I think I'm done with the Army, which is one part of the puzzle. It seems too sudden for me to be making life changing plans, but I have had those thoughts too. I've got some savings and with Pop's savings, we might be able to change this place into some sort of tourist attraction." He heard Crystal think, "What?" "I've wondered if we could create a Heritage Center of tribal art, information, and souvenirs."

"How did I not know about those ideas? They are wonderful," she thought.

Larry continued, "There must be six or eight nations that have lived near here. Done right, I think it would be interesting enough to pull some travelers off the road."

"It's a terrific idea! Why didn't you think about it sooner!" she thought behind her calm mask.

Pastor Joe had a wide smile. "And what about the two of you?" he asked.

"Yeah, what about the two of us?" Crystal thought.

The Pastor continued, "Since the night of your arrival I have hoped that you might become the solution for Crystal's care. She has no family, no job skills or history. I know this seems unnaturally sudden, but practically speaking you are her best shot right now."

"You know, pastor, I have worked for years on the discipline of making decisions based on information rather than emotions. It is easy to be distracted by someone as pure and affectionate as Crystal. I knew the first night I was here that I could lose my heart to her. We haven't had much time to know what is appropriate in this unusual circumstance. I think it would be unfair to take advantage of her distress. So, I think I'd have to talk with Crystal." Larry began a serious thought. Silently he said, "We've only known each other four days." He took a big breath and asked silently, "Would you like to be my wife?"

Instantly she answered "It is the only thing I really wish for."

He continued speaking with Pastor Joe, "But I don't think we should continue to live under the same roof without the blessings of the church. Our control has been pushed to the limit. Pastor would you consider a marriage ceremony?" Crystal threw herself into Larry's arms, demonstrating to the Pastor that they had been having that special sort of silent simultaneous conversation.

"We'll have to wait three days for the marriage license," the Pastor said with a wide smile. "Can you two be strong a little longer?"

"I'm going to have a roof in three days!" Crystal's thought nearly shouted.

"Thank you, Pastor Sharp," Larry said more quietly. "That will give me time enough to contact the folks at home, and Fort Leavenworth. Hopefully they can box my personal stuff for me. I've got about ten grand in cash there too."

The three friends chatted into the afternoon. Pastor Joe had two themes. He reminded them about the ongoing challenge of building a good marriage. "With a sound foundation," Larry thought. "And a really good roof," Crystal added. Secondly Pastor Joe stressed the importance of them having growth goals and plans. He thought Larry's idea of a tourist attraction would be excellent for the community. He also applauded them both for dealing redemptively with the tragic loss of Pop. He trudged away through the drifts before it got dark.

Larry and Crystal sat on the floor near the toasty wood heater. She admitted that she had never been farther away from home than Rock Springs, and knew nearly nothing about geography. So Larry thought about our country, with two oceans and mountains in between, and tremendous cities and vast plains. He imagined a map and pointed out where the nation's capital was located, where they were located right now, where his home was. He imagined a globe, admitting that he was less familiar with it, but could point out generally where Germany was located, and Vietnam.

"There is so much I want to learn about," Crystal thought. "The seasons change, but I don't know why. Do you think the fates choose what we must endure?" she asked philosophically.

"Mom thinks there are many mysteries. By the way, when was your last period?" he waited for an answer that didn't come immediately.

Finally Crystal thought quietly, "I just started today; how did you know?"

"I didn't. I just asked."

"But why do I shed blood if I have not been injured?"

"Your body has a season once a month. Your period means that you are not pregnant. It's part of a month cycle," he thought, hoping that his simplicity would make sense to her.

"Tell me about the seasons, and being pregnant." It was easy to think about a host of intimate questions she had, and some that he had too. Finally the fire was banked for the night. Larry wondered if he could kiss her goodnight after such arousing subjects in the very full day. She moved to him, pushed him onto his back and gently kissed him, thinking "Our roof is going to be beautiful."

Day 5

The darkness was a friendly ally, allowing him to find his place in the new day. He was cozy under his quilt listening to the silence. "Are you awake, my Love?" he thought. He heard a murmur, and then, "Not quite; but I will come to you if you want me."

"I love you. Rest for a while," he thought into the darkness. He got up and as soon as he could, rebuilt the heater flame, shaved, showered and put on the coffee pot. The phone rang before he could pour a cup. "Good morning this is Sergeant Crown."

"Good morning Master Sergeant." The voice was clipped and military. "I'm Corporal Evans calling from Colonel Mann's office. He is interested in your status."

"Thanks for the contact, Corporal. You must have gotten this number from Pastor Sharp. It's good that we are communicating. I'm snowbound just about on the top of the Rockies. That local pastor has been checking in on me by snowshoe. He tells me the Highway department may have a plow in today to open Interstate 80. There are two things you can do for me, Corporal. You can go into my room and box all of my personal items, especially the winter tan coat, and open the desk drawer all the way. Underneath it you will find an envelope with a fair amount of cash. I'm going to need both of those as soon as you can get them here. My suggestion would be to place them on a west bound Greyhound bus, addressed to me in care of Pop's Towing, Reliance, Wyoming. They owe me a courtesy. Secondly, will you advise Colonel Mann that I request Separation Papers be drawn up? My tour is complete at the end of April. I believe I have enough furlough time to complete my enlistment. I will be away from this phone as soon as possible, but will call you in the morning. Is all that clear to you, Corporal?"

"Quite clear, Sir. I'll pass along the message and get right on the other too. Good day, sir." Larry looked up to see Crystal leaning against her door jam, wearing her T-shirt, and a wonderful smile. It was going to be another interesting day.

He found a coal shovel in the shed and was going gangbusters clearing the snow off the driveway, when he heard the phone ring again. Apparently folks were getting his number from Pastor Sharp. He wasn't sure if Crystal would answer it, so he hustled in to say "hello."

"Is this Master Sergeant Larry Crown?"

"It is, but unless this is a military business, why don't you just shorten it to 'Larry'?"

There was a chuckle then, "Works for me, Larry, I'm Pete Houser with the Wyoming DOT Department of Acquisition. I understand you have the power of attorney for the Crandall estate. Are you guys snowed in still?"

"I was just out in the driveway hoping to hear the plow." Larry said, still a bit out of breath.

"It's on its way and should be there within the hour. Our department has been trying for quite a while to get an easement across Mr. Crandall's place. Perhaps you could stop by to talk about that. This is a perfect time."

"Are you in the courthouse?" Larry asked.

"Yes we are. My office is in the basement with several other government offices."

"By any chance is the Department of Interior one of them?"

"Just down the hall from mine. Why?"

"I plan to stop in there to find out about tribal business. Could I see you about 1500, I mean 3 o'clock this afternoon?"

Again he heard that chuckle, followed by, "It will be my privilege, sir."

Larry looked around at Crystal. "The plow is coming," he thought.

"Yes, I heard that, and we are going to town as soon as we can get out. What are your plans?" she asked silently.

"It might be a busy day. I'd like us to apply for a marriage license." She clapped her hands. "Then we should buy some new clothes for you. I would like to stop by the Dept. of Interior to find some tribal contacts, and perhaps get a recommendation about a tribal architect. We'll see what Mr. Houser has in mind. Calling so early, and soon after the newspaper article tells me that he wants something. Then maybe we could stop somewhere for a hamburger. If we get all that done, we will be able to clean up the house tomorrow and get ready for company."

"What company?" she thought.

"It would surprise me if Pastor Sharp doesn't bring the whole congregation to our wedding." he answered with a big grin.

"I love the thought of our wedding," she thought as she embraced Larry.

He was on the last twenty feet of driveway when the plow came rumbling by. Larry waved to the driver, knowing now that their full day would be accomplished.

There was only one other couple waiting to get a marriage license. When it was their turn, Larry got a couple surprises. The clerk took information first, took copies of their driver's licenses, he learned that Crystal's last name was officially, "Bluesky," Then, when the clerk asked them to raise their right hand, and answer: "Do you solemnly swear that all this is true to the best of your knowledge, that you have no wants or warrants, for your arrest, and no other marriage that would prevent you from legally finalizing this agreement?" Both Larry and Crystal said clearly, "I do." He looked at her in surprise.

She thought, "It is just so much more fun to speak this way."

At J.C. Penny's they selected a pair of gold wedding bands, then an attractive tan and blue dress suit for her, tan shoes and a bright blue rayon blouse. Larry also suggested that she get some attractive lingerie. "Why, only you will see them in the dark." she thought.

"Yes, I will see them, and you will feel more lovely in them." he replied silently. She had never been so lavishly treated.

He thought about skipping the Department of Interior. The afternoon was sliding past in a hurry. Crystal, however, silently encouraged him, "We can stop for just a bit of information. You think that is going to be important, and so do I."

The clerk he spoke with listened carefully. "You want to speak to representatives or spokesmen for the tribes?" she asked.

"That's what he just said," Crystal grumbled silently. She apparently was also irritated by obvious questions.

The clerk turned toward a large display of printed brochures, and selected at least a dozen.

"While you're at it," Larry asked, "are there any with information about craftsmen or artists who specialize in tribal art?" The clerk selected another few. "I only have one more request," Larry said politely. "Do you have a recommendation for an architect that might be tribal, or feature that theme?"

The clerk thought a moment. "No one from the tribes comes to mind, but Harris Designs did the Long House for the Cherokee Reservation. It is very attractive." Larry thanked her and they headed back toward Mr. Houser's office; they were only a couple minutes late.

Crystal thought, "She wanted you to ask for more things. She liked you a lot." Her shoulder brushed his, intentionally.

"Mr. Houser," Larry introduced himself, "I'm Larry Crown, and this delightful lady is Crystal, Mr. Crandall's daughter. She speaks very little, but understands everything. She came along to hear your proposal."

"Well, I'm not sure I have a proposal. We're just going to review the situation in Reliance." He spread a topographical map of the area. "Our department thought you may have the key to a great convenience for the towns of Superior and South Superior," his fingers pointed to two dots, "who have been snowed in for well over two weeks. The current road to them is difficult."

Crystal whispered in her thought, "He didn't want to use the words mountainous and expensive to keep open."

"Reliance is directly south of them on the edge of the Great Divide Basin," Mr. Houser went on. "If we could just get an easement across the east boundary of Mr. Crandall's 33 acre property, we'd enter government land. That would open not only an easy way to the highway for Superior, but a recreation advantage to the entire basin."

"He's thinking about a very large plan for development of several ski areas." Crystal thought.

Larry's expression remained pleasantly interested. "Yes, I can see how that would benefit the two towns, as well as campers or skiers. I'm just wondering how that would benefit Crystal. You did use the word, 'easement.' Doesn't that usually refer to passing utilities over, or an ingress egress availability I don't think a two lane highway with ditches on both sides qualifies for an easement. Mr. Houser, what does a quarter mile of straight flat road bed run these days, especially one in a very primary bottleneck?"

"He's thinking about the last conversation with Pop. A hundred thousand is what Pop was asking and Houser said 'no', even though that was a fair price." Having her soft voice inside his head almost made Larry smile more.

Even though they had only spoken briefly, he said, "Pete, it's getting late, and we have a couple more stops to make. You rejected Mr. Crandall's suggestion of a hundred thousand. I don't know why the price would be any cheaper today, in fact with those big plans on the table, the price might go up. You have pressure from your superiors and the ski resort developer to get this done. I think you are fortunate to have this second chance. I'll even allow the harvesting of a thousand cubic yards of fill material from the rest of the property. If that isn't sweet enough I guess we don't have anything more to say to one another. But I would suggest you contact that developer. I'll bet he jumps at the opportunity. Don't they want to break ground this summer?" He rose, thinking to Crystal, "I just made that up, but it makes him think I know more than I really do."

Mr. Houser asked, "Can I call you at Pop's Towing?"

"Yes you may. That's the number that worked this morning." There was that irritation again of nonsense questions.

They were almost back to the car when Larry noticed a book store across the street. "Hey, it's too early for hamburgers. Let's go look at books. They might have one on how to paint." Larry thought.

"Or maybe about roof-making." Crystal thought with a naughty smile.

The only instruction book he found was Bob Rossi's guide to landscape painting. He also found a drawing pad and colored pencils. If the easy step by step process worked as easily for Crystal as the pages made it appear, she would be an artist very soon. At least, the book demonstrated the principles of drawing perspective.

Crystal had scattered happy thoughts, as she finished her French fries, "I don't recall a more exciting day. This has been like Christmas, only lots better. Getting out of the house was terrific. Then the marriage license…thank you by the way, again. All my new clothes, even panties…. Did I say thank you? I'll show you, if you want. Talking to the lady about the tribal information might lead somewhere, and the man from DOT. Was his name Houser? I didn't much like him before, but you handled him easily. Do you think he'll call…" Larry offered her another sip of milk shake, "I'm babbling, huh?" she finally thought silently. "Sorry, but when I'm close to you, I get sort of goofy."

On the way back to Reliance, they stopped at the grocery store to replenish the cupboard and frig. Larry was also mindful to buy some feminine pads, with instructions how to use them. Crystal had been using washcloths that could be washed and reused. Larry tried not to have a thought about that, recalling that Pop Crandall may not have been the best hygiene teacher for a young woman.

"Larry, are you still awake," he heard in the silent darkness.

"I'm awake, Sweetheart," he thought.

"May I come to your bed?"

It would have been so easy to comply, to break down to the delicious opportunity. "Please don't" he thought finally. "I want you more than ever. But I would not be able to have a clear conscience before Pastor Sharp, or my mom. Can we wait just one more night?" There was a lengthy pause.

"I know what the word cherish means now," her thought was a whisper. "I cherish your strength and honor. I rather desperately love you."

"With my whole heart, I love you Crystal." In the night sky the stars were silent witnesses.

Day 6

The morning was still, and Larry was pretty sure that he would find it was snowing again. He hurriedly shaved, showered, and got the heater going. It was snowing tiny flakes. It wouldn't amount to much he was certain. This time he had finished his first cup before the phone rang. Once again it was Corporal Evans.

"Good morning Master Sergeant. I'm happy to report that both concerns of yours have been satisfied. The box is aboard Greyhound bus 331 in route to you today, and in it are your separation papers. Colonel Mann wants me to express our sense of loss. Your nine years were studded with outstanding acts of service. There is a recruiting station in Rock Springs. Please have the separation papers signed and dated by a Notary and returned to the recruiter, who will return them to us. I hope that is clear, sir. Are there any questions?"

"I have no questions, Corporal. You've done a fine job. Thank you, and please give my respects to Colonel Mann. Good day." He hung up the phone thinking what a relief, and at the same time a wave of anxiety about the future. This had been a very sudden shift.

"Is your heart happy or sad?" the words formed silently through her closed door.

Larry went to the door, opened it and stepped next to her bed. He bent and kissed her willing lips. "My heart is one hundred percent happy," he said verbally. Then he kissed her again. Crystal tried to tug him into the covers with her, exposing the truth that she did in fact sleep in nothing. Fortunately, Larry kept his balance and freed himself saying, "I love you in the morning. You are especially beautiful." He closed the door behind him.

"You are a bratty, cruel, teasing man!" the thoughts came at him. "And I love you incredibly this morning. How can I feel that my heart is so full it's about to burst, then you come in and fill it fuller? Come back in here and we can celebrate your freedom."

"You come out here, after you get something on, and we will celebrate scrambled eggs." He felt her laugh joyously.

The phone rang, startling Larry. "Good morning Larry", the voice said, "Its Pete Houser from DOT. I hope this isn't too early." When Larry assured him that it was not, he had already run around the block, Mr. Houser said, "You were correct. My boss is anxious to get this road in, and the developer has offered to pay one hundred thousand dollars for the eastern forty five feet of your property. I have been authorized to invite you back into the office to sign a purchase and sales agreement so we can get the legal stuff started. Who knew a week ago when you boarded a Greyhound bus that all this was going to come about?"

"Life has a way of surprising us, doesn't it?" Larry said as Crystal stepped out of her room in only her new lingerie. "I'll be in before noon," Larry said before he hung up. Instantly he headed for the door vowing to get a snowball to cool her off.

A screaming, giggling Crystal slammed the door to her bedroom. She was convinced he would do it.

When things finally settled down and breakfast dishes were washed and dried, Larry phoned Pastor Sharp to tell him the marriage license was all set. He shared the news that had occurred in the past day. The pastor praised him for keeping his priorities straight. Finally they agreed that Pastor Sharp and other witnesses would be welcome for a 2:00 p.m. wedding ceremony.

Then he called his mom, embarrassed that she wasn't the first one on his list of "must do" chores. He explained that they were still pretty snowbound. "The plow came through yesterday morning, but it's still snowing lightly." "No, mom, we haven't had sex. But if there had ever been a perfect opportunity it was this past week." They talked about the future without the army. "I'm not sure what will open up. I have some ideas." "Yes I miss you too and want you to meet Crystal." "Yes, she is darling, and witty, and full of life." "I'm glad you can tell that I love her. You will too just as soon as you get to meet her" "I don't know. I need to go into Rock Springs today to take care of more legal stuff. When he gave me the power of attorney, he hooked me into a lot of responsibility." "Yes. I'm lucky too. I don't know what the future holds, but as long as I am with her, it is going to be great. Thank you. I am very happy." They talked about Jan and Michael, both of whom had babies on the way. Finally it was time to go do other chores.

First he went through the house mercilessly removing every newspaper or magazine. He started a trash fire a ways behind the house to incinerate them. He added any old book that appeared over worn and out of date. Any clutter that seemed pointless got torched. He took a couple of the black garbage bags into the bedroom and with Crystal's blessing and oversight, all of Pop's clothes were headed for the thrift store, even the two pair of shoes and three pairs of well worn boots. Behind the clothes in the back of the closet, he found three rifles, and a military style 1911 .45 caliber handgun. He would hold on to those.

All the way into town, Crystal's thoughts were nonstop. "Will he like me when he sees me bare? Will the lights be on or off? Who will begin? Shall I touch him? May I? Will he guide me? What will...?"

Larry interrupted her thought by thinking, "Are you frightened by the thoughts of roof-making tomorrow?"

"No, I'm not frightened, or nervous about it. I just don't want to do something that you wouldn't... Yes, I'm very nervous about it. All my teasing, as you already know has just been a smokescreen." She was uncharacteristically quiet. "I have tried to act brazen to impress you, perhaps you would not think I am so ignorant about everything." Her hair rocked as she shook her head.

"Crystal, Sweetheart, we are both anxious about tomorrow. I have enjoyed your brazen behavior. Every man hopes to be wanted by his lover. Will you agree that tomorrow we will be confident that nothing hurtful or shameful will occur, only gentle affection? We will assist one another, especially if it is by our deepest thoughts."

"There, it happened again" she thought. "When I thought my measure of love for you was completely filled, you just added more. What a fortunate woman I am." She reached over and rested her hand on his leg. A sly smile bloomed on her face. "Does every man hope to be wanted?" she thought. Larry moved her hand back to her own side of the front seat.

"You'll put us in the ditch." He silently chuckled.

Their first stop was the thrift store to get rid of four bags of donations. Then Larry signed the papers at Mr. Houser's office. He was told that there might still be a U.S. Federal Bank in the old part of the business district. He was given directions, but no assurance the bank was still there. Happily it was. They went in and with his driver's license, and Army I.D. along with his small bank book, the teller told him his balance after nine years of deposits was \$233,818.36! He asked to close the account with a money order to First National Bank, where Pop had an account. Both of them read the unkind expression on the teller's face, and tried not to respond to it. When they took the deposit into First National Bank, the same teller was there that helped him before. She gazed at the deposit slip and for a brief moment Larry tried to understand the silent thoughts she must be having too. A quarter million dollars can make a lot of dreams come true.

They had been building up their eagerness for the last planned stop, the Harris Designs Architect. Morgan, the senior partner was not available, but Chad, his son was. They were ushered into a comfortable office. "How can I help you folks today?" His voice was cheery, but he was unimpressed by the looks of Larry and Crystal.

"He doesn't think much of us," she silently whispered.

"That is to our advantage," Larry silently answered with a smile that was not understood by the architect. Looking at the young man, he said, "We were told you did the Long House for the Cherokee reservation. Can you tell me about it?"

He hesitated in confusion. "Tell me what your interest is in such a large project." There was no disrespect.

"Well, Chad, we have in mind a commercial multipurpose building that would feature a small café, show rooms for art and tribal crafts, and perhaps four or six guest rooms with in suite facilities upstairs. If you already have a large design, I'm wondering how difficult it could be to adapt it to our use."

"He's trying to understand if you are serious or just teasing him," Crystal reported.

Larry asked, "By the way, do you know who did the construction?"

"I do, he's my brother-in-law, Mountain High Construction."

"Then here's just one more question in this opening round. Ballpark, what was the cost?"

"He's not sure, and is still leery of us," she thought.

"I suppose I can give you a number, but I'm not aware of Bob's financials. I think it must have been in the neighborhood of \$175 thousand."

"He inflated that number for safety," she thought softly, as though she might be sharing a secret.

"O.K. Chad, thanks for your time today. I hope you can do a bit of modification to your existing design, which I know is great. See how close to $130 thousand you can come and I'll get back with you next week. The job site is in Reliance, about a hundred yards off highway 80, easy on and off. It will be a cash job, if it's done on time."

"That caught his attention. It seems the Cherokees haven't completely paid yet," Crystal smirked. They held out their hands to shake on the proposal.

On the way home they stopped at Penney's to get some new clothes for Larry, slacks and a jacket, a couple shirts and ties. He also picked up his tans from the cleaners even though he may never wear them again. They had fish and chips at the Roundhouse and stopped for a couple bottles of champagne, plastic wine glasses, and snacks for tomorrow afternoon. Crystal thought that they might get a bottle of sparkling cider for those who wouldn't want alcohol.

Silently Larry answered, "That's a gracious idea. You're thinking like a hostess,"

She was quiet for a long while, watching the dark shadows passing by. "Larry, I don't know how you keep all the things straight in your head. Again today we accomplished so darned much, and you didn't have a note or anything."

He reached across and rubbed her leg. "Sweetness," he thought, "it's all for you. Each task makes our world a bit more organized, or efficient. At the start of each day, I just think, 'what can I do for Crystal today?'" His hand stroked her thigh, "and then I just do it, as much as I can."

She made a small attempt to pull his hand higher, but when he took it away, she thought, "I was sure you were going to do it."

The house was dark and cold when they arrived home. It didn't take him long to have a warm fire and a cup of tea for each of them. He looked at his watch, thinking, "The bus should be here a little after nine." Larry made sure all the outside lights were on. At 2120 (9:20 p.m.) he heard it approaching and went out to meet it. It was a different driver, but one who was familiar with the drama that had occurred a week before.

"Sergeant Crown, I've got your box right inside. My supervisor told me to thank you again for avoiding the pile-up. This is the least we could do for you." He also had Larry's tan jacket, which he had taken off before exiting the bus.

"That's very gracious of you. I do have this coupon to pay for the box. I'm glad to get my stuff. You better be on your way; I don't want to make you late." The doors closed, and interested faces peered out as the bus resumed its journey.

Inside, the box was opened, first for the separation papers, and then for the manila envelope. Crystal was counting the hundreds," thirty two, thirty three, thirty…" Larry began counting to confuse her, "twenty nine, thirty six, no thirty four." He got punched on the arm as she started over.

"I've been thinking again, Crystal," Larry began silently.

But before he could go on, she interrupted, "I know and I think you are a very naughty boy."

"Listen, Silly, I'm thinking that after the marriage ceremony we might like to leave for a honeymoon of sorts. How would you like to drive to Oregon for a couple days on the coast, and then on the way back, we could stop in and you could meet mom. This is more than enough cash for a little vacation. What do you think?"

She was a bit more serious. "I just want to be by your side, very, very close by your side."

They were in a favorite place, on the floor in front of the heater. There was a gentle kiss, and then another. The next one was more intense and Larry realized the dangerous progression. "Sweetheart," he thought, "easy. We have done so well. Let's not stumble on this last night. Tomorrow night, I promise, there will be no need for restraint" She moved to lie on top of him and Larry eased away, then stood up. "I will be proud of us if we demonstrate a bit of control." A bit shaken, Crystal got up and kissed him lightly, saying, "Goodnight, I have little control when I am in your arms." She went into her room and he was afraid he heard weeping. "I'm sorry my Love, he thought. "I only want to honor you." There was no answer.

Wedding day!

In the morning Larry went through his regular routine. The heater was chasing away the chill, he was shaved and showered and in some comfortable clothes from the box. The coffee was perked and he whispered, "My day will be perfect when I get to kiss you." Her door opened and she came out dressed in her T-shirt.

"Now I can breathe," he silently whispered.

"Me too," she said as she hurried to kiss him.

The morning seemed to be filled with last minute demands. Certainly the most pressing was getting the separation papers signed and returned to the recruiter. They stopped at a florist for flowers, and almost forgot to get a cake, but even that last little detail was covered. At 2 o'clock they were gathered with seven neighbors and Pastor Sharp. Dory spoke for the group when she said she had never seen Crystal more beautiful, or happy. When pastor Sharp finished asking the questions and pronounced them man and wife, he added that if Pop could be here he would give his dearest blessings. Amen! No one wanted to drink apple juice, and the cake was pretty much devoured. Finally at a little past 4 o'clock, everyone wanted to get home before dark. Larry made sure he gave the pastor the "thank you" card he had prepared with a crisp $100 bill, and the happy couple was alone.

"Will you come into my room and take off your clothes?" It made no difference who thought it, or who agreed, it was a joyous idea.

Lovers

In the dark morning Larry heard Crystal think, "Good morning love. You are wonderful." She pulled the covers over her head and was still. He got up quietly, shaved and showered, lit the heater and put on the coffee pot. He heard her get up momentarily and then she whispered, "Come back in here for a morning kiss." Oh my, it turned out so much more than a kiss.

When they were finally at breakfast, Crystal said silently, "I've been thinking about the Oregon coast."

Larry was quick to answer, "Good, we can leave whenever you want."

"Let me ask you, my lover, would you rather be beside me in the car for a couple days or next to me in a cozy bed?" She heard his reply and thought, "Yes, me too! I do want to meet your mom, but the beach can wait." They spent two nights in Boise, at the luxurious Continental Hotel. Larry heard repeatedly, "This is the most wonderful place in the world!"

The first day with his mom was a little awkward. Neither woman knew quite how she fit in, and was unsure what to call the other. But the more time they had to work on it, the easier and more natural it became. His mom said it was uncanny how she could understand Crystal. "Even her unspoken thoughts seem clear to me," Irma declared. "She wants me to teach her how to cook so she can surprise you."

On the second day, Larry suggested they take advantage of some of the larger stores in Lewiston. He needed some casual clothes, and bet that Crystal would like some as well. She was nearly overwhelmed by the Bon Marche; there were so many displays and departments. They had made several selections when Larry heard his name called. "Larry, is that you, Larry Crown?" He turned to see Silvia Shepherd, or whatever her last name might be now.

"Well, hello, Silvia," he said carefully. Turning to Crystal, he said, "Sweetheart, this is Silvia, who was in high school with me." Turning back to her, he introduced Crystal, saying, "Silvia, this is my bride of just a week today." The ladies nodded, but Crystal thought, "Oh wow, is she surprised. She doesn't like me very much." Then they noticed a young girl standing behind Silvia. Crystal asked, "And who is this darling young lady?" She heard quite clearly the child think, "My name is Francine, but they call me 'Fancy'"

Silvia answered, "This is Francine, my ten year old daughter. Isn't she a big girl?"

"She looks pretty fancy to me." Crystal said casually.

Silvia looked sharply at Crystal, saying, "Did you call her 'Fancy?'"

"No, ma'am. I said she looks fancy in her lacey dress and white shoes," Crystal said clearly. But she thought "There is something wrong here. Can you talk to the mom while I talk to this child?"

Larry said to Silvia, "Wow, it's been a long time. Mom sent me some newspaper clippings that you have remarried and are living in Pullman. How did we get lucky enough to run into you here today?" That should get the distraction going.

Silvia obviously relaxed. "That's certainly not news, but yes, we have a new home in Pullman. I'm married to Harvey Waltz; from the class of '49." Her nervous smile asked him not to do the math. Her husband is thirteen years older. "He has a great insurance company there. We're just down for the day. You know it's only an hour and a half drive, so I come down to spend a day with mom every now and them."

"Does Harvey have any family living with you?" Larry asked to stretch out the stall.

Brightly Silvia answered, "Why yes, Robert is nineteen and Jeffrey is sixteen."

Crystal had squatted down so she was at eye level with Francine. "Why are you so sad?" she asked silently. The little girl looked startled, her eyes shifting around to see where the question was coming from. "It's alright," Crystal comforted her. "We're safe right now. Can I help you?" The girl shook her head.

Larry said, "Yeah, mom has kept me up to date while I was in Germany. But when I got to Vietnam things were a lot tougher. Her mail could only get to me every other week." He could see that Crystal was silently talking to Francine. "I think I heard that you have another child?" His gaze was holding Silvia's attention.

"What is so scary this morning," Crystal thought.

"We have to go home today," a tiny voice answered.

"Is there something scary at home," Crystal thought gently.

"The bad boys are there. They scare me all the time."

Silvia shook her head, "Jerry Spooner and I had a son, but Jerry's lifestyle was too Bohemian for me. When we split up, I got Frankie, and he took Jonathon to live with the hippies in California. For a while I thought she was going too. She was pretty fond of Jerry, probably because he was just a big kid himself."

"Wow, do you ever get to see your son?" Larry asked in true surprise.

"No. They've chosen to live with the artists in Quincy, or something like that. It was an amicable split. I'm so much better off now."

"Who are the boys that scare you, Frankie?" Crystal asked.

"The brothers, they are lots older than me." the tiny voice answered

Crystal stood up saying, "What a darling girl. But I couldn't get a word out of her." Silently she asked Larry, "Do you see the tears in her eyes? She's afraid to go back home."

Larry said casually, "What a surprise to run into you Silvia. We're going to get back to mom's and head home tomorrow. Take care." They turned to go their separate ways.

"That woman scares me," Crystal thought, "She is cold as a snake."

Larry said, almost to himself, "I wonder how Francine could hear you. She has no Indian heritage." They completed their shopping, both satisfied with an armload of fun new clothes.

All the way back to Reliance they were thinking about changes that could make Pop's house more livable and attractive. When they pulled into the dark driveway, they were aware of a new foot of snow. Before the heater could chase away the chill, they were cozy under a comforter, breathing words of affection.

Big progress

By the end of February, there was another four feet of snow and the road was closed for four days. Chad Harris had finally agreed to a price of $135 thousand with the inclusion of a large deck on the north side, and had applied for permits. The DOT paid for the strip of property and allowed Larry to make suggestions were the roadway crossed Bitter Creek. If they took the fill material for the roadbed from a specific area, a small reflection lake could be created.

By the end of May the snow was gone and trees were budded, the world was a verdant green. Larry found a carpenter who would build a new garage and master bedroom attached to the west side of Pop's place, and a bulldozer was hired to scrape off most of the topsoil from about five acres where the lake would be created. At this altitude, topsoil is too premium to waste on the bottom of a lake. It would be used to dress and smooth the area around the lodge.

The bulldozer revealed a unique tree, growing out there alone. In the general area of the lake the driver spotted an Alpine fir that had been contorted by many winters of snow, yet continued to grow bent and beautiful. It was a symbol of tenacity, of perseverance in the face of great adversity. Larry asked the driver to protect the area around the tree, turning it into an island of sorts.

A state operated construction team began clearing a straight road bed due north. At Bitter Creek, which was flowing vigorously with the snow melt, they carefully applied three large concrete culverts. On the north side of the creek, they began excavating the fill for the roadbed. Right now it looked like a complete mess, as expected. They had a generous notion of how much fill they could take, but Larry was confident that within a year the lake would be a tourist highlight.

As all of that construction activity was going on, Crystal was busy too. At the library she had used a typewriter to compose a letter to the tribal councils, explaining the intent for the new building and hoping this could be a new day of understanding. She also wrote a letter to craftsmen who might have carvings, paintings, or fabric creations that they would sell on consignment. She reminded them all of a time when the tribes came together in the Great Divide Basin, which was to be the very location of Heritage Center. She made enough copies of the letters to be mailed to the Cherokee, Cheyenne, Apache, Nez Perce, Ute, Comanche, and Kiowa nations. The work she most enjoyed, however was the practice drawings she was making in the sketch book she had been given. She was getting pretty good.

By the end of June the foundation had been poured, and the main support beams were being installed. A deep well had been drilled and tested. There was more than enough fresh water. In the darkness one night, Crystal thought a tender thought for Larry; "I have never watched a large house being built. Now I can see what you said so many times is true: first the foundation, then the frame, and finally the roof. I'm so glad we finally get a roof." She snuggled into him in a most pleasant way.

"Yes, I'm impressed too by this building. But I am more impressed by ours." She didn't understand what he meant, so he explained. "We were strangers thrown together by a terrible accident. In a very short time, because you can speak to my soul, we were more than friends, and not yet lovers. We wanted more, but were strong enough to build the frame. Today I feel more complete than any description of life I have ever read. You are my breath, my laughter, my deepest satisfaction. I have no satisfying life apart from you. I would wither and blow away like dust."

Her thought came softly to him, "Are you trying for more roofing? That was the most tender thing you have ever said to me." She wiggled herself under him, saying, "O.K!"

By the end of July the green metal roof was on, double pane windows installed and a septic tank in place. Built on almost solid granite, there was not enough soil to perk a drain field. A septic pump out was required at least monthly. Since it was so convenient, Larry had another attached to Pop's place for the new bath off the master bedroom. A large propane tank was installed for the forced air furnace, fireplace, hot water and kitchen appliances. Since it was so convenient, Larry had another installed for Pop's place too.

By the end of August, the parking lot was black-topped, the cupboards, counters and shelves were installed; doors and display cases were in place. The lights were installed and a permit to occupy was issued. Aspen were beginning to turn golden and Larry asked Crystal when her last period had been. With a quizzical look, she answered, "It just started today, how did you know?"

By the end of September there were frosty evenings and a tiny snifter of snow. Larry asked Crystal if she wanted to spend another winter snow-bound or would she rather visit his mom for a while. They placed industrial quality electric heaters on low, enough to prevent harmful freezing, in both the center and Pop's place, and left for Clarkston. He promised that if this experiment wore thin, they would return immediately.

Back in Clarkston

They were at his mom's in time for Crystal to sign up for a fall painting class at the Community College in Lewiston. Life seemed tranquil. Larry ran each morning, and they both helped around the house. Cooking lessons were very welcomed by Crystal. There was ample time for long conversations and Larry's mom was even more convinced that Crystal was the perfect match for her son. They often didn't even need to speak, the other already understood.

October crawled by and then November. December was filled with decorations and holiday food. Crystal loved the idea of presents, both to give and get. She presented Larry's mom with a beautiful painting of a mountain lake, with two wolves in the foreground. It was the best present of the season. Larry asked if he could have copies of it made and matted, to be sold at the center. It was an accepted compliment to both ladies.

In the second week of January the evening news carried the story of a young girl from Pullman who had mysteriously disappeared from her home. A sliding door was found open and there were signs of a struggle. Blood stains on the floor were being examined. When her name and picture were shown, both Larry and Crystal were alarmed. It was Francine Waltz.

Crystal thought, "We know her! We should do something!"

"Easy Sweetheart. We can't just barge into an investigation because we had a five minute conversation several months ago." he counseled.

"But she told me she was afraid of the brothers," Crystal thought with force.

"Let's listen to the news tomorrow. They might find more evidence." Larry was trying to understand a strange feeling.

"If she is running, she's trying to get to Queezy, where her other step-father and brother can protect her." Crystal nodded to punctuate her thought.

Irma had been watching the movement of the two. Now she asked, "What is going on with you two?" She looked into Larry's eyes, asking, "Are you listening to one another?"

"Sort of mom," Larry answered. "It is how I knew Crystal was a special person. She was able to speak to me in a way that got through. Think of a date."

Without hesitation, Crystal said, "May 5th, Larry's birthday. Is that your birthday?" She paused a moment and said, "October 17th would have been your wedding anniversary. I can hear your thoughts, but since you are non-Indian, you can't hear mine, but Larry can."

"Mom, do you have a map of California, or an atlas?"

"Your dad kept a stack of maps in the living room, just in case," she said.

Larry found a map and scanned the index. Could it be Quincy?" he asked.

"Yes, Quincy, that's where her step-dad, Jerry Spooner lives, with hippers or something." Crystal was sure. She said, "I can remember his name because I like to spoon with you." She was remembering what Larry had let slip out of his recollection.

Irma continued to listen to the silence between them. She was mystified.

Larry thought, "I can imagine doing something that would make things worse for the police, but I can also think of something that would be easy and correct." "Mom, may I make a long-distance phone call?" He dialed the operator, then asked for the number of the Quincy California Police station. When he was connected he said, "Officer Mars, my name is Master Sergeant Larry Crown, U.S. Army. I have information that might lead you to a missing child from Pullman, Washington. She disappeared last night under suspicious circumstances. I have reason to believe she may be trying to get to her other step-father in Quincy. His name is Larry Spooner; hers now is Francine Waltz, and she is eleven years old. With a twelve hour lead, she may be getting close to you there. There was blood at the scene so she may have been assaulted. I'm assuming that if you make contact with her, you will follow protocol and get her to a hospital where they can do a rape test. If that occurs please call me at this number. I will drive down to bring her home. Or you may contact the Pullman PD. I would advise against calling her mother, since that home is what she is running away from in the first place. I am her natural father."

The kitchen was in stunned silence. When he ended the call, he heard, "Is that true?" They both asked, one silent, the other hushed.

Larry looked at Crystal saying, "I have no proof of that, except she can hear you. Non-Indians can't hear you. I'm pretty sure that neither her dad or mom are Indian. Process of elimination suggests that one careless senior night may have been pretty important. If it comes to that, I'll take a paternity test. If it helps to urge that officer to find her, it's good misinformation."

Irma asked Crystal, "Can you show me how this works? How did you begin to speak with Larry?"

Crystal took Irma's hand and rolled it palm up. With her fingertip she made a little squiggle motion, then another.

"Yes I know he is very bra… Oh my goodness, I can hear your thought. Tell me more." With a smile, once again Crystal wrote. "And he made sure you didn't have sex the whole time?" Crystal wrote. "Even though you tried to win him over, so to speak." She sat back with a curious smile and the beginning of understanding.

Larry said, "Once we started speaking that way, we talked about everything, for hours every day, things that most folks are too timid to talk about. I don't know as much about her because I didn't think of the questions. She knows my soul; she knows about Jan and my distrust of Michael. She said she likes you because you are very wise."

"But she doesn't use your hand to write," Irma pondered.

"That's because I'm half Indian, and I can hear her; you're not."

Crystal held up her hand, as though listening. "There is good news," she said quietly. The phone rang.

Irma answered, "Yes he is. Just a minute." She gave the phone to Larry saying, "It's the police." But she was looking into the depths of Crystal's mysterious eyes.

"Mr. Crown, this is Officer Mars again. I contacted Larry Spooner who had just had a phone contact with the little girl. She was stranded in Portland, at the bus station. I contacted the Portland PD and as luck would have it, they had a black and white at the scene. They made contact with your daughter and are transporting her to Sisters of Providence Hospital, as we speak. I suppose you can pick her up in the morning. Do you have any other questions, sir?"

"No, Officer Mars, you've been the right man for the job tonight. Thank you for your involvement. I'll take care of the rest," Larry said quietly.

"Yes, sir, I hear that." The phone call ended.

Crystal asked, "Shall we go to Portland right now? How far is it?"

Larry shook his head, and thought, "No, it will only take about three hours in the morning. She can get some rest, and have an opportunity to give her statement. We can be back by early afternoon and I can be in Pullman after that."

Crystal asked very softly, "Do you plan to hurt them?"

"Yes, but not the way I would like to. They do not deserve to live another day. But that would ruin our future, and nothing is worth risking that. I will use the law to come down hard on them." Larry gave them both a reassuring smile.

"I just wish I knew what was going on in your minds," Irma said with admiration.

Larry said aloud, "Mom, I need to iron my tans. I thought they were put in the attic forever, but now I think they will carry a degree of authority, and remind me to hold to the high ground."

At 5:30 p.m. Larry and Crystal arrived at the Waltz home. Three Pullman police cruisers were already there. When they were ushered into the living room there was something of a crowd gathered, Harvey Waltz, his sons Robert and Jeff, Silvia and four Pullman police officers, one of them a woman. The first thing Larry said was to the lead officer. "For their safety, would you please place restraints on the men, and have them seated. I want to kill them where they stand."

"Hold on, Sergeant, there's no need for threats."

"Sergeant Kindler, I have just spent three hours with a little girl who has been through living hell with these people. Here is a sealed bundle of semen and blood evidence, results of the vaginal examination, plus the signed statement taken at Providence Hospital by the Portland PD. If you read it you will want to join me in their execution." The officers had positioned themselves to protect the family.

"Let me tell you what I know, Officer Kindler. Night before last, the assault was started by the sixteen year old, Jeff. He went into Francine's room, there was a struggle as he tried to rape her. She had a bloody nose and escaped to the kitchen where he caught her and carried her to his room."

"You've got no proof of that! She's never been in my room.!" Jeff said defiantly.

Larry's body gave an involuntary flex toward him, and the youth flinched and sat down. "Oh but I do you filthy piece of trash." To the officer, he said, "In his bed, pushed between the mattress and the headboard, you will find her pink trinket bracelet. If the sheets are clean, there was enough blood to soak through to the mattress cover. Robert joined the assault and carried her to his father's room where there is a video camera. It seems Harvey wanted pictures of yet another rape. Behind the false books you will find quite a few tapes that Harvey has collected, including one of three people having sex. Silvia, you may not have even known that you were on camera, with his sons." Larry's voice was trembling with emotion.

Jeff said hysterically, "He made us do it!" The police officers had turned to stand in front of the three accused men.

"Officer Kindler, I'm confident you have more than enough evidence here to throw these snakes in prison. My self-control is pushed to the very limit right now. I must leave. But I would ask you to spare my daughter from further abuse by allowing her custodial care in her paternal grandmother's home in Clarkston. My wife and I are wintering there while our Wyoming home is snow-bound. We will care for her and help in any way to see the guilty brought to justice."

An outburst from Silvia interrupted Larry. "You can't do that! You have no right! She isn't yours!!" She sobbed, "She isn't yours."

Larry took a big breath, knowing what was coming next. "Many folks have told me what I can't do" His voice was quiet and threatening. "I can count from October 7th, the night we played Southfield-Lathrup, and I drove you home. July 9th is just nine months and two days later. My family wasn't as wealthy as Steve's so you rode on the Lucas' gravy-train. Getting knocked up by Larry Spooner was a poor move. You screwed the golden goose, because Steve was in WSU when you became pregnant, and you couldn't blame him again. You were locked into the wealth of Harvey before Larry moved out of the picture. Did you even care what was happening to Francine? But I can guarantee she will be safe with me. I hope the bunch of you have a long and very uncomfortable confinement." Looking at Silvia, he added, "I doubt that this model of motherhood will try to work any sort of custody maneuver, since she is also a contributor to Francine's abuse."

A new plan

Larry and Crystal left, confident that the wheels of justice were in motion. Her first question was, "How do you feel? I was afraid you were about to attack the kid."

"Yes, you know I wanted to hurt him as he had hurt Francine. But I'm pretty sure that is going to happen to him in prison, where payback is a bitch." Larry was quiet as the car headed south. "I wonder what will happen to her."

"Larry, are you serious?" Crystal erupted audibly. "She is going with us. She is ours!" She switched back to thoughts. "We can make sure that she is never afraid again." Her thoughts were so loud; however, Larry was convinced they would be audible.

He smiled, admitting silently, "Those are my thoughts too. I just wanted to hear you say it first."

Crystal continued, "I am so happy you got her away from that woman, though. She is a witch! When you were explaining to the officers what Frankie has been through, that Sylvia woman was calculating what she would do with the house when the men were in prison. She thinks it's worth a lot of money and she can go to California and be famous in adult movies. She doesn't want to see Frankie ever again"

Larry answered, "Frankie is a cute name, sort of boyish, but cute. It sounds like our mind is made up."

She slid close to him allowing her hand to rest on his thigh. "Our mind is made up, and you are going to be so happy."

They enrolled Frankie in Clarkston Middle School with the agreement that she could mail in her reports and tests for April and May, when she would be in Wyoming. She took Larry's old room, and the newlyweds moved upstairs to Michael's old room where there was more privacy and another bathroom.

One night Larry overheard a silent conversation. Frankie was telling Crystal how frightened she was still after the bad people had been put in jail. She said there was something like black shadows that were hiding behind the bed, or in the closet.

"I can remember when I first came to live with Pop that I had bad dreams too."

"What did you do?' the silent little voice asked.

"I imagined that I could take a big heavy rock and drop it on them." She chuckled, "Can you imagine how frightened my fears were of being squished? They ran far away and hid." Placing her arm around the child's shoulder, she asked, "Do you think your scary thoughts would run away too if you dropped a heavy rock on them?"

"I like that idea, but they are pretty mean, ugly and stubborn."

Crystal replied softly, "Whenever I would feel one coming back, I would find a big rock. Now I have Larry who chases all my fears away. He will take care of you too."

Toward the end of March, as they were preparing to leave, Crystal asked if she could see some of those old paintings Irma was keeping in her sewing room. They opened the crate of larger ones. She agreed that they were abstract, and definitely not her style. But the one named, "Dancing on the Rhine," was different. It was of moonlight reflecting off the river. The sweep of blue in the dark and white reflections seemed happy to her. In the lower corner, almost lost in the motion was something that reminded her of a couple, twirling and free. She liked it enough to ask Larry if they could hang it in the lodge lobby. There was a nice large space that needed some color.

The leave-taking from Grandma Irma's was more tearful than Larry expected. He was surprised to see how sad Frankie was to go, but Crystal was the most moved. Those three clung to one another until Larry reminded them that they would return in just six busy months. "Do you promise?" his mother asked through tears. "Yes, do you promise?" both Crystal and Frankie silently asked.

Laughing, Larry answered audibly, "Yes, I promise. I live in a funny farm!" As the two ladies got in the station wagon, with Frankie in the middle of the bench seat, he noticed they were holding hands, and understood that a silent conversation was already engaged. He could listen in if he wanted.

A new year-- with new direction

They probably could have made it home in a very long day, but Larry thought it would be kindest to stop in the Boise Continental Hotel again, and make the trip more enjoyable. They stopped at the grocery store in Rock Springs for a couple big boxes of nourishment, and the post office for another large box of held mail. A glance told Crystal that many of the letters were in reply to the information she had sent to the tribes. It was well before dark when they pulled into their driveway, with enough snow still left in the yard to indicate a heavy winter. Larry was eager to see how quickly the new forced air gas furnace could warm the place. They hadn't been home an hour before there was a knock on the door. Pastor Sharp had been watching for their return.

"Come in, Pastor Joe," Larry invited. "Meet the newest member of the family." Frankie was introduced, and a very brief account of how she came to be in Reliance was given.

The smiling pastor said to her, "Ever since your dad has come to us, he has been helping folks. Have you noticed?"

She shyly nodded, "Yeah, I was in a pickle when he came to my rescue."

"And you couldn't pick a sweeter mom than Crystal," the pastor said warmly.

"She's a lot sweeter than the mom I know. Crystal is my best friend." The girl was comfortable enough with these people to speak honestly. "I've got hope if I can stay with her."

Crystal leaned over her and said, "What do you mean, 'if.' There is no 'if' in this house. You are mine, little sis, and I am not letting you go, even if you beg." A wide smile underscored her certainty. The four chatted until Pastor Sharp said it was time for him to check on some other folks, but he was happy to see lights on here again.

So began the leisurely springtime of continued growth. A beautiful sign was hung on the front of the lodge that had the dimensional look of carved letters identifying "Heritage Tribal Center." Crystal began to accumulate an inventory of crafts to be sold on consignment: arrow heads, dream catchers, wooden carvings of animals, deer hide vests with beadwork, fur caps, lamps made from deer antlers. She carefully recorded each donor and price requested.

Larry made a couple sandwich board signs saying "Free coffee 6 – 9." A fresh pot was in the lobby every morning and afternoon, along with a tray of cookies and a basket for donations. The first three days he tried to "salt" the basket by putting in a couple dollars, but the money disappeared along with the cookies. All the inside doors had locks to protect the merchandise on display. But Larry started a vigilant visit to the lobby pretty regularly. The good thing is that folks began to stop. By May Crystal and Frankie were busy most of the day in the store, and the donation basket was frequently full.

By the first of June Larry hired two local ladies to alternate a soup and sandwich lunch from 11 – 2. He got a liquor license to sell beer or wine, and it was fun to see how full the deck became in the afternoon because it had a territorial view of the reflection lake, the Basin and the Teton Mountains. By July all the display space was filled, Crystal's 'Wolves' painting had its third run of copies, and business was brisk. Larry asked Crystal and Frankie if they thought he should hire someone to take their places if the task was overwhelming. They answered that it was fun, and they were just getting the hang of the job.

Crystal shared with Larry that the new member of the family was afraid no one would know that her birthday was approaching on the 9th of July. She would be 12 years old. He made plans for a surprise hamburger dinner at the Cattle Club in Rock Springs. Isn't it wonderful when a good thing leads to a bigger moment of growth? When Larry asked Dory Fisk if she could lock up for them, he learned that her husband's retirement fund was running out, and she would very much appreciate a part time job.

"Dory", Larry began, "I've been too wrapped up in the store to think about another feature we could offer at the Heritage. There are four bedrooms upstairs that we could use as a bed and breakfast, if we had someone to run it. We could take care of the scheduling and expenses in the store, but we would sure need someone to do breakfast and the laundry every day. I'm thinking we should be able to get $40 per room. How would you feel about going halvers with that. If all four rooms are booked that would be $80 for each of us. Breakfast would not need to be fancy, maybe pancakes and eggs, a couple slices of bacon and a bit of fruit."

There were no takers for the first two days the sign was out. But almost every night of August there were folks in all four rooms. When it was time for Frankie to be in school in Clarkston, Larry closed the store, but welcomed Dory to continue to operate the Bed and Breakfast until the snow fell. That was nearly two months of extra income.

Another summer

The following summer was just as lucrative. There was pressure to offer some sort of evening meal on the deck, so more folks were worked into the service family. Perhaps the most interesting thing that summer was the offer from the ski developer. He needed a sales office with highway visibility. Larry turned down the first two offers, but as they returned to Clarkston for Frankie's last year in middle school, there was a substantial offer made that had Larry thinking about it. But when they returned in March, with beautiful snow still on the ground, and work to be done, the offer was shoved aside.

A crucial discovery

The store was restocked and busy every day, the bed and breakfast was equally busy. The free coffee had to be refilled hourly. On July 1st just eight days before Frankie's 14th birthday, a well dressed man asked if he could speak with the manager. Crystal thought he might be from the ski developer so she immediately got Larry out of the kitchen.

"Good day, Mr. Crown. My name is Gunter Klein, I'm Curator for the Denver Art Museum. Yes, many have pointed out the acronym DAM. It is still good for an ice breaker. I stopped in last week, and noticed you have a most unusual decoration painting." He pointed to the "Dancing on the Rhine" hanging in the lobby.

"I purchased that when I was in the Army in Germany," Larry explained.

"Then it is not a print or copy?" the man asked.

"I bought it from the painter, Mr. Laven. He was quite ill at the time," Larry explained.

A very serious expression clouded the face of Mr. Klein. He said, "If that is an original Laven, it should not be hung in the light or elements like this. Do you know what that is worth, Mr. Crown? It was assumed that all his work was destroyed in the war."

"I think I paid 25 Deutsche Marks for it," Larry answered casually.

"Sir, I will gladly pay you ten thousand dollars for it right now."

"Gunter, you are not supposed to do that when you are wheeling and dealing. You have just told me this is much more valuable than 10K. Excuse me while I get my wife. It is really her favorite. She might not want to let it go." He walked into the store and told Crystal a tiny bit about the conversation, and his need for her to come out and listen to Gunter's thoughts.

"Now Gunter, I purchased this painting in the Palace Square market in Wiesbaden." He wanted to give Crystal time to focus. "The signed card on the back says the title is 'Dancing on the Rhine.' It just seems like moonlight on water to me, but my wife believes she can see a dancing couple. I think it might be an illusion, myself."

Crystal thought, "He is very excited that you are ignorant to the importance of the painting. It is very famous. And the personal information from the painter makes it even more special. Are you really going to sell him my painting?"

"In the late nineteenth century and early twentieth," Gunter was sounding like a lecturer, "the material of the frame and the canvas were quite inferior, or the painting would be worth much more."

"Wow," Larry said mockingly, "think how valuable the Mona Lisa would be, if it had better material."

Crystal thought, "He's thinking that if he can't buy it there should be a way to steal it! He is almost desperate for this painting."

"Would you consider selling it for fifteen thousand?" Gunter said quietly.

Larry answered, "You know, if I had been aware how valuable this thing is, I wouldn't have dangled it out here where a thief might want to get his hands on it. I'm thinking that what I should do is send it to the auction company in New York. What's their name? Souter… Suther…"

"Are you thinking of Sotheby's" he asked painfully, knowing that if this secret was widely known he wouldn't stand a chance to get it.

Crystal thought, "He knows if you take the painting there you will get much more for it."

"O.K. Mr. Klein, I'm not going to play with you anymore. One or both of us might make a lot of money today. What would you say if I told you I own thirteen more Laven paintings this size and nearly one hundred smaller ones? All painted between the late twenties to late forties, and all with names and annotations from the painter. You have told me that I can receive more money by selling them at auction, but you are thinking how beneficial to the Denver Art Museum an entire wall of Cubist paintings would be. It would be a major coup for you."

Larry held a long look into Crystal's eyes until she nodded her approval. Then he said to the curator, "Here's the deal. I'm something of a gambler. I'm going to give you a week to talk with your board, or investors to get a ballpark guess at what one hundred and fourteen original, previously thought destroyed paintings would do for the Denver Art Museum. If your opinion is enough to get me to take the next step we can bring the paintings to Denver and have them appraised. That will be the price I will receive. Otherwise they go to

Sotheby's and I will be richly rewarded, and the paintings will belong to someone new."

"He's thinking," Crystal thought, "that you are really lucky that he stopped here, and that he is even more lucky that you are giving them a chance. Your suggestion might work."

Fresh start

In September they didn't return to Clarkston, but to Denver. The ski developer had finally offered a million four for Heritage, and the Museum had offered seven point seven million for the paintings. The Crowns had fallen in love with a delightful home above downtown Denver with a spectacular view of the mountains. Crystal had several paintings being featured in a local gallery. Frankie was excited about the Colorado School of Graphic Design; and Larry had a final interview at the Mercedes-Benz dealership as Service Manager. The car folks were impressed with someone who had been in Stuttgart diesel training repeatedly, and drove a 300SDL coupe.

One beautiful autumn morning after Frankie had gone to school, Larry thought, "I love you, Sweetheart. Are you happy here?" There was no answer even though Crystal was standing on the other side of the kitchen. Larry moved closer and thought, "The house is quiet. Let's take off our clothes." Still no reply. He stepped behind her and stroked her back. She turned to greet him with a gracious smile, a bit startled.

Larry asked audibly, "Sweetheart, how long has it been since your last period?"

"MMmmm, about six weeks," she answered audibly. "Why do you ask?"

Finis: "I Hear You!"

I Just Know!

His little life began in crisis. He was not due for another seven weeks but his mom knew something was very wrong. She called Larry's office.

"Larry, come quick! My water just broke and there's a lot of blood in it!" Her voice was on the edge of hysteria.

"Lie down, Sweetie. Elevate your feet if you can. I'll be right there." He tried to make his voice sound reassuring, but instead of hanging up the phone he called 911 and requested an ambulance. He gave them instructions that if they got there before he did they should break the door if she didn't answer. It was an emergency.

When Larry arrived he found the ambulance backed up to the side door by the kitchen,

"We found her on the floor by the open door. She must have feinted trying to get outside," the lead EMT explained. "We're about to transport her. My advice is Porter Memorial. It's the closest hospital and has a terrific labor and delivery unit." Larry was alarmed to see the ashen face of his unconsciousness bride, strapped to the gurney.

"I'll follow you. The baby isn't due until the end of next month." The bitter taste in his mouth was an expression of his anxiety. In the following four hours he received updates from her surgeon. They had stabilized Crystal, given her a transfusion and a sedative for pain. The status of the baby was still unclear, but it was probable that delivery would be necessary. Larry called his boss at Miller Mercedes-Benz to explain his sudden departure. He called Frankie at her high school and he called his mom. Then he waited.

Finally the doctor came out with a genuine smile as he reported, "We've stabilized your son, who is resting in an incubator in the nursery. Crystal is pretty sedated, but I'm sure she is going to be fine. We are going to watch the baby closely because we just don't know what effects he may have from oxygen deprivation or the drugs we had to use to bring Crystal around. Give her another couple hours to shake off the effects of her anesthesia, and you can see her. I'll tell you, it was close for them both. I'm glad we saw them when we did.

A few more minutes and the results may have been much worse." The doctor shook his hand and Larry felt he could finally catch a full breath. It was the 5ᵗʰ of July, 1975, a real reason for celebration, and just four days before Frankie's. Larry called a cleaning service that could make sure the kitchen floor was sparkling clean again, removing any bad memories that Crystal may have.

Crystal was released from the hospital on the fourth day. After that there was at least one family member each day looking in on the nursery, sometime all three. Crystal had liked the name Daniel Walter because it honored both Larry's grandfather and dad. The regular reports they received from the nurses were positive. For the first two weeks there was little movement or vocalization. Then, instead of the usual crying, which sounded like squeaking, Dannie grunted or growled. At first the nurses thought he was making a diaper deposit, but then realized he was calling for attention. It was delightful. He was released from the hospital on August 24ᵗʰ, five days after his original due date.

A family of four

According to the usual growth markers Dannie was perfectly ordinary. Turning over, crawling, cutting his first tooth, first steps, first word, which was "mom," potty training, all were on the appropriate markers. The only time he would cry was if pain was involved with an accident. Almost always Crystal or Frankie was immediately there to comfort and quiet him. The only unusual thing about Danny was his unmanageable black hair. Try as they might, no comb could make it lie down. It insisted on standing up haphazardly, so it was always in a buzz cut.

When the preschooler was five, however, something very unusual captured the family's attention. They had been working on some separation anxiety that Dannie displayed when his dad left for work each morning. They had learned that if Larry placed his car keys in a bowl on the table near the front door, the chore of retrieving them seemed to allow Dannie's participation in the leave-taking. When his dad said, "Well, I guess it's time for me to go to work," the lad would say, "I'll get your keys, daddy." There would be no problem. On a gray day in late October, as Dannie picked up the keys, he complained that they were hot to his touch.

First sign

"Daddy, I don't want you to have your keys today. Please don't go to work this morning. Your keys are very unhappy," the child said in surprise. "Don't go. Stay home."

Larry considered the outburst and assumed that it was another manifestation of his little son's anxiety. "Let me feel the hot keys," he said.

When they were handed to him, he said, "They feel pretty cool to me. Take them over to mommy and see if she thinks they are unhappy."

Several minutes were taken up with gentle assurance that the keys were not unhappy. Even Jackie got into the discussion. Finally Dannie said, "Daddy, if you go to work, you will be hurt."

"Son," the dad said softly, "are you worried that something bad will happen to me?"

"The keys don't want you to be in the big accident that is happening right now." There was a sense of relief in his voice. He had stalled his dad long enough.

Frankie turned on the morning news just in time to hear that the 265th freeway was being closed. It had just turned hazardous by an unexpected ice storm. It began with heavy hail then the road froze a glare ice covering. Dozens of cars and trucks were in a crash with multiple injuries. Had he left the house on his regular routine, Larry very well might have been part of that mess. The family exchanged amazed glances, then they studied Dannie's contented expression. The keys were cold now. The danger was past.

Yes, he was just an ordinary boy, interested in climbing trees, building forts and getting dirty like any other. His dad took him fishing which required more patience than the lad had. He did have an aptitude for learning though, so by the time he was in the second grade he was reading with comprehension the fourth grade textbooks.

Second sign

One spring day as the class was coming in from recess, Mrs. McClendon, his teacher, met them with an accusation. "Someone got into my purse and took my wallet. Dannie, you were the first one into the classroom. Did you take it?"

He shook his head saying, "No ma'am."

She made her way through pretty much all the students, receiving the same answer.

Finally, Danny said, "If you think about this logically, you can see no one has it in their pocket. It must either be in a desk, or a back-pack, which have been locked up since lunchtime". She immediately asked everyone to open their desk tops. A hurried examination was futile. Still she looked to young Dannie for a suggestion.

"If it is in a back-pack, I know I can help you find it." He seemed far too matter-of-fact to be fibbing to her.

She unlocked the closet where they were all neatly hanging. It was obvious that he wasn't touching or inspecting any back-pack. He had simply raised his hands three or four inches away from them and was slowly passing along beside them.

"Wait a moment, Dannie," the teacher ordered. "Go back to the purple one. It moved." She wasn't sure it had moved, but she was sure he had not touched it. Once again the back-pack moved ever so slightly. He, on the other hand had felt the warm rush as he had passed it and was hesitant to tell her. It was already more weird than he could explain. The purple back-pack and its owner, Sandy Buttons, was off to the principal's office and then suspension.

Later that afternoon he was trying to explain to his mom and big sister the event. "It was very weird," Dannie said. "Remember the morning when dad's hot keys kept him home? It was just like that."

Frankie smirked, "Did you really tell Mrs. McClendon to think logically? Second graders don't use such a big word."

"Well, she wasn't being very smart by just asking every kid in the room. Maybe she could have just asked the stealer to step forward." He shook his head. "Someone needed to get the truth out."

Crystal had been listening with her half smile. She joined in by wondering, "Did you say you could feel warmth coming from the back-pack?" Her tender expression assured him of her positive conviction.

"Yeah, but this time there wasn't any danger. It was more like her wallet was lost and wanted us to find it so it could be where it wanted to be. It was a good thing." His smile was so wide his dimples appeared.

Frankie looked at her mom and wondered, "Mom, do you ever miss that silent talking we used to do?"

"Yes I do," Chrystal said softly. "That stopped when I became pregnant. If somehow Dannie is blessed with the ability to be safe and honest, it was a good trade. Have you tried it with your dad?"

The teenager shrugged, "Yeah, lots, but he has never heard me. I think it was something you brought to us. Maybe it will come back."

With a rosy blush her mom answered, "Maybe. And maybe I am pregnant again."

Frankie squealed, "Really? Oh, I'm so glad for you. Does dad know?"

"It is so strange. I think he keeps track of my periods better than I do. A week ago he asked me when my last period had started." The blush deepened as she drew in a big breath. "I said that it hadn't started yet. Yeah, I think he knows."

Dannie felt that warm rush invade his body. He didn't say a word about it because he had no way of explaining it. But he was delighted that he was about to have another sister. He remained silent with the knowledge.

Third sign

The start of the spring break began just before Holy week. Once again Dannie sought out his big sister for information. "Frankie, how can I take flowers to a friend in the hospital?" He was satisfied that the question would begin a desired process.

She answered, "Who's your friend, and what is he there for?"

"Shirley is in school with me. Mrs. McClendon told us to pray for her because she is going to have serious surgery. I just want her to get all better."

When Crystal was given the information she made two phone calls. The first one was to Mrs. McClendon, to verify Dannie's information; and the second to Barb Wilcox Shirley's mom. She learned that Shirley had been born with a congenital birth defect, a faulty heart valve. She had received corrective surgery as an infant with the possibility that it might need to be repeated. That apparently was now the case. Shirley was in the pediatric ward of Porter Memorial for a couple days, awaiting a Monday morning surgery. Barb said, "This would be a wonderful opportunity to comfort a young girl who was feeling pretty overwhelmed at the thought of heart surgery."

At 7 o'clock they were given directions to the appropriate elevator. On the fourth floor they followed the numbers to Shirley's room. She looked small and delicate against the white sheet, but there was a large smile that welcomed Dannie and his mom. Jerry and Barb Wilcox introduced themselves and thanked them for thinking about their daughter.

Looking at his friend, Dannie began, "Mom said every girl appreciates roses." He was trying his best to encourage her, "but I guessed that you like daffodils more." He presented a happy bundle of yellow blossoms.

Jerry chuckled saying, "What a good guess. Daffodils are her favorite flowers." Barb placed the flowers in a vase and set them near Shirley, who held out her hand toward Dannie.

The patient said softly, "Mom told me that Mrs. McClendon told the class I was about to miss some school. I didn't expect anyone to bring me flowers." She wiggled her fingers, inviting him to hold her hand.

To call it an uncomfortable moment for an eight year old boy would be an understatement. But when their hands touched there was a barrage of information.

Dannie's first experience was her very warm hand. That was a happy thing. Her eyes were bright and clear, and oh so happy. Secondly, Dannie sensed the room getting very warm, and that was not a good thing. He felt it was a warning. He said to his mom, "It's very warm in here." She understood the meaning, although Jerry wanted to say it was quite comfortable. Dannie continued to hold Shirley's hand and hold her blue eyes in his gaze.

That's when the burning pain began in his chest. He groaned and placed the side of his face on the bed. Once again he groaned, mystifying the adults, but Shirley understood and held his hand more tightly. Dannie raised his head looking directly at Jerry he said, "She needs to see her doctor now." Another groan forced its way out, "Right now! Push that button thing for help!"

A nurse was the first one to respond; after just a cursory question, she called for more help, lots more. Shirley had been uncomfortable all afternoon, but didn't know how to express it. For the past two hours her breathing had been labored and no one noticed. The burning chest pains had started when she tried to eat some supper. Holding Dannie's hand had given her the understanding that she had to tell her doctors that she was in trouble. When she released his hand he stood up, symptom free. Fortunately there were enough doctors that she didn't need to say anything more. Crystal and Dannie had stepped out of the room when the crowd arrived and quietly they made their way home. They had a lot to talk about.

Shirley's surgery was successful and just in time, Barb reported. After three days in intensive care, she was back in her room and Crystal and Dannie visited three times during the week before she was released to convalesce at home. It was also agreed that Dannie would keep her current on class assignments and tests. He looked forward to seeing her regularly.

The suggestion made by Mrs. McClendon was less welcome. She and Principal Scott had agreed that Dannie should take some summertime tests because he might skip the third grade and go directly to the fourth. He was, after all reading all of those textbooks. June was pretty much consumed by daily visits to the school district office. He passed with ease.

Fourth sign

June was also an interesting month for Jackie. Her dates began on Saturday night, but soon became far more frequent. It was not uncommon for Larry to announce that it was time to turn out the lights. "The working folks need their rest," he usually said lightly. But as the month went by the amorous activity was becoming uncomfortable for the dad. He was far too protective to allow a twenty year old Jackie to be hurt again. Just before her birthday, Jackie received a marriage proposal! Sean, whom she had met at the Colorado School of Graphic Design, and who had tried unsuccessfully to go to work with Continental Creations where she was employed, presented her with a gorgeous diamond ring. He had planned a most romantic dinner, which concluded with him on one knee and the other guests applauding the moment. As he slid the ring on her finger, he had urged her to never remove it, stressing their unbroken love for one another.

However, when she was delightedly showing the ring to her family, Dannie had another of "those" moments. The instant his finger touched the ring he knew something was not right. It felt very hot to him. He waited until he was alone with his dad before he asked, "If I know something is not true, and it's something real important, do you think I should say something?"

"I suppose each situation is different," his dad replied thoughtfully. "But the truth is always correct. Do you know that something is wrong?"

"Dad, do you remember when your keys were hot? I was afraid to tell you. Just now when I touched Jackie's ring, it feels real hot to me. I know something is wrong. But I don't want to say anything that will take away her happiness." The lad looked steadily into his dad's eyes.

"I remember once hearing my grandfather say that as long as you stand with the truth you won't fall for something less," his dad finally answered. "Frankie has been through a lot. I think she is tough enough to accept the truth, and I'm sure she doesn't want to fall for something less."

A relieved son said quietly, "Then will you tell her so I don't make her sad?"

"What a Wiley Coyote you are," Larry chuckled. "You have given me a challenge you stinker." But there was a very satisfied smile on his face. "I'll bet if I ask her to go with me down to Benson's Diamonds to have her ring cleaned and appraised for our insurance policy, she may not be too offended. I'm not sure what could be wrong with it."

As it turned out, the inscription on the inside of the ring said, "Forever, Jonathon." The jeweler identified the two carat ring as one of the items listed from a recent burglary. The police were contacted and arrests were made. Jackie wept a lot at first, then she became angry, and finally she was really grateful for a little brother with a strange gift. She vowed that before she would ever consider a marriage proposal again the prospective groom must have permission from her father and approval from her little brother.

Probably the best part of that summer was the Tuesday and Thursday afternoon visits he had with Shirley. At first he read some fun books to her. When her mom said it was O.K. for her to be out of bed, she played the piano for him and they played checkers. She got tired of losing all the time so they learned how to play chess together. After a couple weeks they quit because she got tired of…. you know. They were just super happy friends. Several times he accepted Barb's invitation to stay for supper. He didn't tell Shirley about the class change until just before it was time to go back to school. Then they had a serious conversation and he promised to see her regularly after school.

Dannie's dad tried to help him anticipate his new class. "Some, probably boys, will resent you because you are smart. Most of the others will not care one way or another. But you can count on some being nice to you because they know you will soon be a leader. They might also be jealous, but they will help you. If you get a chance, choose a seat in the front row; most of the trouble makers sit in the back. Sit near the windows if you can. That will give you something else to look at or think about if you need it. Just know how proud I am of what you are accomplishing." Larry gave him a hug which neither of them expected.

Runners

The next morning as Larry was preparing to take his morning run, a sleepy son joined him in the kitchen wearing shorts a tank top and his tennis shoes. "Dad, if I can keep up with you do you mind if I try?"

"I was just wondering what would make this sunny morning better. You bet you can join me. Let's stretch those muscles and take an easy first time." There was instruction for preparation and then an easy loping introduction to distance running. By the second half, Larry thought it wise to slow the pace, which the new student appreciated. A very satisfied smile was on their faces by the time they finished their three mile circuit. Next time they would work on technique and the importance of deep breathing, and they would continue with the other half. By the time school started they were running at least three mornings a week, and Dannie was keeping up the pace.

The fourth day of classes something happened that his dad couldn't have foreseen. Dannie was just putting his cafeteria trash in the container when right by his elbow someone said, "Blabbermouth!" and he was struck in the face by a food tray. Some folks nearby laughed when they saw the mustard and catsup splattered all over him. As Mr. Evans, his teacher, ran toward him, however the laughter stopped and they saw the nasty cut on his eyebrow made by the sharp edge of the tray. Even Sandy Buttons, the attacker, was stunned when she saw the trickle of blood run down his cheek and onto his shirt. He was taken to the infirmary, and then to his doctor's office for stitches. Once again Sandy went to the principal's office and then into suspension.

At supper when his dad got home, Dannie was shown a scar in his dad's left eyebrow, just like this new one. "I was smacked by a sucker punch too. A guy by the name of Thomas, I think, was sent to the stockade and then out of the Army for mine."

Dannie said he would work on a better story than a girl in the cafeteria hitting him with her food tray. "That is just lame," was his only response. For the next week he wore his stitches like a badge of honor. He actually believed it deflected some of the comments. But if anyone asked, he would reply nonchalantly, "Oh it was just a cafeteria scuffle."

The best part of the incident was Mr. Evans allowed him to remain in the classroom during recess. It gave Dannie an opportunity to become acquainted with the Wall Street Journal, which his teacher had as a subscription. He had never imagined there were so many opportunities to make money.

The Registry

One article in particular caught his attention. A Senate committee on Indian Affairs was voting on holding in trust for the Moapa band of Paiute Indians a portion of Nevada totaling nearly seventy thousand acres. The concluding paragraph stated that the Deputy Director of the Bureau of Indian Affairs as part of the U.S. Department of Interior was compiling a list, in conjunction with the national census, of all federally recognized Indian tribes. It gave the address and process for registration. Dannie thought his dad would be pleasantly surprised.

Using a typewriter at the library, the application was carefully completed. Dannie even had a copy of his birth certificate. Under ancestry, he put:

Father: Larry Crown; 50% Nez Perce; Mother Crystal Bluesky; 100% Washakie Shoshone; Grandfather; Walter Crown; 100% Nez Perce; Grandmother; Alice Bluesky; 100% Washakie Shoshone; Great Grandfather; Daniel Crow; 100% Nez Perce.

There were quite a few N/A for not available on his page, and when the form asked what claim he was making, he simply put "none." So that simple Washakie Shoshone application made its way across the country, down dark hallways, through stacks of boxes, across several desks until a weary secretary noted that with no claim, a simple solution was available. A registration number was created. The Crown family was awarded Shoshone tribal status with no entitlement for the four surviving members. It would be a long while before that meant anything. But eventually it would be of significant importance.

The fourth grade was pretty much like the second. Dannie was always ahead in his reading and Mr. Evans anticipated his tests would be all correct. He began reading the fifth grade books. Lunch was always his anticipation because he could sit with Shirley. In fact, their table became popular with other students who wanted to be seen with the girl who had heart surgery and the smart kid with a scar, who got to skip a grade. Most of the time Dannie and Shirley just ignored everyone else and chatted about their own agendas.

Baby Opal was born just before Thanksgiving, and Grandma Irma came to visit for a week to help out. Dannie wondered what she was going to help with, since the cook was there every afternoon to prepare supper and the house keeper cleaned up every Monday and Thursday. The fun benefit of all that supervision was during the long holiday break, Barb Wilcox brought Shirley over to spend time with Dannie.

The first week of December Frankie brought Charlie home to meet her folks. She tried to make it sound like no big deal, but everyone understood that it was the first level of approval. They had a fun Italian dinner with plenty of laughter. Perhaps the most unusual part of the evening was the invitation for them to attend the church's Christmas Eve service. Charlie was a member of the choir and very excited about the beautiful music planned for the evening.

Afterward, Dannie told his big sister that the handshake from Charlie was a friendly warm one. "He's a nice guy, I know. He looked me square in the eyes and I could feel that he was truly pleased to be with us all. I hope we go to hear him sing"

A new faith

When that special night rolled around there were several surprises. The first one was that his folks didn't attend. They said that they wanted to keep baby Opal safe from the cold and the cold germs from the crowd. But Dannie felt that wasn't true. They didn't want to go because they had never learned to love the message of the church. They didn't know what they were missing.

The second surprise was that when he and Frankie went in to find a seat, they were invited to sit up front with Shirley and her dad. Barb sang in the choir too. When Shirley clutched his hand in happy greeting she said, "I didn't know you attended and I didn't want to offend you!" Her warm hand helped him understand her care. Jerry Wilcox also shook his hand. It was the first time they had seen each other since the hospital time. His wide smile and warm handshake were eloquent affirmations too.

By far the greatest surprise of the evening was the content of the inspiring story sung beautifully by the choir. Creator God, in one supreme moment sent the Revelation of his Son to be among us, to inspire, guide, protect and direct us. There were tears in Dannie's eyes as he tried to grasp the depth of the beautiful story's meaning. He was sure that a whole new area of study was dawning for him. During the following week, Dannie read the four Gospels, and badgered Barb with a multitude of questions.

The springtime snow melt meant that once again the dad and son runners could return to their morning circuit, even if they had to wear a bit of warmth at first. By Easter, Larry was praising his young partner for his growing endurance, and helping him develop the concept of a two part stride. By activating the first part of a running step by pointing his toes and landing more on the ball of his foot than his heel, he could then pull his stride back to be in position to trigger a stronger drive forward. A smoother more powerful technique was created.

The proof of his growth was demonstrated in the Father and Son May Day 10 K. The rule was the team had to cross the finish line together. Dannie was sure his dad was holding back for him, so when they had about a half mile to go, he took it to his top speed. There were only two pairs who finished before them, and those sons were much older than 9. One of the time-keepers happened to be the track coach for a local school. He was full of praise for his new prospect.

Mr. Evans was also praising his young student as he was speaking to Principal Scott again. Dannie was consistently ahead of the class and a candidate for the new Hill Middle School. With all new students, there would be less attention on a younger one. Together they agreed that with acceptable scores on all the necessary testing in June, he could move on to the sixth grade. Fortunately, his body was growing taller, even though the corresponding muscle development was yet to happen.

A job

It was an unusual Friday night when everyone was home, watching Lawrence Welk. Larry and Crustal had chatted a bit about his job and some needed updating in the big bathroom. During a commercial break, Danny asked his dad how the golf lessons were going. His dad answered that he didn't have a lot of time, but it was pretty relaxing.

"I've got a suggestion that might help," his son said. "It usually takes you a couple hours to mow the lawn. For $5 for the front and $5 for the back, I'll mow. Then you could play golf more often." His smile suggested an honest offer.

Larry thought a bit before he answered. "Do you have a need for some money, or are you just being thoughtful?" He liked the idea of not mowing the lawn, but he tried to make it sound like he was doing Dannie a favor by letting him earn some money. The reason surprised him.

"Mr. Evans has let me read the Wall Street Journal at school. With summer coming on, I'd like to have my own subscription. I think it is a good way to start earning a bunch of money."

"How much does a subscription cost?" Larry had anticipated some frivolous need. This was completely unexpected. Who the heck reads the Wall Street Journal? "I can pay for your subscription," he offered.

"Thanks dad." An unusual frown rippled across Dannie's brow. "I think I should pay for it if it is part of my future success. If you pay it will seem like your helping me. I think I'd like to take this on myself."

"Well Pal, would you like to mow only our lawn or would you like me to find out how many other guys in the neighborhood would like a little more golf-time?"

Until school let out for the summer, Dannie had two yards on Saturday and one after school on Friday. In June he had the testing at the district office in the morning and three afternoon appointments plus his two on Saturday. On top of those if the homeowner wanted extra garden work done, there was extra pay.

In July he attended the Hilltop Christian Vacation Bible School. It was just five mornings, but was a terrific opportunity to learn about

"Bible Heroes" with Shirley. He recalled how sad it had made her when he waited until the end of summer to tell her he was skipping a grade. It made her even sadder when he told her as soon as he found out that he was moving into a different school. But he promised they would continue to see each other often and be best of friends.

That was a difficult promise to keep with later school hours. Dannie didn't get home until 4:30. Crystal and Barb agreed that the friendship was worth helping, so most Sunday afternoons Dannie and Shirley were together at one home or the other. The telephone would eventually become another communication tool for them.

By the end of September, Dannie had over eight hundred dollars collected. He knew what he wanted to do with it but he just didn't know how it could be arranged. It was time for another conversation with his dad.

"Yes, Pal, I have a broker at Merrill Lynch; his name is Pat Darnell. I can make an appointment for us to see him together. I'm pretty sure the law is you must be 18 years of age to open an account. But something called the Uniform Gift to Minors Act allows my name and social security number to be on it with yours. It will be your account. The deal is he can buy or sell any share for you for a 50 cent commission per share. If he manages your account, buying and selling when he believes he can make you more money, you will be charged about 1% per year for the value of the account." Then he told Dannie about the paintings he had purchased in Germany and the reason they had come to live in Denver. "Mr. Darnell does not manage my very large account, which is deposited in long term federal bonds" Larry realized this was a maturing moment for his son. "Shall I make an appointment with him?"

"I think we should. I also want to visit the Denver Art Museum and see our paintings. Maybe Shirley could come with us."

It was a memorable moment for Dannie as he signed his name as "the investor." It was equally memorable for Mr. Darnell who had never imagined selling 38 shares of the new Microsoft stock to a ten year old. His $19 commission certainly wouldn't be the largest of his day. He just hoped that the opinion of a child wouldn't prove to be a total waste. At least it wouldn't be a large loss.

Dannie really liked the Middle School program. He had different teachers every hour! While he didn't have a choice in the class selections, it was an introduction to the style of education he would enjoy for several more years. No class was his favorite, yet none were what he would call a waste of time. Math was easy. History was fascinating. His English class had a terrific teacher, who made writing seem exciting. A music teacher helped him realize that singing would never be his strong suit, but appreciation for classical music certainly was. There was so much to learn! And PE was a snap because of the morning running with his dad. And he was doing it at a fantastic pace!

His teachers realized that he was reading far ahead of the class, already. Now instead of moving to a new grade, he was shifted into an accelerated group of students. They continued with the same subjects, but now with a much deeper engagement. True to his dad's prediction, some of the boys thought a ten year old had no business in this class with them. Curiously the girls thought he was admirable and made sure they were a buffer for Dannie.

He was not even aware of the first two rescues that happened. Then at lunch the boy seated next to Dannie spilled his chocolate milk right in Dannie's lap. The wet spot was strategically embarrassing and impossible to hide. Dannie stood up to brush off as much as he could, to the hilarious laughter of the other boys around him. To their shock and total dismay, however, four girls spilled their chocolate milk in the laps of those offenders. There is nothing a young man hates more than the derisive shrieks of laughter from women! It was the closest the cafeteria ever had to a food fight, and the end of any hazing for Dannie.

Sign five: A moral dilemma

The Wall Street Journal had predicted a meteoric rise in Microsoft stock. There was a healthy initial increase, but then the newness wore off. The little evidence of development caused the value to become stagnant. Danny was afraid he had made a big mistake. In November, he read that Microsoft was offering a promotion to stimulate their new stock. A founder's block of 13 hundred shares was being offered one time only in conjunction with the introduction. Those founder's blocks were 25 thousand dollars each, and he so wanted one. He thought for a moment about asking his dad for some financial backing, but that was out of the question.

The nefarious solution presented itself when he read that the Colorado Gaming Commission was offering a lottery to raise the matching legislated twenty five million dollars to build Mile High Stadium. Each ticket cost $5, which was very doable. The winner would walk away with two hundred fifty thousand dollars. He only needed six correct two digits numbers. In the privacy of his bedroom he took a deck of playing cards and lined up ten numbers, one to ten. They were separated a few inches apart.

"The first number is…," he held his breath as he passed his hand over the row of cards seeking a sign of warmth. "Nine." He wrote it down. The second number is…." Once again he felt definite warmth. "One." "The third number is…" Seven."

He compiled the twelve numbers, and then repeated the trial. When he compared the lists they were exactly the same. Now he had to determine what he was going to do with it. He felt it was pointless to ask his mom or dad. He already feared what they would say. But how could this possibly be cheating? The numbers had not even been drawn! The most he could lose was the five dollar bill from his lunch money, and the opportunity to be a Microsoft founder.

He found Frankie alone in her room so he asked, "I have a big favor to ask you. It's a secret, but I wonder if you will drive me to the market and buy a lottery ticket for me. I'm not old enough to do either. It's sort of a math test on probability." He wasn't sure if that fib was believable, but at least it was a reason.

She looked at him with a great deal of misgiving. "This doesn't sound like something dad would be too happy about," she answered with a squinty eye. "Is that why you are coming to me?" He nodded, but didn't say anything more.

"Is it something illegal or dishonest?" she wanted to know.

"I don't think so. We are just going to buy a lottery ticket. Lots of people are hoping to do that." Dannie tried to keep all emotion out of his face.

"O.K. let's go do it, since you are only losing five bucks. It will only take a few minutes and if I think about it anymore I'll figure out what you have up your sleeve," At the store she repeated the numbers for the clerk to enter, checked them again and paid for the ticket. Dannie was very quiet for once.

Saturday night when the lottery was revealed the first ball to roll down the rails was a nine. The next was a one. There was a space and then a seven. Frankie looked at Dannie with a mixture of awe and guilt. They were both sure what the following numbers would be.

"Dad I did something I must tell you about", Dannie began before the rest of the numbers were revealed. "I so wanted more stock that I bought a lottery ticket. I'm pretty sure I have the winning numbers. I begged Frankie to drive me to the store and buy the ticket because I'm not legal." Frankie was watching the numbers, and nodding with each announcement. "If you think I should, I'll rip up the ticket. I'm sorry." A contrite son couldn't look his dad in the eye, which told him how wrong the entire ploy was.

Frankie had an enormous smile as she said, "Yup, all six numbers in the very order you gave them. That's amazing!" The rest of the room was silent.

Larry said quietly, "I wish your mom could silently tell me what to say. I can remember a time when I got a wad of Deutsche Marks that I didn't earn and a car that I didn't buy. I used them anyway and wasn't very happy about it. Your mom and I took advantage of a special way of speaking to each other, so I sort of understand what's going on." The challenged dad took a deep breath. "My advice is that you not rip up the ticket as long as you followed the rules. Cash it and use it for what you want. But I believe the knowledge of how you got it will forever be a blemish reminding you to use the gifts you have in their proper way, like warning me when my keys were hot…"

"Or when my ring was hot," Frankie added, the large smile gone.

"Or like telling Shirley's dad to get the doctor," his mom added.

Larry continued, "Dannie, I don't know how special you are, but I'm convinced it is considerable. This family has so much going for it we need to stay completely open and honest with each other and make sure all of our actions are righteous. By the way, how much are you going to win?" His countenance was so relaxed that his son did too.

"I think the prize is two hundred fifty thousand dollars," he answered. "I think it depends on other correct answers." Dannie shrugged. "We'll see in the next few hours."

On Monday afternoon, Larry drove Dannie to the Gaming Commission office where a forty two thousand dollar check awaited. There were three other winners. With the taxes prepaid it was more than enough to do what Dannie wanted. They went to Mr. Darnell's office to purchase the Microsoft founder share. The broker advised Dannie to divide the seventeen thousand dollar balance in other new technology stocks. He added seventy shares of Hewlett-Packard, and McIntosh to his account. His dad had been correct. When it was accomplished, Danny felt very little satisfaction in what should have been a fantastic accomplishment. It seemed tarnished and he knew it would be quite a while before he did anything more with this account.

The highlight of the Thanksgiving holiday was that Dannie and Shirley got to spend two afternoons together. His folks took them to the Art Museum where Dannie had a rather overwhelming experience. As they made their way from room to room, examining the masterpieces, he had a sense of warmth, happy warmth coming from the paintings. Sometime it was modest and sometimes impossible to ignore. His smile grew and faded a bit with each display, but it never left his face. They stood in a room dedicated to Cubist paintings. His mom found Dancing on the Rhine and told them the whole story behind its presence. The little group left the museum pledging to come back soon. There was just so much more to see and learn.

The Saturday before Christmas, the Wilcox invited the Crowns over for dinner. It was a really nice meal, and an opportunity for Jerry to share the news that the company he worked for, Boraxo, was moving to California. He wasn't sure what the future held, but their friendship was too important to leave. The news only magnified the tenderness of the following little gift exchange. The dads traded some golf stuff and the moms' gifts were for the kitchen. Dannie gave Shirley a red and white scarf with matching knit gloves. She gave him a red and white stocking cap with matching knit gloves. There was plenty of laughter over the fact that they had spent enough time together to begin thinking alike. Crystal smiled at Larry for they knew exactly how pleasant that could be.

Later at home, the family was enjoying a cup of hot chocolate. Crystal asked each person to identify something they were looking forward to in 1987. Frankie was the first to answer. She said she hoped the relationship with Charlie might hold a marriage proposal. Crystal said she was looking forward to painting again, especially after seeing the museum. Larry said he was looking forward to another visit to Stuttgart for more Mercedes diesel training. There was a long pause while everyone looked at Dannie. Surely he would say something about Shirley. Instead, he said, "I'm really looking forward to meet my new brother." Everyone caught their breath.

Larry was the first to speak. "Sweetheart, are you…" He didn't finish.

Frankie squealed, "Mom, are you…?"

Finally Crystal answered, "I don't know. I'm only a couple weeks late." Looking at her smiling son, she asked, "How do you know, Dannie?"

The lad shrugged his shoulders. "I just know. I can feel your warmth and another little guy too." They loved it when he smiled big enough for dimples.

It was hard to top that evening, but when the family sat with Jerry and Shirley at a Christmas Eve service that promised the birth of a savior, everyone's heart was full to overflowing.

In the week before school started again, Dannie was once again sharing lunch with Shirley. He really liked the way Barb grilled cheese sandwiches. She put a little horseradish sauce in them. He hadn't known how much he appreciated that special little snap to it.

Even though there was snow on the ground, the sunshine flooding the kitchen nook was toasty. Shirley looked at Dannie and said, "I know you are really smart because of what's happened at school.

Dannie, do you know what you want to be? What are you going to study?" Her eyes searched his in that way he knew she was looking deeply.

"I haven't thought about it much," he answered. "I have been happy to earn some money and that doesn't seem very hard. But I'm guessing because you asked, you have been giving it some consideration." Now his eyes searched hers, while Barb marveled at the closeness these two children shared.

In a soft voice Shirley replied, "Since the day in the hospital when I couldn't identify why I felt so bad and you knew as soon as we held hands, I think I've wanted to be a children's doctor. I want to hold their hand and know how I can fix them." Her mother's smile bloomed in satisfaction. "But I also see how smart you are and I know I'm not like you."

"Kiddo, you are real smart," he said immediately. "You spent a lot of time learning to play the piano. I just used the same amount of time learning from books. I'm not a lick smarter than you, and I think you would be a great children's doctor. I'd even get sick just to come see you." He chuckled at his own corny humor, but Shirley wanted to hug him. That was an urge she would not do, but her mom might, and did before Dannie went home.

Track

By the time school started again there was a couple feet of snow on the ground and a new schedule of classes. Dannie had indicated that he would try out for track, so his PE class was sixth period so he could stay after school for training. There wasn't much of that at first, but as soon as the track was cleared they began to run. There were two or three days that were bitter cold. Dannie was especially warmed by his red and white stocking cap and gloves.

Mr. Perry, the track coach who was also the timer for the 10K race, had them run the 220, the 440, which was a quarter mile around the track, and the mile, which was four laps. Dannie had that sweet smooth stride that looked like he was just cruising. But when he ran the mile against his teammates, he nearly lapped the slower ones.

In April they had their first official track meet. A student could only be entered in a maximum of four events. Dannie was scheduled to run the first leg of the mile relay each runner going one lap before passing the baton. He gave his team a fifty yard lead. He was scheduled to run the first leg of the two mile and gave his team more than a half lap lead. When he ran in the finals of both the mile and two mile individuals, he established new school records for his times. Running with his dad had given him such a decisive advantage.

After the meet, he was getting dressed in the locker room when an eighth grader pushed him into the locker saying, "Get out of my way Punk!"

Dannie staggered to his feet with his hands in a fist ready to defend himself. A voice from the other side of the room shouted, "Hey, Glasgow, knock it off you fat dummy!"

The bully answered angrily, "Shut your trap Brass or I'll clock you too."

"Yeah, you're all mouth now. What did you win? Zip! Crown won all four of his events. That's why Hill won. Now quit being such a pain in the ass. No one appreciates your shit!"

Glasgow squared up on Brad Buttons whom everyone called "Brass," but immediately remembered the last time he had done that and got his clock cleaned. With a snort he turned and left the locker room. Dannie wasn't sure if he should thank Brass or forget the whole thing.

Finally he was in control of his voice enough to ask, "Brass, do you have a little sister named Sandy?"

"Yeah, be carefully what you say about her," he snapped still a little charged up.

"I know," Dannie said with his big grin going. "She's the one who smacked me with her food tray the last time I saw her." He pointed to the scar on his eyebrow. They both shared a chuckle that defused the moment.

Just then Coach Perry came in saying, "Great meet fellas. Dan was that a fluke or can you run like that at every meet?"

Dannie liked the shorten form of his name. He answered, "I love running in those spikes. If I do a better job warming up, I think I can better my times, especially on the two mile."

"Then we are going to have some fun this season", the coach said jubilantly. "We are going to set some middle school records."

All of a sudden it was the end of the school year and Hill Middle School had a lovely collection of trophies for their new display case, and Dan Crown had set two records that would last quite awhile. It was time to get after those lawns!

When Jerry Wilcox learned that Dannie's Friday folks had moved, he asked if he could take their place. Along with the mowing, he hoped that Dannie could stay for supper. It felt pretty contrived to Dannie, but actually he welcomed time with Shirley and of course, her folks.

Sign six: Antique whisperer

By the middle of July, everything was rolling along as planned. Dannie had happy customers and his mom's tummy was pretty round. Barb Wilcox asked Dannie one Sunday afternoon if the kids would like to go to an estate sale with her. She had a fondness for antique furniture and thought they might be interested too. Actually, with Jerry in Chicago for his new Westinghouse job training, she was a bit uneasy leaving two youngsters who were so fond of each other alone in an empty house. Dannie understood the motivation of the invitation. He remembered his dad saying that he should always choose the righteous way, so they agreed to go along.

It truly was an estate; a huge old house set on a large property on the outskirts of the downtown. Only a few cars were there, which seemed to be a good sign to Barb. "There might be some undiscovered treasures here," she said trying to generate a bit of enthusiasm.

They walked into a place that had the fragrance of wax and elegance. It also at one time had been a family's pride and joy. A man sat at a sign-in table making sure that everyone registered and understood that the purchase price was clearly marked and would be by cash or check with no return. He showed little interest or awareness of the value of items; his task was simply disposal. Barb seemed drawn to some stately antiques while Dannie strolled into the library. Shirley followed her mom.

It was like a summer morning when the sun begins to push away the chill. Dannie felt a warmth from a painting of a sailing ship. He was having a moment and didn't know what to do with it. He looked at the $25 dollar price and felt the heat spread through his body. He turned to look at the picture of a hunting dog and felt the same heat. Its price was also $25. He strolled into the dining room, wishing he could run somewhere. A painting of an Italian looking villa and vineyard made him feel like he was blushing. It's price was the same. He realized that all the paintings were priced at $25; even the frames were worth more than that.

Dannie found Barb and asked her if she would come into the sitting room where there was a picture of a wishing well and a sunny path through the trees. She had a questioning expression as he took her hand in his. Shirley trailed behind them puzzled at her friend's behavior. "These paintings are trying to tell me something," he said softly. "I have never tried to share this with anyone except Shirley. Do you feel the heat of the paintings?"

The mom was somewhat embarrassed holding his hand. Then the expression on her face changed. She could feel the heat radiating through her. It wasn't uncomfortable, but it was undeniable; she felt feverishly warm. She pulled her hand away and immediately the sensation was gone. A frown wrinkled her forehead as she trembled and took his hand again. Almost immediately she felt the rush of heat. It wasn't unpleasant only unnatural. She sensed that there was no danger, but closed her eyes trying to understand what this meant; instead she clearly saw them all, the pictures where vivid, bright and illuminated. Dannie released her hand. The sensation stopped.

"This has not happened to me often, but I feel it is important when it does happen. That's how I knew Jerry should call the doctor in the hospital. I think these paintings want to go home with us. Perhaps that is an immature way of saying I think it would be greatly to our advantage if we purchase as many of these as we can. I have about $500 at home. That's good for twenty. I can call dad to see if he can bring my stash."

Barb was still shaken by the sensation. She said quietly, "I would be happy to write a check that you could reimburse me. Do you think we can get twenty in the station wagon? Some of these are pretty large." She sort of shook herself and asked, "Do you think it would work on furniture?"

"I don't know," Dannie answered, now knowing that Barb was a believer. "But I'll give it a try." For almost an hour the three shuffled from room to room. Barb was enthralled by the awareness of the antique value that was available.

She finally asked, "Dannie, what would you do with all of this? Your house doesn't have enough room for it." She was speaking quietly as though they were adults exchanging a secret.

"I don't know. I think there is a difference between having something to keep and having something to use. If I couldn't keep something of value, I would want to use it to make money so someone else could keep it. Mom has some really nice paintings in a gallery downtown. They will sell them for her and keep some of the money. Maybe I would find an empty store and sell this stuff to folks who are sorry that they didn't come here to buy them for less." He grinned, knowing that his idea was as ragged as his feelings.

Barb faced her daughter and said in that same quiet voice, "I've never made a large decision without your father, but this seems like an urgent opportunity to me and he is not here." She hesitated, knowing that the ground she was on was truly a slippery slope. "But I can't see passing these treasures up, and I don't believe I can lose the investment." As she spoke she was convincing herself. "What do you think, Sweetie?"

It was an awkward moment for a girl who had never been consulted about a family decision of this scope. "I like all these old things. If they were in a store, I'm pretty sure people would buy them," she was quiet for a moment and then concluded, "and I think girls should be able to make some decisions too."

That was enough for her mom to go to the man at the registration table and get some pages of red stickers. They would indicate a sold status. In the rest of the afternoon Barb made her choice of more treasures than the moving truck could handle in one load. Danny chose his twenty paintings, two of which were too large for the station wagon. Barb selected a dozen more when he ran out of stickers. When she took him home, she volunteered to get some Kentucky Fried Chicken for everyone. She was pretty sure that their counsel and support would help her break the news to Jerry that she had spent over eight thousand of their Rainy Day dollars. Larry volunteered their garage space for storage if needed, and Crystal shared that a dress shop in the same block as her gallery was going out of business and would be a perfect place for antiques. Isn't it amazing how simply some monumental changes can happen? Larry noticed that his son never quit grinning all the time they were talking about it.

It took less than a month for their dream to become a reality. They signed the lease, took care of the dealer license, and got a State Farm Insurance adjuster to appraise their inventory for renter's insurance. When Jerry saw the total value, he was convinced that even if it took a year to sell these items, they would make more than he could selling

Westinghouse appliances. He was also openly grateful for such a wise and brave wife. Dannie was more than happy to place nineteen of his paintings in the consignment area. He wanted to keep the Wishing Well for himself. There was something about that one that always made him warm inside. There weren't any of his paintings that the State Farm adjuster appraised for less than Dannie had paid for the whole bunch.

At least half of the inventory of antiques was sold during August. Barb learned of two more estate sales and invited Dannie to come along. They were a little productive, but nothing like the first one. She said they were happy with the consignment side of the store which was quite busy. That was also a pleasant surprise. By the time school started, half of Dannie's paintings were sold and he opened a savings account at First Federal. Barb was a regular buyer travelling to estate sales. Frankie announced she and Charlie would be married in the Air Force Chapel in Colorado Springs. As a reservist he had base privileges. She was gorgeous in her white gown and his uniform was classic. All in all, it was a pretty interesting summer.

Dannie found the new studies more demanding, but also more interesting. The Biology class was entertaining when they had to dissect a worm and then a frog. His rudimentary understanding of the body and its functions was greatly expanded with an introduction to sexuality. The birth of Andrew Garnet Crown was nearly a practicum of what he was learning. Crystal explained to him what "having her tubes tied" meant. It was a time of personal growth and understanding.

A new understanding of heritage

In a way the same thing happened in his U.S. History class. The outline had them learning about the American Revolution for three months. He watched the development of a free nation and felt deep patriotic pride. The rest of the year would focus on the western expansion and the plight of Native Americans, who through repeated broken treaties, were evicted from land they had lived on for ten thousand years. Before the holiday break Dannie began reading: "Bury My Heart at Wounded Knee." It would change the direction of his life. He had never been given the identity of an Indian, even though he was 75%. The subject became intimately personal to him.

The 1988 track season would have been sensational in a town like Clarkston, but it was hardly noticed in a major city like Denver. Hill Middle School had seven track meets, all of which they won. Dan Crown reset records each week, but very few took notice of it.

It was a typical summer, with a couple exceptions. Dan, his family agreed with the shortened form of his name, began growing hair where it had never been before, his armpits, lip, and elsewhere. He noticed also that Shirley's shape was changing; she was blooming. Perhaps the most unexpected change was at the gallery where Crystal's paintings were being shown. The owner said he was ready to retire and for a reasonable price he would sell it to her. She contacted many of the artists who had consignments with her at Heritage, and was surprised at the positive response. She hired a college girl who could nanny Opal and Andy. Her name was Paige and she was both startled and then pleased when Dannie asked to hold her hand a little. He smiled broadly at the warm response he received. "She is a really nice person," he announced even though she didn't know why. The last big change was that Crystal began taking Dan with her to art auctions. He had a way of detecting works that would sell for double their auction price. Before the start of the next school year she was set up with a thriving business.

It was fun to be an eighth grader, even if he was the same age as the sixth graders. He felt taller and the weight room had been productive with some muscles. The really good part was he was able to have lunch with Shirley again. Dan was surprised to learn that the next Thursday and Friday would be dedicated to taking the Scholastic Aptitude Test. He was told that his future school curriculum would depend on the test results. He was convinced that the test would show his aptitude for business or finance. Then it was business as usual until his mom wanted him to go with her for a two day auction in Chicago. Top end paintings would be available and she wanted as much advise as he could offer.

Sign seven: Auction inspector

"Welcome to Schaeffer's Autumn Auction," the over-dressed man crowed. "Again this year we have assembled the finest collection of American art available for your selection." His smug smile was ingratiating to some and irritating to others. "You have three hours to browse and plan your purchases. The auction action begins at 4 p.m. promptly." There were four large banquet rooms filled with art and potential bidders.

Crystal said quietly, "I don't think I'll waste our time with the modern stuff." They made their way through a room that had several interested art enthusiasts to one with only a smattering of folks. "Since we already have a western theme going in the gallery, I think we are looking for some fine western art to go with it." She studied the face of the boy who was rapidly becoming a man. They strolled down an aisle with several paintings that caused a bit of warmth to radiate in Dan, but nothing outstanding. He asked his mom to hold his hand, thinking that if it had worked with Barb, it would certainly work with her. When they came to a Kenneth Wyatt, a warm glow began.

"Do you feel that?" he asked. "I'm pretty sure this is a top western painting. But I'm only getting a small sensation from it because it is going to sell for more than you can get in the gallery." Crystal nodded in understanding. They walked past it even though she thought it was an outstanding candidate for their shopping list. He also walked past a Fredrik Remington of a bucking bronco. "I'm getting nothing from this one," he said in a whisper. "I think it is a bogus one in spite of the signature."

They found a cluster of Grace Carpenter Hudson paintings of Native American women in casual village settings. Dan said that he was getting a warm rush and Crystal felt the transmitted heat. "I'm pretty sure these would be good for the gallery."

Then they came to a whole row more of Kenneth Wyatt's work. The first two were devoid of any response. The third and fourth ones had an immediate reaction for both Dan and his mom. The rest of the display was once again nothing.

"What's happening?" Crystal murmured. "I don't feel anything."

"I don't either," her son said behind his hand. "I think these are counterfeits, except the two tan ones."

"What do you mean tan ones?" she asked for clarification.

He pulled his hand away from her in frustration. "I don't know!" His voice was more audible. "Look at the pictures with your eyes out of focus. Can you see how soft and dusty these two look and how hard bright the rest are?" Crystal was trying to follow his instructions because he was responding with unusual strength. Then she recognized what he was saying. There were two paintings that looked old and five that were definitely different.

Their voices had come to the attention of the curator who strolled over to them asking, "Is everything in order here? May I help you in any way?" His tone was condescending.

"No. Everything is quite all right," Crystal said sweetly.

But Dan was less civil. "I think you had better bring in someone who knows the difference between an authentic painting and a phony." He said it loud enough for several nearby to stop and turn toward a word no buyer wants to hear.

"Oh my," the curator said in alarm. "I can assure you that every art work in here has been examined thoroughly. Please rest assured that we would never offer any inauthentic painting."

Dan was too engaged in the confrontation to be mollified. "Well take another look at the one that claims to be a Remington, and five of these Wyatts. We didn't fly here from Denver to look at street fair art." His mom was alarmed at his boldness.

Several of the other buyers were gathering around the scene. The curator hurried away to find reinforcements. He returned in just a few moments with a scruffy man in tow. "This is Patrick Sharpe, our appraiser who will assure you that all of these art works are authentic."

Crystal tried to insert herself as a buffer between Dan and these agitated men, but he nudged her out of the way and said, "Good. Mr. Sharpe, can you explain how a Remington can be authentic painted on a linen canvas? In the nineteenth century they were all cotton. And how in the world can these Wyatt paintings contain a whiter white that was developed after the Second World War?" Crystal had no way of explaining how those words came from her son.

The appraiser produced a magnifier and studied the paintings in question. After only a few moments he looked at Dan saying, "Amazing! The lad is correct. This is not an authentic Remington. It has been painted recently, a very crafty forgery that I couldn't tell from the original." The curator's face paled and he shook his head in disbelief.

After another close examination, the appraiser responded, "And these are imposters as well. They are painted with Titanium white, which was developed in the 50's. I don't know how you detected this when I didn't, but we are in your debt. Had we sold these we would have been liable for a lawsuit." The appraiser patted Dan's shoulder asking, "I wonder if you can look at the other inventory for defects." His voice was sincere and appreciative. Crystal was speechless. "We will be happy to pay you an inspector's fee for your trouble." Now Dan's smile was enough to produce dimples.

As it worked out, each painting, before being placed on the auction tripod, was closely examined by Dan. His nod was more than an approval, it was a signal to his mom that if she wanted to bid, it was at least a money making candidate. When he nodded twice, the painting was authentic, but would sell at a significantly higher price. He found one more counterfeit, which was pulled from the auction items. They went home with three crates of work she had purchased, a smaller crate of western copies she promised to dispose of by selling them as "reproductions," and Dan had a pleasant check for his perceptive help. His savings account was growing to the point he rethought his reluctance for buying more stock. It had been a trip that most of those involved hoped would happen again soon.

They got back home too late for him to visit with Shirley. The family was sitting together in front of a cozy fireplace. "I couldn't believe it when he explained why the paintings were bogus," Crystal said with a wide smile. "I thought he was bluffing, and he nailed the truth. It was incredible." Her smile was more praise than Dan felt he deserved.

Paige, who was grateful to be included now that the kids were in bed asked, "Have you studied art in school?" She wasn't sure how old Dan was, but he seemed pretty adult to her.

He answered, "No, none. But it was like the paintings were telling me about the problem and all I had to do was repeat what they were saying."

"Wait! No, you can't be saying that the paintings talked to you really!" It was so much like having Frankie speaking with him that he almost called her name. Since Frankie and Charlie were married, Paige was staying in her room during the week and going home on weekends.

Finally he just said, "I can't explain it. I just seem to know when something is true or false. That's why I held your hand when mom was about to hire you to take care of Opal and Andy." His shrug indicated there was nothing more he could say.

She sort of giggled, "Wow, a walking lie detector!"

It was a white Christmas again, which was fun to look at, but restrictive in many ways. Dan could only spend two afternoons of the long school break with Shirley. Something was changing. She seemed more serious or guarded. There wasn't the usual laughter and joking. Had he been brave enough to bring the topic up, she would have agreed and said that he was changing. He was more serious or guarded. They weren't children anymore, but on the verge of adolescence. All sorts of changes were going on.

The SAT results were of little surprise to Dan's teachers. Once again he was in the top bracket. His subject of greatest agreement with the test, however, was not business or finance, but Anthropology and he was scheduled to have a chat with Mrs. Sanders, the Social Studies teacher at Lincoln High School. All he was told in preparation was that the accelerated program had an unusual relationship with Denver University. He would have another bright opportunity, while taking high school requirements he could also accumulate college elective credits.

The track season of '89 would be remembered as a clean sweep by Hill Middle School. They dominated their seven meets. Once again Dan Crown set school and city records in his events. He was visited one May afternoon by the Lincoln track coach who had been following Dan's successes. He wanted to make sure that Dan knew about the outstanding program at Lincoln. The graduating student told him he loved to run, but was unsure of the time demands. "I don't plan a future in sports and there may be some afternoon classes that claim me," he said noncommittally. The coach tried one more shot at getting the runner to reconsider. But Dan was pretty sure that his competition days were over. And then middle school was over too and it was time to mow lawns for the final summer. He was retiring to give more time to summer school, and to help his mom find new paintings, of course. She was doing so much business, however, a lot of really good art was coming to her for consignment.

Lincoln High School

There were eight Lincoln students in the accelerated program that rode the little bus over to Denver University. Fortunately the program was so well constructed and received that the handful of younger students were nothing out of the ordinary. Dan had three classes each day. His favorite was the Introduction to Anthropology taught by Dr. John Wesley Lawrence. Dan was careful to write the first words he shared with the class: "Anthropology studies physical and cultural differences among human beings across time and space. It helps students understand the nature of those differences, why they exist, and, most importantly, why they matter."

Dan realized that this accelerated session would be more important than he had even hoped. As the first class was closing Dr. Lawrence gave them an assignment to write a brief paper demonstrating their understanding of the Kroeber quote, "Anthropology is the most humanistic of the sciences and the most scientific of the humanities." (Alfred L. Kroeber) It took Dan several hours to finally say succinctly that the area in which the passion of human experience intersects the patience of examination is the study we call anthropology. An objective look at the various methods humans deal with the environment and opposing cultures allows for the selection of techniques most likely to survive.

Time is a relentless river sweeping us through the seasons. Dan had hardly missed the two high school track seasons. He felt real satisfaction with his use of time. If he continued at this pace he would be finished with Lincoln just in time to get his driver's license and he would be a junior in college. To celebrate he decided to let his hair grow. Achievement was running in the family; his dad, who had made yet another trip to Stuttgart, was now the General Manager of Miller Mercedes-Benz dealership. Dan felt like the accelerated program was amazing.

An unfortunate encounter,
and another sign

He was Christmas shopping in the new mall, happy for the warmth and convenience of these shops. He had already found some nice gifts for his mom and Frankie when he heard someone call his name.

"Dannie! Hey Dannie Crown, is that you?" The female voice was not one he recognized; and when he turned to find the source he did not recognize her either.

"It's me. Sandy. Maybe I should hit you with a food tray."

The young woman in front of him was smiling as though they were old friends. Her face had far too much makeup, and her hair was about the same as his unruly fuzz. Her skirt was way too short and her blouse seemed to be a button or two short of covering her chest.

"I remember you, Sandy. Sandy Buttons, isn't it? How's your brother?" He was speaking to a stranger.

"Yeah, I don't know about Brad. I moved out last year. I'm really glad to see you today." She moved toward him, far to close toward him. Dan backed up a step. She reached her hands toward his waist and Dan caught her wrists and held them gently. Whatever was going on was a mystery and not a pleasant one. "Listen, Dannie, I'm in a kind of tight spot. I need to move back home but I don't have enough for the U Haul. Do you think you could lend me about twenty dollars?" She had again stepped into that too-close-for-comfort circle, and his back was against the wall.

He could feel the heat of alarm from contact with her arms, and to him her breath smelled like rotting flesh. He understood that what she was saying was not true. She needed money for a drug fix. This was a dangerous moment.

From the other side of the mall walkway, though, the encounter looked far different. Shirley and her two friends were also Christmas shopping. Trisha asked, "Isn't that Dannie Crown?" The trio turned their attention to a couple standing against the far wall.

Pam said, "I think that's Sandy the Tramp he's holding. Wouldn't you think some people would have the sense to do that in private?"

Trisha added, "Get a room!"

Shirley could only stare in disbelief. Granted, they had never been romantic or made promises to one another. Since he had started at Lincoln they had spent much less time together. But this seemed so unlike the Dan she knew... and loved. Tears formed in Shirley's eyes as she turned away, followed by her two confused friends.

"Sandy, I don't have any money for you," a frustrated Dan was saying.

"Come on," her voice was becoming desperate. "Brad told me you've got all kinds of jobs and a pocket full of money." There was a quiet moment and she said, "I'll do anything that you want for ten bucks."

The heat radiating from his grip on her wrists was a clear warning. Dan released her and spun away. He said softly, "You're really ill. Sandy, go see your doctor. You are high and infected. Please get some help." She would have continued to plead with him but he held up his hands and slowly backed away from her. She also turned away, looking for someone else to ask for money.

A few hours later Crystal received a painful phone call from Barb, who reported the sad experience Shirley had at the mall. Barb thought an apology from Dan would help restore a friendship that seemed fractured.

After listening, Crystal said, "Oh my; that explains the conversation I eavesdropped on. Dan called Brad Buttons to tell him that Sandy confronted him at the mall asking for money. He pleaded with Brad to have their parents get her to the doctor, that as he held her hands away from him there was a stench on her breath like death. He said she was in danger of hurting herself and infecting others. I'm not sure what Shirley saw, but I will assure you it was not a romantic moment. I'll tell Dan that she saw him with Sandy, but I am pretty sure that he will not be inclined to apologize for anything he has done. I'm a bit surprised that as close as you all have been you would think so little of him." It was a moment of destiny that swept two people in opposite directions.

More stock

Just before the 1991 New Year, Dan received a call from his Merrill Lynch broker, Mr. Darnell, to inform him that a new stock was just going public. "Starbucks is a coffee company in Washington State that has all the indicators of being a great investment. Right now the initial offering price is twenty one dollars a share. Are you interested?"

Dan thought about the twenty four thousand dollar balance in his savings account that drew 2% interest. He was glad for those Schaeffer inspection checks and those old paintings that had sold. Now he thought it was time to take advantage of them. "Yes, sir, I'm real interested. May I buy nine hundred shares?"

"You realize that is eighteen thousand nine hundred dollars?" the broker asked quietly. "And there is a four hundred fifty dollar fee."

"Yes sir. I can bring you a cashier's check in the morning," the happy lad wanted to sound grownup. His net worth was growing, righteously.

In Lincoln's class of '92 there was only a tiny mention of an acceleration student by the name of Dan Crown who had satisfied with honors graduation requirements and was currently completing an on-site study of Reservation Politics at the Wind River Indian Reservation in Wyoming. He had 60 Denver University credits from seven electives: Slavery Issues, Trail of Tears; the Politics of Internment; The Power of Nonviolence; the effects of Political Action groups; White Flight and Urban Renewal; Reservation Politics.

An exciting dawning

Dan boarded an early morning bus, June 3rd, bound for Casper Wyoming. A second one in the afternoon took him to Riverton, the largest town on the Wind River Reservation. After a noisy night at the YMCA, he was met by Willie Longroad, who would be his guide for the next week.

"What brings a fella all the way up from Denver to learn about our res?" He was probably thirty years older than Dan and those had been hard years. His gray hair was receding and there were pronounced crow's feet wrinkles around his eyes. "Most folks who do the Denver U study just watch the video. I don't suppose there is anything new up here since that was made." He squinted a bit and added, "Well there are three casino groups that are tryin' real hard to get permit approval. Four, if you count the Smoke Shop, but that's just a card room." Dan was feeling friendly warmth from him.

"You know, they did offer that video to me" the student responded, "but I thought as long as I could see Wind River for myself I could better understand it." Dan gave a little nod for punctuation.

"Well brother," his guide chuckled, "it's about 2.2 million acres or thirty five hundred square miles, which is a bunch to see in a week."

"Wow, maybe I'll need to stay an extra day or two." Dan laughed at his own humor. "I'm in no hurry. This is sort of a graduation trip. It would also be good if I can learn about some of my ancestors. My maternal grandmother was Alice Bluesky. I don't know much more than that about her." He was watching the beautiful countryside sliding by.

"I seem to recall a family near Ten Sleep that was named Bluesky. Their youngest daughter ran off with a Shoshone shaman. I'll see if I can find out something for you." Several quiet minutes passed before Willie asked, "Do I recall that you are on the federal registry?"

"That's right. My dad is Nez Perce from Idaho, and mom is Shoshone from here. Dad was in the Army." He wasn't sure why he thought to throw that in, but it was important to him anyway.

"I'll make sure Mr. Trosper knows that. He is Chairman and Director of the Chief Washakie Foundation. He's also the great great grandson of Chief Washakie, which makes him the closest to celebrity that we've got. Most folks feel there is a difference between the Foundation and the res Council. I don't think there is a lick of difference. They just meet in different buildings is all."

Dan could see that there was a cluster of buildings ahead and he thought there might not be another chance to ask a probing question again soon. "Willie, what would you say is the number one problem on the reservation?"

"That's easy. It's poverty. Most of us are rattling around between two dimes. The legs of the problem are liquor, no jobs to speak of, no education, and nothing to bring tourists in to be a source of hope. All of which feeds our high crime and divorce rate." He took a deep breath. "We live in one of the most beautiful parts of the country. The potential is here. It just seems to always be out of our reach." They pulled into a weary town with old buildings that had never been attractive. Age hadn't helped Fort Washakie. The one exception was the federal building that housed the Board of Indian Affairs for the Department of Interior, and the Washakie Foundation. It had been an ugly box when it was built fifty years ago. Age had softened the ugly of it.

Willie parked the car and invited Dan to meet some of the members. It was dawning on Dan that there was no schedule for his visit to the reservation. It was a little like an ad hoc tour. They would just see what developed. He was introduced to Mr. Rowe the Director of Finance and next door was Mr. Jansen, Director of Operations. The Offices of Instruction, Development and Safety were dark and unoccupied at the moment. Willie identified himself as Director of Transportation. Mr. Ferndale was introduced as Director of Human Resources and Assistant Director. The corner office was that of Mr. James Trosper, Executive Director of the Wind River Indian Reservation. He was wearing a tan western shirt, jeans, western boots and a large smile. Dan received a warm greeting and handshake.

"We are honored to have a young scholar so interested in our reservation," he said. "Willie has probably told you that in the past a video is adequate information for the average class. I'll be happy to hear of your perception by the end of the week. Willie has energetic plans for your tour. Please feel free to bring me any questions or insights you might have for us." Again he offered his hand indicating that the brief greeting was complete. It had just been a formality.

In the car, Willie said, "I expect you want to see the graves of Chief Washakie and Sacajawea. They are on the way to Lander, where we can get a good lunch. I didn't ask if you want to go back to the Y at Riverton tonight. We do have a Motel 6 here, but the Best Western in Lander would be more comfortable for you." He hadn't started the car and seemed in no hurry to leave.

Dan turned in his seat so he could address Willie directly. "You know, I'm not so interested in graves as I am in our future. My heart broke when I read about Wounded Knee and again the Trail of Tears. Our people have been shuffled, abused and marginalized for a couple hundred years of broken treaties. Isn't it sad that the preferred lodging for a guest or a decent lunch is off the reservation? I'm just a kid, Willie, but I'm convinced that if my generation doesn't step up, that miserable treatment will continue."

"Well hold on," his guide said, "I'm not convinced that we have it all that bad. We get paid from the IA, that's the Board of Indian Affairs. We get an allotment from the Department of Interior; we get residual payment from the oil companies and the white ranchers who run their cattle on our grazing land. We don't have it so bad."

Dan nodded apologetically and said, "Willie your right. I came to Wind River believing I could offer some help. But I'll tell you because we are proud of our home, which we are not given, we work for it. We mow the grass and plant flowers. We don't dump our trash in the front yard or leave our dead cars to rust there. We take pride in it." He was pointing at a house across the street from the federal building that he had described. "Perhaps our people will never regain their lost pride," he concluded softly "and we'll have to go off the res to get a good lunch."

The car was silent until he continued, "I thought there would be more to the reservation than these sad echoes of the past. You can take me back to Riverton. I'll go back to Denver tomorrow and watch the video."

Willie said, "I'd hate to see you leave so soon. What you say is true. Most folks around here live in an old double-wide and pride

199

is not a word I would use to describe us. It just stings to hear an outsider remind me of it." He shoved Dan's shoulder good-naturedly, "especially such a smart young one. Let's go over to the Smoke Shop and get an early lunch. Maybe there is still something around here you would like to see." His smile was more playful than the words merited.

Carly, and another sign

They drove toward the mountains to the edge of town. Willie pulled into a muddy parking area. A low rambling building with a lot of beer signs on the front and neon "Smoke Shop" sign on the roof offered little invitation. About a dozen cars were parked in the gravel lot. "They usually have a really good daily special here," Willie said as they got out. Not surprising, the inside was old and pretty heavy with a tobacco smell. Card tables were on one side of the room and a few dining tables were on the other.

"Hi there cutie," Willie said to the young woman who greeted them. "Are you serving my favorite for lunch today?"

"No road-kill yet this morning, Willie. Sorry, you'll have to settle for the meatloaf sandwich again." Her eyes twinkled with mirth and it was obvious that she was glad to see him. Her black dress accentuated her cute shape and her black hair and eyes finished the lovely picture. "Who's the cute guy you have with you today? He looks like a bureaucrat; are you in trouble again?" She giggled.

With mock anger Willie answered, "Now listen; you can insult me all you want, but this is a real college student from Denver." Then in a voice loud enough for the card tables to hear he said, "I don't want you to corrupt him or take advantage of his innocence!"

The woman hooked onto Willie's arm, saying in a raspy sort of voice, "Oh I really like the innocent ones."

Willie was having a good time. He chuckled, "Dan, meet Carly, my daughter. Carly this is Dan, the student from Denver U I told you about." They shook hands and Dan was startled by the warmth he felt coming from her, happy, positive warm. Finally they released their hand clasp, but neither of them wanted to. They were seated and Willie said he would have a coffee and Dan asked for a diet coke.

"Dan, do you play cards?" Willie asked to get some conversation going. He had watched Dan's eyes follow Carly behind the counter.

"Our family plays some games, but just for fun, you know Pinochle or Cribbage. But I never gamble. I believe that is a losing situation."

Willie said, "There are sure a lot of folks who believe they are going to strike it rich."

"Yeah, they believe that because the ones running the games are perpetuating the notion while raking in the tokens," Dan said with a shake of his head. "The odds are always in the house's favor. Sooner or later the player loses and the house wins."

"Don't you think the fact that people keep gambling is proof that they occasionally hit the big one?" Willie really liked talking with Dan because they so quickly got into deep discussions.

"Look," Dan said playfully, "I'll bet all the money I'm carrying right now that I can make up a game that will clean out the pockets of everyone here right now." His grin was too challenging for Willie to pass up.

"You are going to make up a game?" Dan nodded. "You are going to win everything they have on them?" Dan shrugged saying, "Someone may be packing several thousand dollars that would shut me up. But I'll bet the average wallet has less than a hundred dollars in it." He waited a moment before asking, "Shall we see?"

There were nine men who thought they were going to teach the college kid a lesson.

"O.K." Dan said confidentially. "This game is called Sequence." He was separating the hearts from the deck. He then showed them the ace through ten, plus the joker.

"These are placed face down and our lovely dealer will shuffle them like we do dominoes. You will ante up a ten for your draw. You may not touch or move any card but your selection. The object is to turn over the ace. If you turn over the joker you are out of the game. If you turn any other card, Carly will reshuffle and the next person has a shot at it. The pot grows until someone turns the ace and takes it. The remaining cards are reshuffled and he can then try for the two. If he turns the two we all pay him twenty and after the cards are reshuffled, he tries for the three and when he turns it we pay him forty. The winnings increase double each time. When he fails the sequence, we reshuffle all the cards and start over. It's a simple game. You could win or lose thousands." Almost all the men were smiling at the thought of easy money.

The third man drew the Joker and had to step away. There were ninety dollars in the pot when Dan anteed in then, without touching any of the cards, turned over the ace of hearts. Everyone else groaned. He missed the two and the circle began again. The second man turned the ace and frowned that there was only twenty dollars in the pot. When it was Dan's turn he said, "Well, some of us are about even and some of us are a bit behind. Do you understand how this game is played?" They each nodded. "Do you want to continue?" More nodding.

He anteed another ten and then turned over the ace. Before he removed his winnings he said to them, "I do not gamble because I hate to lose and sooner or later we all will." He turned over the two and then the three, and then the rest all in sequence leaving the Joker to the very last. "I have no way of knowing how they do it, but some people have an uncanny way of beating us. I would rather be your friend." He tossed the handful of tens on the table saying, "Carly, I'd like to buy these fellows lunch. Thanks guys."

When they got back their table Willie couldn't wait to ask, "How in the world did that work? You said you just made that up? Are you some sort of street con artist?" His smile was assurance there was no malice intended. "That's the best magic trick I've ever seen."

"I did it to prove a point. You cannot go against ten to one odds and win. I could have taken their cash a little at a time or all at once. Ten doubled to the tenth power means they would have lost $7,680 each. I imagine that would have cleaned them out. The mysterious thing to me is that if that had happened, one or two of them would have tried it again thinking they might win."

Willie looked deeply into Dan's dark eyes and asked, "So, do you have some master plan for us?"

"Good grief no!" he answered, hoping that he didn't sound too much like Charlie Brown. "I have no idea what you want to do. I'm just sad that you don't want to do something. With all this charming potential you are willing to just sit and live on tokens and residuals. That's a losing hand I do believe."

"You've talked about potential," Willie said with a shake of his head. "What do you see that we don't?"

Before Dan could answer, Carly brought their food. She sat down next to her dad so she could face Dan and asked, "How did you do that. You had me so convinced that was a righteous win. How did you do it?" Her smile was dazzling.

He said with a shrug, "Like I said, some people have an uncanny way of getting to us. Would you believe me if I said it was a fluke and that was the first time I've ever done it?" She was shaking her head. "But that is the gospel truth." He shrugged again.

"They are over there wondering how you did that." Carly said with a snort. "They are sure you pulled some sleight of hand stuff over on them, and just want to figure out how." Some new guests entered for lunch so she said as she was getting up, "You can get back to me later on this. I'd like to talk a bunch more with you."

As they watched the attractive lady walk away, Willie whispered, "I can't figure her out. She's usually pretty stand-offish. I think you caught her attention." After just a brief pause he said, "You were about to tell me what potential you see that we don't."

"Where to start?" Dan mused to himself. "Let's begin by pointing out that millions of people pass by to your north and west boundaries on their way to Yellowstone the nation's first and finest National Park, but do not come into Wind River because you have no hotels, motels or RV Parks. You want casinos, but suffer from the same restrictions. Think of Las Vegas. They certainly don't have the mountain splendor all around but they are an enormous success there in the empty desert because they made a reason for people to come to their casinos. Think about the hunting and fishing that is not happening because there are no guides, permits or camps for them to stay in. You could have conference centers where students could come and learn about a proud heritage instead of watching a video. Those centers would not only be a source for employment, they could also be opportunities for learning new technologies that are about to rediscover the world. When not scheduled they could be leisure centers for hikers."

"I remember a quote I had to learn in school: 'If a man builds a better mousetrap or preaches a better sermon, though he build his home in the woods, the world will beat a pathway to his door.' The point is people won't stumble into you without a reason. They will come in droves if you give them even a little reason. I'll bet energy people would be all over solar panels, wind generators and geothermal heating here on the res. And this is the potential I've been able to think about in just in the first five hours. Wait until I have been here a week."

"Then I take it you are not going back to Denver tomorrow?" The happy smile on Willie's face already knew the answer.

"I'd still like to see Thermopolis and the Hot Springs. Maybe on the way back we could look at Boysen Reservoir. If there is time later in the week maybe we could visit Bull Lake and Sinks Canyon state park, even though that's by Lander off the res. I would be fascinated by a river that flows into a cave and disappears for a half mile.

"I'll give you this," Willie said with fresh respect. "You sure did your homework before coming up here. You sound like a better guide than I'm tryin' to be."

As it turned out, they had enough time to go out to Bull Lake and then follow the Wind River up to the little community of Crowheart. Willie was glad to tell his guest the legend of the warrior chief Washakie. On the way back Dan smiled and said, "There is more of the potential that I see. River rafting from Crowheart down to Bull Lake would be such a hit. That's the sort of thing that families with bigger kids would love to share; it would be safe, spectacular scenery and a real moneymaker without a lot of investment."

Willie nodded, more convinced that Dan really was here to help. These constructive ideas just seemed to continuingly appear. He wasn't sure what the Council would think about them, but for sure they had better consider them carefully. They were back in Fort Washakie in time to check Dan into the Motel 6 and have a soup and sandwich dinner at Ruby's Café. Before going to bed, he called his folks to report what a successful day he had.

In the morning the late spring sunshine warmed his run back out highway 287. He calculated he had covered about three miles, he turned back and increased his pace. When Willie joined him for breakfast, the first thing he asked was, "Were you out running this morning?" As Dan nodded, his guide said, "I got a call from Mrs. Morton saying that some stranger was galloping up the road. How far did you go?"

"I try to get in six miles to start the day," Dan grinned. "If I was a bit more familiar with the area, I'd use side roads. But there wasn't much traffic anyway."

Willie chuckled, "I figured you were just making your point from yesterday, because 287 is the busiest highway around here."

"So I guess my question is still the same. Does anyone want to do anything about that or is everyone happy with empty roads?"

It took them two hours to get to Thermopolis, which was just outside the northeast corner of the reservation. Dan noticed several highway signs advertising spas. When they drove up to the parking lot of the world's largest mineral hot spring, there was raising steam even on such a warm morning. There must have been a couple hundred people walking about the grounds and gift shop. The restaurant had a waiting line.

Willie mumbled in defense, "I think they have an all-you-can-eat special on Wednesday." There was that playful twinkle in his eye. "I promised Carly we'd stop in for a late lunch." They joined the folks strolling around the steamy lake that smelled a bit like boiled eggs.

On the way back down highway 20 they passed a camping area when Dan noticed a forest service fire road that went off to the right. He asked Willie if they could take a look at what was at the top of the hill.

"I've been out this way several times, but I never turned onto the service road," he said as they left the paved highway. He slowed down on the rough road. There were no signs that anyone else had driven up here recently. They climbed a pretty steep pitch for about a mile with four switchbacks before cresting onto a very wide plateau, with a fork that turned into a canyon meadow. Dan asked him to go just a bit further into the meadow. He was certain it was the most lovely mountain vista he had ever seen, so Willie finally stopped and they got out of the car.

Dan was hushed as he said again, "This is what paintings try in vain to capture; it's so vast and quiet." At the far side of the meadow a deer rose out of the grass and trotted toward the trees. "I can't believe how wonderful this place is." Looking at Willie he asked, "What's the name of this?"

Willie was just as pleased with their accidental find. "I think these mountains are the Owl Creek Range and those out there beyond are the Tetons of course. I doubt if this spot has a name."

Dan asked another question, "Has there been a fire in here recently? That hillside seems to have bare trees that look dead." He was studying the far side of the meadow which seemed to be a pretty sheer rock wall.

Willie answered, "There's a boring beetle that invades the trees sometime, but that looks more like a steam vent to me. Gases have probably destroyed a handful of trees. Do you want to go take a look? I think the road goes right to it."

All the way back to Fort Washakie they talked about the amazing opportunities and the gorgeous day. Willie said jokingly, "If you were here in August you'd think it was hotter than a chili pepper, and January and February are colder than a mother-in-law's kiss." Both chuckled at his humor.

She was just as stunning today, but Carly looked more formal in a black party dress with vertical satin stripes and red accents. "Well you boys look like you have stayed out of trouble so far today," she said playfully. "Do you need some help with that?" Dan wasn't sure which way to understand that so he just smiled and nodded.

Willie gave a recap of their travels before asking, "I don't suppose you have any more of those meatloaf sandwiches left?"

"I was hoping you'd have time for me on this busy day" she replied with a wink. "I saved you a couple in anticipation." She looked at Dan and asked, "Were you just running home at sunrise this morning? Someone told me you were out on the highway just chugging along."

Dan grinned enough to reveal his dimples. "Yeah, a bunch of the guys wanted to play a new card game called Sequence. It took me a little longer than I expected to clean them out." All three enjoyed the humor of it. She hurried away to place their order.

Willie leaned over and said softly, "I think she really likes you. I haven't seen her flirt like this for a long time." He straighten and said more normally, "On a serious subject, the Council meets tomorrow afternoon. They would like you to attend and share the thoughts we've talked about. Director Trosper was surprised at the scope of your ideas. I told him that's what happens when we allow college students to just run wild."

Their food arrived and they were both eager to enjoy it. After a bit of quiet, Dan said, "I think I've had enough touring for today. If you can direct me to a quiet road where I won't disturb the neighbors, I'll take another run to organize my thoughts and turn in early."

When his guide dropped him off at Motel 6, he pointed to the road that went north from the building. "Just follow that. I'll see you at Ruby's for breakfast around 8 o'clock. Oh, by the way, if you get to a blue double-wide with a Ford pickup in the front yard you have gone four miles. That's my place. I hope you have a restful night with high mountain memories." He drove off with Dan pondering his attitude about the condition of local homes.

His morning run was even more satisfying than last night's. Breakfast was great and then Sinks Canyon State Park was much more than he expected. The river really did flow into a cave and disappear for at least a half mile. Willie explained it as a lava tube from an ancient volcano. It was still mysterious.

Before the Council

At lunch Carly had said she was sure that Dan would do a wonderful job for the Council, which alerted him to the possibility that this was more than a chat about what he had seen on the reservation. When the time came, Willie led him to a one story building that was the modest Reservation Long House. They entered a room where six other men and a woman who was taking notes waited. Yes, this was more than a chat, in fact, it was a report to the Reservation Council. Willie introduced Mr. Dan Crown from the Anthropology department of the Denver University. Dan felt nauseous with that erroneous introduction. But he had prepared a presentation and even though he was not an official consultant from DU, he could give it.

He looked up at the seven as though he was surprised and asked excitedly, "What would you like to do with your reservation if price was no issue?" He thought that was a good way to get things started. "If you knew you could not fail, what would you like to do? Those are planning questions aimed at setting your goals. The who and how questions are simply problem solving. The plans are the significant consideration."

"Thank you for the hospitality I have received this week. I came here with the instructions to simply learn about Reservation Politics. Your form of government is different than I am used to, but obviously it has worked well for you, and will continue. However, my youth and exuberance saw so much that goes beyond politics, things that could be done in this magnificent setting. There are so many possibilities all around you, I became something of an irritation to Mr. Longroad. I imagined dozens of ways the reservation could capitalize on the multitude of tourists that are at your border and at the same time offer greater services and financial benefit to your residents. Wind River Indian Reservation could become as well known and visited as Yellowstone, America's original national park."

"I won't bore you with my babbling about the possibilities of hunting, fishing and river rafting guides who could be useful to outsiders, and the management of cottage stays, or the revenue from permits. I can only guess what dozens and dozens of new jobs would be like, which is not to mention the hotels that would welcome casino guests to the gaming tables, dining tables, and entertainment concerts which are a prerequisite to the casino permits you are currently seeking. Tourist Information centers at all border crossings onto the reservation could give a friendly welcome and distribute helpful information about entrance permits, lodging or RV parking, recreation opportunities and sightseeing points of interest."

Dan shook his head as though trying to avoid telling them this last part. "Just yesterday Mr. Longroad took me to a high mountain meadow. I was charmed by it and then I thought about those words, 'What would you do if you knew you couldn't fail?' I envisioned Echo Lodge: a learning and leisure center with twenty two-bedroom suites for fishermen, hunters, hikers, or event attendees; a dining room, conference room and indoor swimming pool; built on a 99 year lease in Wind River Reservation, heated by geothermal steam and featuring a water slide down a thrilling course that would be a toboggan run in the winter. It would be a taste of the past; the ecology of the present with nature hikes and lectures; and the possibility of future financial security." Again Dan shook his head in disbelief. "It is so easy to get carried away in this glorious place, a place of beauty and pride." He was silent and his listeners were stunned.

The note-taking woman said softly, "I'll have what he's having." The laughter broke the tension.

Director Trosper looked at Willie and said, "My Lord, you guys have been busy these three days. I thought you were going to just look around." Then he looked directly at Dan and asked, "Can you do even half of that for us?"

Dan responded with a startled, "Oh no that's problem solving! I came here just to learn. But if my sense of opportunity is a tiny bit contagious, if you see things in a fresh way, if there is some change that helps our people, this time will be even better spent. But I would love to walk along with you when those changes happen.

Director Trosper leaned forward and said directly to Dan, "Are you interested in a job, son?"

Dan was shocked but managed to maintain a quiet demeanor. "Mr. Longroad is driving me back to Riverton this evening so I can catch the bus to Denver in the morning. I have a job offer in a Chicago Art Auction gallery that I must honor."

The Director, who was not accustomed to being turned down, went on as though he had not heard Dan, "We need a Director of Development if we are going to get to that brave new day. You would be the perfect man for the job. It would be outstanding on your resume."

"Thank you for your wonderful compliment, sir. You have given me something to pray about on my way home." Dan was ready to stand.

The Director said, "And you are a man of God to boot! It just keeps getting better." His enthusiasm was showing. "I want you on our Council, so pray hard on that bus." Looking at the others seated at the table he asked, "Does anyone else have questions for Mr. Crown?"

Mr. Rowe, the Director of Finance, asked with a bit of a frown, "You talk about hunting and fishing on the reservation. We cannot simply open our land for others to use or abuse."

Dan eased back onto his chair. "Certainly not. In Alberta hunters need to present their proof of housing reservation, a valid hunting license and game tags to the border patrol before they can enter. Those are all prepaid revenues. A licensed hunting guide is required for each two hunters; that's also new revenue and assurance that your land will be respected. When we went in, we were given a four day pass that had to be validated by another border guard as we left Alberta. It was carefully controlled and helped us appreciate our hosts. There is no room for neglect or abuse." Heads were nodding in understanding.

Mr. Rowe asked again, "You mentioned Border Guards, how does that work?"

Dan smiled widely. "Now you are talking about problem solving again. That's great; it's the next step in growth. Border Guards mean a more formal ingress egress to the reservation. You can style it as relaxed or rigid as you would like. I've noticed that we could drive on and off the reservation without inspection. Border Guards recognize our national status and would mean jobs for your people. They would mean a stronger economy and a reason for some of your young men to stay here rather than going to Casper or Cheyenne for work. It may even be reason for some, especially military, to come back for a job here. That can bloom into a reservation security police. If you are proud of what you've got, you'll guard it." Dan stood up, signaling the end of his time. Another man asked, "But who will certify…" Dan said softly, "That's just more of the problem solving. The real question is, 'If you knew you couldn't fail, what would you do with your reservation?'"

Willie's game-changer

When Dan returned home he was more energetic and enthused than his folks could remember. He offered to take a regular shift at the art gallery, and when they returned from the Schaeffer Summer Auction he was glad to have a substantial check to restore his depleted savings account. Instead he opened a new account in the name of Washakie Investment Foundation. He asked his folks to be co-signers, and explained that he wasn't sure how but he wanted to do something constructive for their people.

He found a small pile of letters waiting for him from folks in Fort Washakie:

From Mr. James Trosper: "Hello Mr. Crown. Your all-too-brief visit with us has created quite a stir. The Council has made an energetic list of improvements that would be beneficial to our reservation. We found it stimulating to take the first step of planning. We are now in a bit of a quandary. We need a guide to walk with us through the problem solving process. Will you consider being our consultant for the month of September? Our stipend will be fifteen hundred dollars, plus your living expenses while you are with us. We are praying that you will get us going in the right direction. Yours prayerfully, James Trosper, Director."

From Willie Longroad: "Son, I miss you. Our Foundation and Council meetings are not as quiet as they were before your visit. Folks are thinking in more excited ways than I can recall. You lit a fire, yes indeed. Here's the problem that you already figured out. We need you to help us. I'm pretty sure there are fellows who could get the job done, but they aren't one of us, and you are. I'll make you a deal. If you come up and help us for a month, (I'm thinking the Chief has already asked you) I'll go over to Ten Sleep and find out about your ancestors, the Bluesky people. Seems like a fair deal to me. I sure hope I hear from you soon. Cheers, Willie L."

There were two from Mr. Rowe that raised problem solving questions about funding.

There was a very sweet "Thank you" note from Margie Flowers, the secretary of the Council.

From Carly: (The one he saved for the last was written on pink paper and smelled like flowers.) "Hey you! How come you left without saying goodbye to me? I sort of had plans to make sure you'd remember me when you got back to the big city. Do you believe in love at first sight? I don't either. But there was some very unusual connection in our first handshake. Did you feel it too? It felt electric, or toasty warm to me. I can't figure you out, but I'd sure like to have a chance to work on that.

It's easier to write this instead of telling you face to face. I fell in love in high school. He was a couple years older than me and wicked handsome. He was athletic and played the guitar. Yeah, I fell hard and was all ready to be his Mrs. We spent two hot years together before I found out he already had a kid from another woman who was ready to be his Mrs. too. I was devastated, outraged and crushed. This is the truth just between you and me. It's been a while since I wanted to trust another man. But with you it is different. I found you to be an honest and a purely loveable man. Please don't think I'm trying to get you back for the Council. I'm not that politically minded. I'd just like to have a little more time to see if my heart can really say hello, and mean it. Thanks for listening. Your friend Carly."

The rest of June passed in routine. Dan saw Shirley at church one Sunday, but by the time he could shuffle out the crowded aisle the Wilcox family had gone and Dan wondered what he would have said to them if he had caught up. There were a couple more auction safaris that were semi successful. On the 5th of July Dan's dad presented him with a fairly new Jeep Wrangler. It would come in handy with his new driver's license. And Willie called from Wind River.

"May I speak with Dan Crown at this number" he asked politely.

"May I tell him who's calling?" Larry answered in the same way.

"This is Willie Longroad from the reservation. I have some information about some of his kin folks I believe he will welcome."

"Willie, I'm Larry Crown, Dan's dad. I want to thank you for taking good care of him on that recent visit. He came home as excited as a summer storm."

"I hear that! Our Council is still all worked up about his ideas for us. I hope we'll get to see him in September," Willie said with a hopeful voice, "Maybe sooner."

When the phone was handed to Dan and courtesies were exchanged, Willie reported, "I went over to Ten Sleep for you and asked around about the Bluesky family. I was right. They were important people in the past. The granddad was either a chief or a powerful shaman. Alice ran off with a guy and died not long ago in a Cheyenne nursing home. The folks didn't know anything about her having a baby named Crystal. But they told me how to get in touch with the little girl Alice left with her sister. Pearl still lives in Ten Sleep and has a couple boys and a girl. They are all pretty grown up but still live near the town too. I've got Pearl's phone number if you want to give her a call. I'll bet that will be a surprise for everyone. You've got some cousins, son." He gave Dan the phone number.

A grinning Dan responded, "Willie, I've never known much extended family. We've had my half-sister for as long as I've been around, but she was old enough to be another mom to me. My little sister and brother are just kindergarten and preschoolers right now. We'll get to know each other in time. I'm really excited to know about this. I owe you, friend! If the folks are as thrilled with this news as I am, I think you will see me before September, and I'll bring reinforcements."

More family!

As soon as he hung up the phone he shared the news with his folks. His mom had tears in her eyes as she murmured, "I have a sister and a family."

It was a bit awkward at first, but after a few minutes of explanations and assurances the women on both ends of the conversation were laughing and making plans to greet one another in person. Crystal said, "Is next Monday too soon? I can close the gallery and Larry has a couple years of vacations coming. We'll leave the kids with Paige. Oh I am so eager to see you, Pearl."

They drove the Jeep north on 25 to Buffalo Wyoming. A Howard Johnson offered both good food and clean rooms, and they were just an hour away from Ten Sleep. Larry asked Dan, "What's your plan for the visit?

"I don't know," the son replied. "How do you say hello to a family member that is new news?"

"No, I mean, what is your ideas for the reservation?" Larry had watched Dan's face and posture and knew that he was working on something big.

"It's going to be a difficult sell. I need to convince them that they can't nickel and dime their way into this, and they can't do it all at once. So there is a narrow middle ground of progress that needs careful thought and bold vision."

Larry was constantly proud of his son, but perhaps now more than ever. He was showing maturity that was beyond his years.

"Dad, you told me that in Reliance you built a tribal center. Would you mind, when I introduce you, to tell them about the center and the architect that designed it? We need information that is grounded to excite them. The guard stations will be easy to design. But a casino hotel with a couple dining rooms and a gaming plaza is going to be a challenge. These folks are not accustomed to dreaming big dreams."

"Dannie, those big dreams cost big bucks. Where is the money going to come from?" Larry studied his son's eyes.

"You can tell me if you think this is wrong, but I've been thinking about the lottery again. Those folks don't care who wins. They've already made their big cut. It feels wrong because not everyone can anticipate the numbers, but it is for a cause. It will help this tribe and all the people who will be nurtured by it to find their dignity again. I don't want a dime of it for me or us. I want to make up for the broken treaties and promises these people have endured for the last hundred and fifty years." As he spoke Larry thought he was becoming stronger.

His dad smiled and shook his head saying, "I've never thought about it like that. You know, your great grandfather Daniel would be giving you a big hug if he could right now. I'd argue with you if I could see a problem with that. But you'd better let me talk to your mom before you tell her your idea." He gave Dan an embrace instead.

It was mid morning when Dan pulled into the Standard station in Ten Sleep to ask about the Gunner residence. They were told to take the first right and go two blocks. They were the white house with brown trim on the corner.

Folks must have been watching for them because greeters were out the door before the Jeep stopped. A tall woman with salt and pepper gray hair wore a huge smile. "I can't believe you found us," she was saying laced with laughter. As Crystal stepped out of the car the woman embraced her and said, "I would recognize you in a crowd!" She hugged and kissed Crystal on the cheek, as two men and a young woman joined her. "Thank you, thank you, thank you!" The tears were beginning to flow on both faces. Larry and Dan joined the group to begin the introductions.

Pearl's husband's name was Cliff; he worked for the highway department as a driver and mechanic. Their oldest son was Ben; "he's a forest fire fighter stationed right now in Sheridan." Kit offered his handshake to the two fellows saying. "Hi I'm Kit. I have just one more year to finish at the University of Wyoming in Engineering. My field is renewable energy studies." As he was finishing the young woman offered her hand to them saying, "And I'm Sue. I'm the receptionist for the dentist, Dr. Friesen. All the while the two sisters clung to one another. Larry introduced himself, "I'm Larry Crown. I manage the Miller Mercedes-Benz dealership in Denver." Dan, who had been staring at his new cousins, said, "I'm Dan; I just graduated from High

School." Larry added, "We left Opal and Andy in Denver with Paige their nanny."

Cliff asked Dan, "Do you have more school plans, or are you going into the service?"

"It's a long story Uncle Cliff." He nearly chuckled just saying those words. "Dad's military career might be enough for our family and I have a good start at Denver U."

Crystal and Pearl joined them and they had to do it all over again.

Inside the house when all who wanted some fresh coffee were served, Pearl asked. "How in the world did you find us? I didn't even know you existed."

Crystal replied, "I guess it started with Dan going out to the Wind River Reservation to finish a Social Studies assignment. His guide was a man named Longroad." Cliff interrupted, "I know Willie. He's the Transportation Director on the Council." Crystal continued, "I'm not sure if it was just a kindness on his part, or if he is trying to pressure Dan to return to the Council meeting, but he made inquiries about the Bluesky family and discovered you. I didn't know much about mom. She dropped me off at a man's service station and never came back. There is so much I'd like to know about us."

"There's not a lot I have to tell you," Pearl answered. "Mom left me too, when I was just a toddler. Dad was not much for parenting so he didn't come home one Friday night and Aunt Beth took me in. She died when I was nine and then the Catholic School took me in. I met Cliff when he was home on furlough. We were married in the base chapel as he was finishing his enlistment in Virginia. Ben was born in '63; Kit in '66 and Sue in '71. You have doubled the size of our family. I am so deeply grateful." It was time for a couple more tears.

Cliff sought more information asking, "So Larry you were in the service? What branch."

"Army, just like you," came the brief answer.

"Where did you serve?" The question was asked softly just to keep the conversation going.

"CID sent me to Wiesbaden for a year, then Vietnam for five, the Philippines for a couple and finally Leavenworth Kansas," Larry answered with a bit of satisfaction.

Crystal added, "That's where I came into his life. The Master Sergeant was on his way home on furlough to Clarkston Washington when he was faced with a snowy highway pileup. My foster dad, I guess we would call him, had a little tow truck business. He was trying to pull a car out of the ditch when there was a problem, and he got hurt really bad. Larry jumped in to help him. It was a mess. Pop didn't make it to the hospital but left a power of attorney for Larry. His last thought was concern for me." She was still.

So Cliff broke in, "That sounds real familiar to me. Was there a picture in the newspaper?" When Crystal nodded, he said, "I remember a fairly dramatic photo of a soldier in tans all covered with mud and blood."

Larry agreed, "That photo even got back to my command at Leavenworth. It didn't work out the way I thought that's for sure. Looking at Crystal he added, "My life in tans came to an end and real happiness with Crystal began."

Cliff was enjoying this new family information. He asked Dan, "Your mom says the Council wants you to visit them again. Did you raise their hackles the first time?"

There was the grin with the dimple. "Yeah sort of," he chuckled, "I got a little too charged up about the changes that could bring the reservation up to the twentieth century. They are trying to get casino permits, but they have no supporting system to allow that to happen. I merely pointed out a half dozen or so opportunities they could capitalize."

"What sort of suggestions did you raise?" Cliff shook his head. "That's probably the most conservative group of leaders I know."

Dan shrugged, now embarrassed by the attention, "Oh, you know, I pointed out how Alberta runs its hunting and fishing program. I showed them how an RV park would add to the number of casino visitors. I talked a little about hunting, fishing and river rafting guides."

Cliff moved forward in his chair, "My gosh, that's amazing that they would even consider one of those."

Dan wasn't quite finished. "I think the frosting was when I suggested that they build a major hotel convention center to host at least one of the casinos."

Cliff started to swear, "Son of a …" he caught himself, and said instead, "The Wyoming Gaming Commission has been running a lottery for three years called 'Mega Millions.' They have a televised drawing every Saturday that no one has won. There are a handful of little prizes every week to keep folks interested, but they require eight two digit numbers plus a three digit magic key, so the pot just keeps getting bigger, more enticing. I personally think it has been designed to be mathematically possible but practically impossible. Each week is a new set of numbers. Sooner or later someone will get it. Like they say, 'If he tries long enough, even a blind squirrel will find a nut.' The winner right now would get almost a hundred million dollars, half of that if they want the lump sum payoff. There are no other gaming stations except card rooms, and sure enough, no casinos in the state right now. That's why the reservation is so hot to get into one."

Dan and his dad were sharing a long gaze. That was motivating information.

They talked to and through lunch before Larry reminded them that they still had a three hour drive to Fort Washakie. Before they left, Dan asked if he could use a deck of cards. He also found out where they could buy a lottery ticket.

There were promises that the Gunners would visit Denver soon. Kit had never been there, and Sue admitted that she had never been out of the state. She said it would be refreshing to meet a young man who wasn't trying to beat the record of beers consumed in one evening and the number of women insulted. Their parting had lots of promises, laughter and tears.

One last sign

They stopped in Worland so Larry could buy a lottery ticket in the name of the Washakie Investment Foundation. They had an early supper in Riverton and were able to get a couple rooms at the Motel 6 in Fort Washakie before the sun set. Dan called Willie to see if he wanted to join them at Ruby's for breakfast. They wanted to thank him for the introduction to their extended family. Dan also offered to bring his mom and dad in to meet as many of the Council members as might be available. His dad could refer the architect that had designed the Heritage Tribal Center in Reliance, and his mom had brought the list of artists she welcomed in her consignments part of the gallery. "I know it is a day early for the Council meeting. The Mid Mountain Air only makes one round trip a week to Denver on Thursday. They are going to fly home and I'm going to hang around for a while." That was very welcome news.

Willie said it was a deal if he could also throw in a lunch at the Smoke Shop. There was a young lady who hadn't been the same since he left town without saying goodbye. Dan giggled agreement because quite frankly he was curious how he would be greeted. Willie guided the visitors to the grave sites and a general tour of Fort Washakie.

When the four entered the Smoke Shop, however, there was only one person Carly spoke to: "Hey you in the gray shirt! Yeah you! What are you doing coming in here for lunch? We reserve the right not to serve rude people! You ignored me and now you expect service?" She had walked straight over to Dan. "I ought to punch you one," she said as she hugged him tenderly and kissed him on the cheek. "But I missed you way too much to do that."

Willie introduced Larry and Crystal, Dan's folks, who were finally able to enjoy her humor.

Carly regained her decorum and said, "He was only here three days and we're all still talking about him." Then looking at Dan she said, "You made a pretty large impression, sir." Talk about impressions, she was wearing her black party dress with a yellow scarf. Her warm smile was all the accessory any girl would need. She didn't mention that electric warmth she experienced again when she touched Dan.

"Did you save us some meatloaf sandwiches?" Willie asked. Dan felt a happy comfort in the familiar setting, now that he had recovered from Carly's unexpected greeting.

It was not surprising that all the Council members were available and Margie Flowers was there to take notes. After introductions, Larry described the tribal center, with its display rooms, café, and bed and breakfast rooms. "With only a bit of change, this could easily be a model for your Visitor centers." He described how they had started slowly but by the second summer were serving a full house every day. Then Crystal described filling the shelves and display cases with tribal items that were an easy sell on consignment. They both answered several questions and Dan promised to be back in time for tomorrow's Council meeting.

There was still time in the afternoon to show his folks Sinks Canyon State Park and have dinner at the Rancher restaurant in Lander. Finally, Larry had an opportunity to say, "No wonder you have been so eager to return up here. That lady is fantastic!" His mom agreed.

"Come on, guys," Dan began his defense. "Yes she is darned cute, and I have never been greeted so special, but she must be, what, twenty two, or twenty three? She is going to faint when she learns that I am just sixteen. I want to introduce her to Kit. Now that could be a match." His winning grin reappeared. "I haven't shared my age with any of them. Here the council wants to give me a job like I'm an adult or worse a professional something or other. I'll take care of that before I come home." He took a big breath before continuing. "The thing that excites me about the reservation is that they are so behind the times and I have a chance to help them launch something that will change the future for hundreds or thousands of people."

His dad changed the subject, saying, "Speaking of getting home, did you bring enough cash to carry you for a month or so plus gas for the drive home?"

"Well, I brought about three hundred dollars. That should do it, especially if the council wants to cover my expenses and pays me a stipend."

Larry pulled a couple credit cards out of his wallet saying, "Here's a bank card for emergency and a Shell card for gas. I noticed the Jeep doesn't get great mileage. I've got my expense account card that I can use for the flight home. I feel better knowing you have a back-up."

It was one of those moments when Dan hoped he would one day be such a thoughtful and generous dad. "Thanks dad, I'll take good care of them."

Larry heard the flush of the toilet next door. When he looked at the clock beside the bed he smiled, thinking "Dannie's up before 5. I'd better get going." When he stepped into the warm morning he found his son stretching and ready to run.

"Morning Dad, Are you ready for a Rocky Mountain high?" the happy lad asked. "How much gas do you have in your tank? We could do six or eight if you're up for it. I recall that you said your morning run is not a race but a meditation." When his dad nodded, Dan finished, saying, "That's a good thing because we have a lot to ponder."

When they came to the blue double-wide, Dan stopped to stretch and catch his breath. "This is Willie's place. He's probably still under the covers. We have four more to get back to breakfast."

"Lead the way. You set a very good pace." The dad was trying to keep his voice steady instead of panting as he would rather do.

When Willie joined them at Ruby's, he joked, "Larry did you let that rascal play a trick on you? He probably told you that you were just going around the block. Helen, my wife, said she saw two guys this morning running on our road. She wondered if we were having one of those marathon races. My dog went under the porch and won't come out. He quit speaking to me some time ago after I left him in town and he had to run all the way home. I tried to reason with him saying that some people have to run both ways." It was very pleasant to have a humorous beginning to the day.

Willie offered to show them the quickest way to the Riverton Regional Airport. There was not a lot of time to get there, but since there was only one other passenger flying to Denver in the twin engine commuter, there wouldn't be much of a crowd. That way he and Dan could lay out their strategy for the Council meeting on the drive back and still have time to work in a lunch at the Smoke Shop. Dan was suspect that the only strategy his guide had was getting him together with his daughter. Yup, it is very pleasant to have a humorous beginning to the day.

Carly looked at the only other table with lunch folks. She had just served their food and could now pause for a conversation. She slid in next to her dad with a concerned look on her face. "Is there going to be trouble at the Council meeting?" she asked. "I heard a couple of the card players talking about the 'hot shot' from Denver U being back. It didn't sound very friendly." She looked into Dan's dark eyes and saw nothing but openness.

Dan answered, "I'm sure not expecting any trouble, are you Willie?" Her dad simply shook his head. "On the other hand I haven't been here for nearly a month and I've stored up a whole lot of new ideas, so there might be some sparks." He chuckled, trying to lay aside any anxiety.

"Will you come back after the meeting? I would rest easier if I know it went well for you." She held his gaze just a bit longer than his comfort.

"I'll make sure your dad gives you a full report," Dan said gently. "I need to make some weekend plans back in Ten Sleep, with my new family. I think my cousin Kit is going to be a very valuable resource for us. If these plans start coming into focus it will be clear that we need more people. One of my questions to the Council will be where do we house and feed them."

"Sounds like I'm going to be busier," she said lightly, trying to hide the disappointment in his avoidance. But she stood up to return to her duties.

The Council was running over with enthusiasm. Each member greeted Dan as though it had been a long while since his last visit instead of a short month. When order was established and two minor financial issues dealt with, Director James Trosper said, "Mr. Crown, our Council has had a month to digest your thoughts about Wind River growth. When you left us last, we were pretty stirred up. Today it seems we are even more excited by your presence. We hope this means that you are accepting the position of Director of Development." His smile was one of confidence.

"Thank you, sir," Dan said with his best smile. "I'll tell you truly that this project has been on my mind constantly in my absence. As you know from yesterday my parents are also quite thrilled with our progress." He opened a notebook so he could have information available. "The Tribal Heritage Center which they built in Reliance was designed by Harris Designs Architect in Rock Springs. The total cost was $135,000, which included two display rooms, a large commercial kitchen a dining room, rest rooms and four bed and breakfast upstairs units with in-suite facilities. It also had an over-sized deck for outdoor dining and a bar with territorial views of the Tetons and a reflection lake. Imagine, if you will, four of those constructed prior to our security stations. That way folks could get information, enjoy some food and beverage, and pick up any appropriate permits before coming onto the reservation. Any questions or thoughts about that?"

Mr. Rowe, the Director of finance asked, "Are we locked into that design or is there possibility to downsize for cost savings?"

Dan chuckled to keep his response light. "Oh my, we are only speaking about the vaguest concept. And before we cost-cut, we must agree what is the scope of the project." He turned a page of his notebook and said, "That brings up another subject. I must remain completely separate from reservation funds, so I have formed a foundation to identify available construction funds. The Washakie Investment Foundation, which will be used for donations and fund raising currently, has a balance of only three thousand dollars. That's all I had to start it. But by my next report I may have something more noteworthy." He turned another page.

Mr. Trosper asked before he could go on, "Dan, are you telling us that you formed a foundation with your own money on our behalf?" There was a hint of incredulousness.

"Yes sir," he responded brightly. "My folks make up the other officers and have signature rights. It's only a way to keep track of available funds and help us monitor progress."

Mr. Rowe asked without recognition, "What happens if we need funds for reservation salaries or utilities. Are those funds available for general use?"

"The foundation funds are stipulated for construction only," Dan said gently. "We must protect it to insure a complete project."

The Director of Finance may have been feeling a bit invaded. Or perhaps he was being testy by nature. In a more aggressive voice he snapped, "Well how much do you expect to have and who's making the deposits?"

Dan stayed positive in spite of the snarky attitude. "At this time there has been only one deposit. I made it from my savings account." He waited for some response but none came, so he added, "There are federal matching funds, and any number of private investors who may want to donate. I expect to receive enough to complete the project. The rest will be problem solving."

When there were no further comments, he went on to a new subject. "I have one new item for our planning attention," he said looking around at the members. "We haven't talked about staffing for the project. If all goes by the script we will need five or six employees at each visitor center; that's two dozen. The guard stations will need at least six each, that's another couple dozen. I have no idea how many would be required for the hotel and casino, three or four dozen more at least. I can imagine a real influx of employees. My question is: do you plan to staff all those jobs from reservation residents, or recruit them from outside?" He let the question sit for a bit then added, "I can imagine a couple apartment facilities that could house a lot of folks, and retrieve some of the funds spent. It would be a better idea than having most of our work force living in Lander."

That got discussion rolling along with about as many ideas as there were folks in the room. Willie noticed that Dan never lost his big smile. They were doing the first part of the project. They were planning, sort of. Before they adjourned Mr. Trosper suggested that by next week's meeting they should begin to build a proposed time-line. If they had a goal to guide there was a greater probability of success.

Disaster!

Before going to Ruby's for a bowl of stew, Dan called Kit. "Hey Cousin, it's Dan Crown." "Yeah, I'm in Wind River for a while." "Well, that's what I'm calling about. How would you like to drive over in the morning? I could show you some of the reservation." "Yes. I'd like to go up to the meadow again. I think there is a steam vent that would supply heat for a lodge." "I don't know about that. You're the expert. But I could also introduce you to the sweetest lady I've met here." "Yeah, she's really lovely, smart and funny. Isn't that a full house?" "Yeah, I'm so sure you will like her a lot that I'll buy lunch if you don't. O.K. I'll buy either way." There was enough laughter to affirm a growing family connection." I'm staying at the Motel 6. There's an extra bed in my room if you want to spend the night. I'll see you here about ten."

When the cousins finally got to the Smoke Shop, they were still talking about the possibilities of a river raft business. They had driven to the little town of Crowheart, and then followed the river back to Bull Lake. "It was about fifteen miles," Kit reported. "At an average speed of five MPH it would take about three hours for the rafts to navigate that. You could have three or four groups in the river at the same time." His voice had become more enthused as he saw the potential. They were in agreement that a rafting business would be a real draw.

She was in a turquoise dress with a bright red flower in her hair. "Well I never," she began with a chuckle. "Two city slickers lost on the res without a guide. How did you find your way back to me?" Her smile was radiant as she approached them.

Dan placed his hand on Kit's shoulder as he said, "Kit, this lovely lady is Carly Longroad. I believe you are acquainted with her dad." Kit held out his hand. When Carly touched him there was a moment of warmth and attraction as the surprised couple looked into each other's eyes. Before Dan removed his hand from Kit's shoulder he said, "I can't tell you how happy I am to introduce you two." The handshake lingered a moment longer like a kiss. Dan was aware that he had taken advantage of a couple innocent people. He was not in the least sorry for it however.

"Carly, has your dad been in yet today?" Dan asked "I'm wondering if you might still have a couple meatloaf sandwiches in the kitchen?"

"You are in luck. I don't expect him for another half hour. By that time you can eat and run."

She was joking but Dan was serious when he said, "I'm hoping we can meet him today. Kit is just finishing his Engineering degree at UW. He might be a real help when it comes to energy application in the new project." Before they sat down, he said, "I'm going to get a notebook out of my Jeep, but sooner or later I'd like a diet coke with my sandwich." As she watched Dan make his way toward the door, Carly noticed Colt Border get up from a table and head in the same direction. He was the villain she had been in love with in high school.

Having retrieved his notebook, Dan was approaching the door when he noticed a fellow finish a cigarette, and flip the butt into the gravel. He glanced around the parking lot, sensing warning warmth.

"Hey, Slick," the man said casually, "I'm Colt; the one she dumped." It takes less than a half second for a strike to be made from the waist to shoulder height. It takes more than a half second for reaction time to trigger danger and to take some defensive action. Colt's fist slammed into the side of Dan's unsuspecting and unprotected face. Bones broke and he was knocked unconscious. The force of the blow drove his yielding body backwards and he slammed the back of his head against the porch pillar. Perhaps Colt was surprised at the devastating assault, but he was not about to pass up an opportunity offered by the crumpled form. He bent down and fished Dan's billfold out of his back pocket. Wow, there was over three hundred dollars and a couple credit cards in it.

At that moment Carly, who didn't trust Colt's absence, opened the door to see what was taking so long. Gasping, she shouted, "Colt, what the hell?" He threw the empty wallet on the ground and raced for his car. Carly spun and shouted "Terry, call 911; we need police and an ambulance quick!" All the patrons rushed out to help if it might be possible.

Kit was the one who said, "Don't move him; he hit his head and maybe his neck is broken." His face was ashen white with shock.

Someone brought a sleeping bag to cover the unconscious form trying to keep him warm.

It took ten minutes for a Highway Patrol car to arrive and twenty minutes before the ambulance from Lander could get there. All the while Carly sat beside the still form of Dan, holding his cold hand hoping for that spark.

The patrolman was asking questions: "Do you know the name of the victim?" Kit offered Dan's wallet, which was empty except for his driver's license.

"This says his age is sixteen. Is that correct?"

Kit said, "I'm his cousin, and I believe that is correct."

Carly said, "What? He's only sixteen? He's just a kid!"

Kit answered nearly under his breath, "He wanted to tell you but didn't know how. He likes you very much."

When the patrolman learned that Colt Border had committed the assault and robbery, an APB was put out on him, last seen driving an '83 Chevrolet Malibu with Wyoming plates headed southeast from Fort Washakie. He was arrested before he made it to Casper. His possession of two credit cards belonging to Larry Crown was firm evidence of his guilt.

Willie arrived at the scene before the ambulance team had stabilized Dan on a backboard. He volunteered to notify the family, and he tried to help Carly make sense of this horrible turn of events. Both of them were feeling guilt and loss in the tragedy.

There were ample hardy hands to ease the board bound Dan into the ambulance. For him the days of mystery had begun. There were two days at the Lander Medical Clinic where no one knew what to do with him. He was officially labeled as "in a coma". An IV drip was started and a nurse looked in on him twice an hour to record, "no change." On Monday Larry ordered an ambulance to transfer Dan to the University of Colorado Medical Center where a team of neurologists were prepared to look more closely into his injuries. They also had state of the art equipment to help them diagnose a plan for his recovery. Kit promised to bring the Jeep and all Dan's personal items from the Motel. It was still unreal to all of them that this had taken place.

The depth of mystery

On Tuesday Crystal stood again at the doorway of the intensive care unit studying the tubes and wires connected to her son. His broken jaw had been set and a plastic brace held it in place covering most of the bottom of his face. She had asked the question repeatedly to the darkness, "How did this happen and why?" It was unbelievable that his breathing was now dependant on the machine. She wept again.

The next day Larry was with her as they studied the quiet rhythm of the equipment. Crystal stepped over to the still form on the bed and rested her hand on his shoulder.

"Hi Mom," she heard silently. It was very dear, clear and strong. "Is dad with you?"

Crystal turned toward Larry and whispered, "I can hear him. He's awake." Then she answered silently, "Yes we are both here."

"Good," the voice said. "Hold his hand so I don't need to repeat this." A moment later he said, "Hi dad. This is way weird, huh?" There was a long pause before Dan said, "I don't know how this works, so I'll start with what I do know. At first I was really frightened. The brain injury is like a rock chip on the windshield; it started little and just keeps growing. I can't hear or see; I can't move anything. It's like I'm in a warm mud cake. Do you remember when we saw pictures of the glacier falling in the ocean. Chunk by chunk dropped off. That's sort of what's happening to my brain. Then I realized that I am not alone. The Lord is here with me and has assured me that he will not leave me. I want you to know that I am in no pain at all and I'm not afraid. Then I started getting all sorts of information. Will you tell Dr. Jacobson that I have a Degenerative Cerebral Cortex due to a strong sedative you received before I was born. It is not reversible or repairable. Tell him I was an emergency preemie. That important part of the brain should have been tough, but mine was like wet Kleenex. It's a wonder it has lasted this long. The fragile covering was easily torn when I bumped my head and is still tearing. Every now and then I feel a little less aware. I don't think I have much time left."

After a brief pause when the only sound in the room was the gentle hum of the equipment, he continued, "Before you get super weepy," he continued, "I have learned so much in here. Let's try to move beyond sadness for a while and accomplish what we still can. Tell Dr. Jacobson also that what he is calling 'heartburn' is actually an Aortic Aneurism. He must see his cardiologist right away. If he asks how we know this, tell him that I just know. Tell him to quit making excuses. He should give us a discount for those two diagnoses alone."

There was a long pause in which his folks were worried that the conversation was over. "Tell Nurse Rosa that her son Robert is in a drug rehabilitation program in Redding California and will be home by Christmas." There was a quiet satisfaction in Dan's tone. "And the wrap-up of ICU secrets is that nurse Irma's son will be home soon from the Middle East safe and sound. Those ladies have been praying a lot for me and their sons. If they ask, tell them that I just know."

Dan's voice said softly, "What I've learned in these quiet hours is that gratitude is the most powerful emotion. It leads to our most precious treasures. I am grateful for every moment of my life. We've had sixteen bonus years. I could have died before I was born. Our home has been a perfect model of gratitude. Dr. Blanchard is about to make a terrible investment because he lacks gratitude. He is afraid he doesn't have a large enough retirement. I would love to tell him to get out before he loses the good funds he already has. I am so very grateful for everything you shared with me."

"By the way" he seemed so casual, "have you heard how the lottery drawing went?"

His dad replied silently, "Your numbers were all correct. The foundation is fifty six million dollars richer." The news seemed so paltry in light of these circumstances.

Dan replied, "Maybe you can scrape some off the top to pay for these hospital bills I'm running up. There will still be enough for the Council to get a great start. I've been wondering if the Gunners would like to take my place helping with that project."

Both Larry and Crystal marveled at the ordinary attitude Dan had here in ICU. It was obvious that he knew the situation was urgent and was still relaxed in it.

A nurse came in to replace the IV drip and his mom and dad promised to return tomorrow. Crystal lifted her hand from his warm shoulder amazed that they could communicate like that. She asked the nurse's name. "I'm Rosa Gomez, ma'am"

"This is going to sound crazy to you, nonetheless, Dannie just ask us to tell you that Robert is in a drug rehab in California and will be home by Christmas."

A doubtful nurse responded, "You spoke with Dan, and he told you that?"

"Rosa, it's a complicated family trait. He told us to tell you he just knew. Would you mind directing us to Dr. Jacobson's office. We have some pertinent information for him too." It had been some time since Crystal had seen that confused expression on another's face.

The next afternoon his folks were back, accompanied by Shirley. Dr. Blanchard informed them that Dan had a difficult night and had to be resuscitated. He was shocked when they gave him Dan's counsel not to invest. When they were asked how that information came to them Crystal simply said, "Dan just knew." The three went into the darkened ICU.

Crystal said to Shirley, "This is going to seem very strange to you. Please relax and listen with your heart." She held Shirley's hand and Larry held her other hand while Crystal placed her hand on Dan's shoulder. "How is my brave son?" she thought.

The thought that replied was faint. "Mom, I'm glad you're here. Is dad with you?"

"And Shirley is with us. I hope you don't mind a crowd." Crystal had not thought it could be a problem.

"The feather-light voice responded, "The three people I most want to talk with today. I am still not alone so when I tell you that I have very little time left, you must know I am not afraid. It is all going to be good. I just know. But we have some business to talk about. Can you do that for me?"

Shirley trembled in the strange moment, and Larry said, "We'll try to hang in there with you, Pal." Tears were streaming down Crystal's face.

"O.K. the ICU news is for Nurse Clarice. Tell her she will finally be pregnant before her next birthday. I just know. And tell Nurse Bess that the diagnosis is scary but she must trust in her team. She's going to get through it fine. I just know it. That's the easy part."

There was a lengthy pause before the whispered voice continued. "Shirley this might seem real weird but I have felt for years that you and I would grow old together. I want to help you with your dreams. If you need financial help with med school, I'd like you to have the Microsoft stock. I'd also like you to have the Wishing Well painting. We were together when I bought it. I think I was fond of that painting because I had big wishes for us. Mom I hope Opal and Andy can use the Starbucks and other stock for their college fund. Does anyone have any trouble so far with my last will?"

Shirley whispered, "I'm so sorry I had bad thoughts about you. I love you and wished we had kissed."

"Me too," she heard silently.

"O.K. dad, here comes the tough stuff. In the next few hours you will need to sign the donation papers for my organs" His mom groaned and his dad shook his head recalling how years ago he had made the decision for his own dad. "I think they are in perfect condition and will give several folks a chance for a new life. I'd like the rest cremated and the ashes sprinkled on the high meadow Willie took me to on the res."

"My friend is telling me we need to say goodbye. I am so grateful for the lessons we learned together. I love you eternally. Mom could you say a prayer?"

Before she could say a word his alarm went off. Dan's heart had finished the race. Now it was time for sadness.

Mourning

The following hours were blurred by tears. Larry called his mom, and then Frankie and Charlie to tell them the horrible news. Barb Wilcox called the church and Pastor Curtis Springs came over to pray with the family and comfort their loss. He agreed that the church would be available for a memorial service the first Saturday in August. Then the cards, flowers and supportive visits from friends began. In the midst of an awful time both Larry and Crystal were surprised by the many folks who were offering kindness, even Sandy Buttons who was out of rehab. They were also surprised at the return of their silent communication.

Larry was gazing out the window, watching the evening lights of the city.

"Sweetheart, would you hold me?" he heard clearly.

He turned to see Crystal leaning against the kitchen door jam. "I've never hurt this much," she thought in anguish. He walked to her and gently wrapped his arms around her. For just a moment he remembered the women of Bereavement. Now it was personal for him.

"I know what you mean," he thought gently into her hair. "It seems like a nightmare and we must surely wake up." They stood together for several moments reflecting on the gratitude they felt in having such a remarkable son.

"Your strength will help me get through the next couple weeks," she whispered. "You have been doing that for as long as we have known each other." Each day was a bit less painful until a week had gone by.

Grandma Irma flew in from Clarkston and the next day both the Longroads and the Gunners arrived for the memorial. Kit brought the Jeep back, which triggered another round of tears. He would have been delighted if Carly had been able to join him. He was a bit doubtful of her reason that she couldn't get anyone to take her shifts for five days. His suspicion was that she was overwhelmed with guilt and the shame that her former boyfriend was now in jail charged with manslaughter of a minor and grand theft. Kit was confident he could help her through that, in time. Larry made reservations for the two families at the Marriot and welcomed his mom into their guest room. He also made invitations for the guests to share Roberta's delicious meals in their spacious home, which would become their base camp. Having Pearl there with Crystal was a great comfort. Another week crept by.

"That was the most beautiful service I've ever seen," Cliff said in appreciation. "The beauty of your church took my breath away. I'll be thinking of that for a long time."

Sue added, "And the youth choir was like a bunch of angels. How many choirs does the church have?"

Larry was grateful for something to talk about that didn't cause tears in his eyes. "During the school year there are two adult choirs and a youth choir of about fifty. Today we saw about two thirds of the youth choir. I suppose many of them are travelling on vacation. But several of those who responded at short notice were Dan's school chums." That tender thought allowed the tears to return anyway.

Willie hugged Helen, saying, "This has been a terrible set-back for the Council. They looked to Dan as the idea man." Then to Larry he said softly in respect, "That was without a doubt the biggest most beautiful church I've ever seen. And to think you get to go there every Sunday. No wonder he had such glorious ideas."

Larry needed to redirect the conversation, so he said, "I've rented the big van for the week. Would you folks like a city tour tomorrow?" He wanted to get the conversation onto something other than the memorial.

A deep breath and a fresh beginning

Sunday evening's Italian dinner was their final meal together. There was much praise for their gracious hospitality and Roberta's magic as the family cook. The desserts were just about finished when Willie knew this was his last chance to ask. "Larry, I'm a bit uncomfortable asking this question," he began tactfully, "but it may be my last chance. You must know that the Council is grieving along with us. We've never been so motivated to make major changes. With the loss of Dan, what do you see for our future?" His face reflected the pain he was feeling.

"Yeah, that fuzzy haired rascal had a way of working folks up," the dad said with a wistful smile. "I would hate to see what he started come to nothing. In fact one of his final thoughts was about the makeup of the Council. He suggested that the Gunners take a much more active role."

Willie nodded his agreement, saying, "He sure enough convinced us that we need more workers to get this ball rolling. But what are we going to do about the funds?"

"Did Dan tell you about his Foundation?" Larry had a half smile, as though it was a secret.

"Well, yeah," Willie replied knowing he was in a very fragile place. "We were impressed that he could come up with three thousand of his own dollars. But I'm afraid that's not even openers."

"Well sir," Larry paused knowing that he had to share a bit of the truth. "What would you think about fifty million? His money raising was incredible." Everyone except Crystal was in shocked silence. "His Investment Foundation was more successful than we can imagine. But before you tell the Council that you are rolling in dough, I must tell you there will be major strings and conditions. I need to conference with the Gunners to see how involved they want to be. The funds will be a very empowering loan to the tribe, motivating action and not just talk, and certainly not a gift. Dan's opinion was there are already too many of those on the res. These funds could build the infrastructure that begins to earn major return dollars. Crystal and

I want to see progress so I will probably make adjustments to my current employment and take Dan's place as Director of Development in charge of funding. Mr. Rowe can rest easy, I want nothing to do with his job. Is that vague enough for you to report to the Council?"

Willie asked, "You did say fifty MILLION, didn't you?"

"Yes sir, I did. And I also said loan with strong conditions, which will enable a lot of federal matching funds. That's more than enough to establish Wind River as a serious tourist attraction." Willie could see the Master Sergeant image in Larry.

A huge grin spread across his face. "We've had a group of posers way too long," he said gladly. "I can feel Dan's spirit building a fire under us again."

"I've made an offer to Mid Mountain Air. I'll guarantee a round trip on both Thursday and Friday for six months if they will expand their service. I can be at every Council meeting and only be gone from home one night a week." For some it seemed excessive, for a couple others it was the beginning of profound changes.

Willie and Helen returned to Fort Washakie with both sorrow and bright hope in their future. Willie was eager to give the good news of Larry's proposal to the Council.

The Gunners returned for breakfast on Monday. There was an established sense of family among the six. Shared sorrow was a strong bond between them. There was a bit of conversation about the lovely memorial service. Kit recalled how the pastor had said that some people require sixty or seventy years to leave the memory of a major accomplishment, but in just sixteen short years Dannie had become an amazing force for good. Pearl lifted a glass of orange juice saying, "Here's to Dannie. He will remain forever in our hearts." They all joined her.

Finally Larry said, "I will never get tired of saluting that lad, but I did ask you here for something else." He smiled warmly at his new family. "Have you folks given any thought to how you might like to take advantage of this new opportunity?"

Cliff shrugged saying, "I figured it wouldn't amount to more than Dan running up against the conservative old Council. I nearly had an accident when I heard how much money is available."

Pearl said, "I've been trying to think how I might be of any help after this terrible sorrow. My only work experience was part time at the café; and that was years ago. I can't imagine what I might have to offer."

Larry leaned toward them and said, "I believe the Council's strong desire for Casinos is a chance for us to design some life changing satisfactions for the family. Anything we can do to help them realize that dream will be significant."

Cliff asked, "I don't follow you Larry. What have you got in mind?" He opened the door for the future.

"Well, for example, we don't want to move from Denver because Crystal has her gallery here and we want fine schools for Opal and Andy. But I can continue the job with the dealership, and still manage the foundation loan money by being in Wind River each week for the Council meeting." He looked at Kit and said, "I think it will begin with secure Information Centers. They become the initial source of visitor passes. Dan shared with us how excited you are about the river raft idea. With an easy enabling loan, you could be the point of the new spear of development. I believe an RV park near Bull Lake would allow you to run the business while finishing school. By hiring two or three guides and office help, you could model how potential can be utilized. The Council needs a Director of Instruction, which I believe you could fill easily."

He looked at Cliff and said, "I can imagine you on the Council as Director of Safety, which could manage the security as well as running the hunting program and lodge. A half dozen local hunters could be a great start as guides." To Pearl he said, "Pearl, we will need someone who will manage the Welcome Centers. Crystal could be a very useful helper." And to Sue he said, "We will need someone who can be our receptionist, making reservations for the hotel and bed and breakfast, as well as selling permits for visiting the res or hunting or fishing. You could have an office in a Welcome Center or in your home. I would expect that if you are interested it might be a few months but I would think you'd like to have a new place there in Wind River." He looked at his family and said, "I believe between the six of us, and maybe a stunning lady named Carly, we could become a very positive influence on the Council. Together we could help those huge changes that would bring you a lot of satisfaction and financial security. It seems to me that there is a lot of money waiting to be made here. Someone will want to fill the jobs, why not you?"

Cliff had an embarrassed expression as he said, "Larry, our old place is not worth much. I'm not sure I could dig up enough equity to build a new place."

Larry reached over to rest his assuring hand on his brother-in-law's shoulder. "Dan was thinking ahead," he chuckled. "We'll all need to try to match his positive creativity. A new house must be built on a 99 year reservation lease. With new Council positions and businesses, you could easily afford a deferred payment construction loan from the Washakie Foundation slush fund, and we are going to have a host of eager contractors hungry for consideration. We just need to begin thinking like he did. There is a poster in Dan's room that pretty much sums up his attitude. It says simply, 'If you can dream it, you can do it!' He just knew it could happen."

Finis: "I Just Know!"

Printed in the United States
By Bookmasters